ASH LAKE MURDERS

An absolutely gripping crime thriller with a massive twist

HELEN H. DURRANT

Detective Alice Rossi Book 1

Joffe Books, London
www.joffebooks.com

First published in Great Britain in 2022

This paperback edition was first published
in Great Britain in 2022

ISBN: 978-1-80405-243-3

For Margaret, sadly no longer with us but who spent many happy times with her daughter and son-in-law at their holiday home on a particular country retreat in middle England.

PROLOGUE

Friday Night

The sound of water dripping on stone echoed through his head, unremitting, finally dragging Callum Hilton from his semi-conscious state. He opened his eyes to total darkness, strained to see the faintest chink of light but there was nothing. Logic told him he was in the old boathouse. He had to be, it was the only building around and she couldn't have dragged him any distance.

He'd been fishing from the jetty just in front of it when he'd heard a voice, turned and seen her behind him. Without a word she hit him across the side of the head and felled him with a single blow. He couldn't understand why she'd do something like that. He'd thought they were friends.

He called out into the darkness, "Anyone there?" But there was no answer. It was late and all the fishermen would have left. Of the three fishing lakes on the Still Waters country retreat, Ash was furthest from the lodges. No one ventured up here after sunset. Even if he could get free there would be no one around to help him, he was on his own.

Callum Hilton closed his eyes and rested his head against the stone wall. He was soaking wet from the leaking roof above him and could barely feel his arms and legs, which were bound together with tape and numb with cold.

He couldn't make sense of what had happened. The images in his head were confused. He recalled watching the night gather around Needle Crag and waving to the other fishermen packing up. He'd been about to call it a day himself, make his way back to his parents' lodge before it got too late. But he'd lagged behind, wanting one more go at that elusive carp, which had been playing cat and mouse with him all day.

His mother had arranged a get-together for the neighbours, and had specifically asked him to be back on time. Would she even notice his absence? By now it would be in full swing and everyone would be too drunk to bother about him. So no one would miss him and he couldn't expect anyone to come looking.

The woman's voice came out of the blackness. "Sorry, Callum, nothing personal, but on reflection I'm glad it's you."

Her words made no sense. She liked him, she'd asked him out for a drink a couple of times. They got on. "Let me go, please, I'm not a threat."

"Agreed, you're no threat to anyone, Callum. You're a thoroughly nice lad and that's what makes you perfect for what I have in mind."

"My mum's got folk round, I should be there. They'll come looking," he said.

She laughed. "Sure about that, are you? If there's one thing I know about the residents of Still Waters, a drinking session wins hands down every time."

Her soft fingers stroked his cheek. "You don't really want to go to a boring party with a load of drunken pensioners, do you?"

"Please, I won't say anything."

"You don't like it here at the retreat much, do you, Callum?"

That wasn't strictly true, he liked the fishing. But most of the people who bought lodges at Still Waters were retired, had time to spare. They appreciated the beauty of this country retreat in the Pennine foothills and made full use of the fishing, the golf, the walking. He'd have liked it more if there were others his own age here but the few he'd met worked on the site and had little time off.

He felt a sharp kick to the guts and howled with pain. "What did you do that for?"

"I like an answer when I ask a question," she said, kicking him again.

"Okay, it's too quiet and the people here aren't my sort. That do you?"

She laughed. "My thoughts exactly. Brain dead most of them, particularly your mother."

"My mother's okay."

"She's an interesting watch, I'll give her that. Were you aware that she's making a play for Neil Lewis? They're always walking about together and whispering. Wonder if his wife Gemma knows."

Callum felt her warm breath on his face. "Shall I tell her, Callum? Cause a right stink that would. Gemma is a right jealous cow — who knows what she'd do?"

He didn't like her criticism of his mother. It was unfair, all she was guilty of was having a good time. "I can't feel my legs."

"That'll be the cold. You're sitting on a wet floor and rain is pouring through the roof."

"I'll get pneumonia."

"No, you won't, Callum. You won't live that long."

He felt sick. The kicking, the confusion from the bang on the head, were taking their toll.

"There's a wind getting up but at least the rain's stopped," she said conversationally. "Hear that squawk? It's one of the ravens heading to the trees to roost with the others before he gets caught out."

The moon had risen and was bright enough now to illuminate parts of the boathouse through the gaps in the rotting main doors. The woman stood over him, he could just make out her shape.

"Don't worry, you won't suffer, Callum. I'll make it quick. And don't think I'm not grateful. I am. You don't know it but you're an important part of my plan. To use the fishing vernacular, you're my sprat — you know, like in the saying, *a sprat to catch a mackerel.*"

"I can't stay here all night, I'll freeze."

"You're right. Even I'm not that heartless."

He was too woozy to realise what she meant by this. "You're releasing me then?"

"No, Callum, I'm putting you out of your misery."

CHAPTER ONE

Saturday

The lashing rain and high winds of last night's storm had given way to still air and brilliant sunshine. Clare Hilton stood on the veranda of her lodge at Still Waters, a country retreat in the hills above Glossop, with a mug of tea in her hand, admiring the view. She turned to her friend and neighbour, Liz Webb, who was busy checking her mobile. "That was a damn good night. D'you realise, we got through a dozen bottles of prosecco and two bottles of gin and that was just us girls." Clare laughed.

"Shame you upset Gemma though," said Liz. "Went off early in a right strop, she did. Did you hear the names she called you?"

Clare pulled a face. "Gemma can't take a joke, that's her problem."

"What was she supposed to do?" Liz said. "I mean, you did come on a bit strong. You were all over her husband. You and Neil spent most of the night curled round each other on your sofa."

"I like Neil, he's good company. He's the best looking bloke here *and* he's got plenty of money to spend."

Liz grinned. "You've got no shame, Clare Hilton."

Clare laughed. "She's too young for him anyway. I'm more his age, we understand each other. What's Gemma, forty at the most? Neil is drawing his pension."

"That's not the point. He's her husband, not yours."

"More's the pity."

"No signal again." Liz tossed her phone onto the table. "What about Wi-Fi?"

"There's that hotspot on the other side of the site," Clare said. "Better still, why not give it a rest? That's what we're here for, to get away from all that."

"I know, but work will still email me and I don't want to be out of the loop."

"What loop?" Clare scoffed. "You overestimate your importance. You're only there part-time, so the place isn't likely to go to rack and ruin because you take a week off. Anyway, you were supposed to retire last year. I don't know what you're still doing there."

"Damien relies on me," Liz said. "That new girl he's got in doesn't know the ropes yet."

"Given how young and pretty she is, I doubt Damien gives a toss. I don't know about you, but I intend to have some fun this week. Gemma's off home tomorrow and Neil's already said he's up for a few trips out. He's got a mate arriving to stay with him any day. Our pair," she said, referring to their husbands, "will spend all their time either fishing or playing golf. What sort of break is that for us?"

"We have any sort of day out with Neil and his mate, Gemma will be on the warpath next weekend. It won't stay a secret — you know what this place is like. After last night she's got you on her radar. Take my advice, leave the man alone."

Clare laughed. "I'm not afraid of her. She makes it obvious the retreat isn't her thing."

"Give her time."

"If she wants to fit in she needs to lighten up," Clare said firmly.

"Gemma's got a vicious temper. Minty told me she has a brother who's done time."

Gemma's brother a jailbird, that was interesting. Minty was the manager at Still Waters and a seasoned gossip. "What exactly did she tell you?" Clare asked.

"That this has happened before, there've been other women chasing after Neil. She sorted the last one by keying her new car and having her son beaten up. The lad spent a week in hospital and it cost a fortune for the car to get a respray. A few choice words in the woman's ear and she didn't go near Neil again."

Clare shrugged. "So Gemma's a nutter. I'll bear it in mind. Pity."

"Dave didn't look happy with your behaviour either. He's not daft, you know. He'll be keeping an eye on the pair of you."

"Might wake the bugger up. He's become a right bore these last years, no fun at all."

"He's not that bad," Liz said. "Come on, you love him really."

The women fell silent, Dave had joined them — a balding man in his late sixties who could do with losing a few pounds. "Either of you seen our Cal? His bed's not been slept in. Today's match day and it's nearly time to draw the pegs."

The same old ritual. The fishermen would meet by Oak Lake and draw lots to see who would fish where. There were favourite spots around the water — pegs as they were called — where a good catch was practically guaranteed.

Clare shook her head. "See what I mean? The match is everything. That means another day given over to fishing. Cal will have bunked down with one of his mates. Liam Purvis, the odd job man around here, is my best bet. They'll have drunk themselves stupid and talked fishing until the small hours."

Satisfied with the explanation, Dave nodded, yawned, and went back inside. "Bloody hard work this relaxing."

"There's plenty wants doing," Clare called after him. "After the match the grass wants cutting and the spare bedroom needs sorting. It's full of your junk." Dave swore in response.

Liz grinned. "You are hard on him at times, you know."

"Don't start feeling sorry for him," Clare said. "I was, and look where it got me. Holidays are out because we've got this place. As far as Dave's concerned, we come here or go nowhere."

"You could have said no," Liz said.

"I was too soft. I gave in to that stupid smile of his, didn't I? That's me all over."

"Yes, but you like coming here too."

"When the weather's good. The problem is it's nothing but fishing and golf. That doesn't suit me."

Clare caught sight of Liam strolling past the lodge and waved him over.

"What happened to your Cal last night?" he said. "He was coming back to yours for an hour then meeting me later on in the pub."

Clare leaned over the veranda to speak to him. "We've not seen him. We thought he'd stayed over with you?"

"No. I waited in the pub but he didn't turn up. I gave him a ring but no joy."

"Dave!" she shouted at her husband. "Cal's not at Liam's. Never was."

Dave came out onto the veranda bare-chested, a towel draped round his neck. "Is he with some girl?"

"Nope, he's got someone back home," Liam said.

"So where is he?" Clare asked.

Dave didn't seem concerned. "He's a grown man, he can take care of himself."

But Clare was worried. Her fingers shook slightly as she tapped on his number in her contacts. "No bloody signal as usual." She turned to Dave. "Cal doesn't do missing. Liam hasn't seen him, he hasn't phoned and no way would he dodge the match. Come on, Dave, move your arse and get him found."

CHAPTER TWO

Callum Hilton had been a good-looking boy, tall, fair and well built. She ran her fingers gently down his naked chest. Pity she'd had to spoil him. She had a soft spot for men with blond hair, especially this one. He was nice, always spoke to her politely, flirted a little too. She recalled the time she'd given him a lift back from the bus stop. They'd gone out for a drink and ended up going back to hers for the night.

Shame it had to end like this, but he was the best choice. She'd kept her ears open, and found that despite coming across as such a nice, clean- living boy, Callum had enemies. He had a gambling problem and owed money. The police would have plenty to unravel before they got anywhere with this one. Then there was that toxic family of his. They'd panic, particularly the mother — a spectacle she'd enjoy watching.

She'd brought him to Ash Lake because it was usually deserted. The boathouse was only there because they occasionally had to row out to check over the aerators in each of the lakes. A moorhen had made her nest on top of the one on Ash Lake, and until her brood fledged, no work would be done there. Oak and Birch were some distance away, and dragging the boat over to them was a chore.

She laid the naked Callum out on the cold flagstones and placed two black bags of the type used to hold builders' rubble beside him. Callum was to be divided up and put inside them. She didn't want all of his body being found at the same time, which meant taking him apart limb from limb like a beast being butchered. Messy, but there was no other way. His arms, minus hands, lower torso and legs would go in one bag, the one to be ditched in the lake and found first. All body parts that could identify him, including his upper torso which had a distinctive tattoo across the chest, would go in the other. She'd hang onto this second bag until she was ready. Eventually it would go in one of the skips around the retreat and make its way to landfill.

She went about the gruesome work of cutting him up calmly and methodically, completely unperturbed. She'd done it before, it was part of the ritual. Besides, it was the most enjoyable part of the kill.

Dumping the unidentifiable bits of Callum in Ash Lake was a good choice. There was already a body in there from over six years ago that had never been found. But Callum was different, she wanted him found, she just had to decide when. If they found the old body too it didn't matter. The victim would be too far gone for the remains to be much use. Soon, a detective with a keen mind would look at Ash Lake, spot the clues and send in the divers. And she knew exactly who that would be.

Callum Hilton was the bait in her trap. It wasn't the usual tactics of a killer, but she was no ordinary one.

Within the next few hours Callum's mother would report him missing. The local force would first be involved but they wouldn't do much. If Clare Hilton stamped her feet hard enough they might run to sending a detective out to the retreat but that could take days. Callum was an adult, perfectly free to take off at will with no explanation. Plus, whoever they sent wouldn't be up to the job of finding out what had really happened to him. There'd be nothing to suggest he'd been killed, probably he'd simply left, gone home.

They might look into his immediate past for an explanation, settling on his gambling and the people he owed money to.

She might want Callum finding but that was no reason to make it easy. After dark she'd open the large doors at the end of the boathouse and row out into the middle of the lake where it was good and deep. There, she'd push the bag containing the unidentifiable bits of Callum overboard. There was building work going on at Still Waters. Across the road on another piece of land that had been acquired for the purpose, Still Waters Two was under construction. The second bag would be kept hidden among a pile of other similar bags containing building rubbish. Once the police divers had searched Ash Lake and found the first bag, she'd dump the second one in the retreat's general rubbish skip, from where it would find its way to landfill. As for the mess on the floor where she'd dismembered him, it was easy to swill it down with bleach and drag the boat over it. If the local police investigated they wouldn't suspect a thing. She smiled. The police could be stupid at times.

With Callum dead and hidden, it was time to play her final card, tempt an old enemy into her lair one last time. She was tired of playing games and wanted rid of her old adversary for good.

CHAPTER THREE

Sunday

Clare Hilton woke early on Sunday morning. She'd promised to go for a walk with two of her friends at the retreat, sisters Erica and Emily Cross, but given Callum's disappearance she had better things to do. Despite all her phone calls, all her searching, her son remained missing. She'd done her best but there'd been a match on and no one had shown much interest in finding him. Today would be different. Clare intended to speak to everyone at Still Waters including the staff.

Dave wasn't much help. He'd wasted the previous day at the fishing match and had done nothing but grumble when he didn't catch much. The winner, who walked away with fifty quid, had caught a huge carp which thoroughly pissed Dave off and saw him giving up halfway through, after which he sat in front of the telly and proceeded to drink a skinful. Consequently, he was still in bed.

Clare banged on the bedroom door. "Get up, you lazy sod. There's stuff to do."

"Your Cal shown his face yet?" Liz had arrived, and was standing behind her on the veranda.

"No, and I'm worried sick. Him in there isn't helping either, he won't even get out of bed. This isn't like our Cal. I asked around at the match yesterday and no one's seen him since Friday night. All we know is that he'd been fishing Ash Lake most of Friday. A bloke who left about eight that night said Cal was the last man standing."

"You don't think he fell in, do you?" Liz asked.

"No. Anyway, he's a good swimmer."

"Have you tried his mobile?"

"I keep on trying, but you know what it's like round here, no signal to speak of."

"What about his fishing tackle?" Liz asked. "Your Cal has some expensive gear and one of those trolley things. Has it been found?"

Clare gave her friend a look that said she hadn't thought of that. "Dave," she called, "have you seen Cal's gear?"

"No, leave me alone."

Clare rolled her eyes. "And you wonder why I look at Neil."

"Why don't we have a walk round the site, talk to a few people, ask if anyone's seen him. We could go up to Ash Lake, see if we can find his gear," Liz suggested.

"Good idea," Clare said. "We'll speak to Minty too, tell her to keep an eye out."

In addition to being site manager, Minty ran the shop and retreat office. She knew everyone and generally had a finger on what was going on. She'd been at Still Waters a while and was the 'go to' person for queries about the retreat or the lodges.

Clare followed her friend out, grateful for the support. "If we do the rounds and no one knows anything, I'm calling the police."

"Before you do that, ask Minty if you can use the landline in the office. Ring your home number, see if Callum is there."

It was a good idea. Liz was a real help. The two of them made their way through the site, stopping to speak to everyone they met. The lodges at Still Waters didn't come cheap but the people who bought them weren't snooty. Generally, they were a friendly bunch, only too pleased to help. However, no one had seen Callum, apart from Bert Hodges, the man who had seen him fishing on Friday night.

"When I packed up he were th'only lad left."

"Did you speak to him?" Clare asked.

"No, he were on th'other side of the lake. It were almost dark and I wanted to be off."

"Would you show us exactly where he was fishing?" Clare asked.

Of the three lakes on the site, Ash was by far the largest and the furthest away. As Birch and Oak were nearer to the lodges, most people fished from those. Clare knew that Callum liked to fish Ash as it contained the biggest fish and he'd have the place to himself.

It took them ten minutes to climb the hill to a spot just above a sloping bank leading down to the water. "He were about here, on one of these pegs," Bert said, pointing at the wooden planks at the water's edge. "I waved as I left, and he waved back."

"Did he look okay?"

"Yes. He was drinking by the looks of it."

"Was anyone with him, no one hanging about nearby?" Clare asked.

"No, it were just him and me."

"Thanks, Bert. We'll have a look round, see what we can find."

Liz pointed at something metallic lying in the grass. "Look. There's a lager can. It's Callum's brand too."

Clare had picked up a stick and was poking around in the reeds by the water's edge. "No sign of his gear." She stopped and looked around. "I don't understand it, Liz. What's happened to him? Why didn't he come back Friday night?"

But Liz wasn't listening. She was bending over a patch of grass. "Clare! Over here. I think this is blood."

* * *

Clare took one look at the blood and lost it. Clutching onto her friend, she called out Callum's name. "He's hurt, has to be. Oh God. I have to find him, find out what's happened to my son."

"We'll go and see Minty like I said, use her phone," Liz replied. "Before you do anything, you ring home and make sure he's not there."

"Why would he go home and not tell me?" Clare cried. "If something upset him, if he got hurt, Callum would say so, he wouldn't just disappear."

Liz led her friend back down the hill and into the office. "Speak to Minty. She knows everything that goes on here."

But Minty didn't know anything about Callum. "He passed by here on Friday afternoon, heading for Ash, I think."

"There's blood on the grass up there." Clare's voice shook. "He must have had an accident, but where is he now?"

Minty picked up the phone and dialled the number Liz gave her — Clare's hands were shaking too much. "Answer machine," she said. "Anywhere else he could be?"

Clare handed Minty her mobile. "Try Andy on there, he's Cal's best mate."

Another dead end. Andy hadn't heard from him since Thursday night. Minty looked at the two women. "He says there were some blokes in the pub asking for him, the same lot he owed money to."

Clare grabbed the phone from her. "What money?" she yelled to Andy.

"I've no idea. Anyway, they didn't seem too bothered, just said they hoped he was well," Andy said.

Was that a threat? Had Cal taken off because he was scared of them coming after him? "Did you tell them where he'd gone?"

"No, I didn't say much at all. I just bumped into them in the pub in town and they asked about him. Said they hadn't seen him in a while."

"Did you recognise them?" Clare asked.

"They're from that casino Cal used to go to."

"Name! D'you have a name?" By now she was screaming.

"Look, Clare, all I know is that Cal told me he'd sorted it. But the blokes are still hanging around, so maybe he didn't."

"I can't stand this." Clare looked at Minty. "Ring the police, tell them Callum's disappeared and that he could have been set upon and injured."

CHAPTER FOUR

"You're bloody mad, you. Why involve the police?"

"Our son is missing, Dave. There's blood on the ground in the place where he was fishing and I'm worried sick. Anything could have happened to him. I've spoken to everyone on the site and no one's seen him since Friday." Clare paused, giving him time to take this in. "Did you know he was in debt?"

Dave gave a sigh. He knew all right. "He asked me to lend him money a while ago."

"Was he gambling again?"

"Yes, despite all the promises. The lad has a problem, he can't stop."

Clare was about to give her husband a piece of her mind, tell him he should have done something to help his son, but at that moment she caught sight of Minty standing in the open doorway with a uniformed officer in tow.

"This is PC Taylor, he wants a word."

At last, now she might get something done about finding him. "Come in," Clare said. "Our son Callum is missing. We found blood at the lake where he was last seen, so I think he's been hurt."

"But you don't know that for sure," the policeman said. "The blood might not even be human. You've checked all his usual haunts, spoken to his friends?"

Clare was taken aback at his lack of concern. If she was him she'd be straight on it. At least he should want to take a look. "Yes, of course I have. I've tried everyone, and no one has seen or heard of him since Friday. I went to where he was last spotted, by Ash Lake, and that's where we found the blood on the ground."

PC Taylor wrote this down in his notebook. "How old is he?"

"Twenty-four."

He stopped writing. "Old enough to take care of himself then. Are you all on holiday here?"

"We've owned this lodge for five years now. We're here a lot since me and my husband retired. Cal comes too, on and off."

"Any reason he came this week?"

Clare looked at Dave. He obviously wasn't going to say anything, so she'd have to. "He's been staying here for a few weeks this time. He lost his job, so until he gets his head together we thought he might as well." She paused. "There is something else you should know. A mate of Cal's told me there's been some blokes looking for him, saying he owes them money."

The policeman cocked his head. "D'you know who these blokes are?"

"Look, I don't think the money has anything to do with this," Dave said.

"You don't know that," Clare retorted. "They could have scared him, threatened him with God knows what."

"No, they didn't, Clare," he said firmly.

"How can you be so sure?"

"Because I paid them off," he said. He looked at the PC. "My son did owe money to some rough types and they did threaten him, but it's sorted now. I'm positive that whatever happened here, if anything did, it wasn't down to them."

"I'd still like some names," the PC persisted.

"Well, I'm sorry but I can't oblige. That would start things up all over again and it's cost me enough already. Callum is safe from those thugs now and I want it to stay that way."

PC Taylor put his pocketbook away. "He's an adult, free to come and go as he wishes. I'll list him as missing but there's not a lot more we can do."

Clare started to cry. "You haven't even looked at the blood up at Ash Lake."

The PC turned to Minty. "Can you see that the blood or whatever it is gets covered up and I'll ask scenes of crime to take a look." He returned his gaze to Dave and Clare. "But I have to warn you, that could take a day or two. The local crew are busy with a spate of robberies in Tameside."

Dave was right, the police weren't interested. As soon as the PC and Minty left, Clare turned to her husband. "Why didn't you tell me you helped Cal?"

"It was a lot of money and he asked me not to, he didn't want you worried."

"So, there was something to worry about," she said. "This isn't just me being melodramatic."

"He had a bunch of morons after him. He got mixed up with a gang who run a casino down Cheetham Hill way. I met these people and believe me, if I hadn't paid the debt for him, he'd have had no choice but to do a runner or end up in hospital. But it didn't come to that. He hasn't been near that casino in weeks, and the gang are no longer interested. But to be on the safe side I insisted he come here with us, to keep him away from all that."

Clare gave him a weak smile. "Sorry I've been so awful to you, Dave. I had no idea. You should let me in, share stuff."

"Cal asked me not to. He didn't want you knowing how familiar he was with Manchester's gangland."

That made Clare wonder what else Cal was into. What else didn't she know about her son?

"Are you all right, Clare?" The voice at the doorway belonged to Gemma, Neil's wife. "I waited until the copper left. I have to say, he looked a bit young for such a responsible job."

Ignoring the comment, Clare said, "I thought you were going home today?"

"I heard about your Callum and knowing how upset you'd be, I decided to stay." She stepped forward and gave Clare a hug. "I know we've had our differences but a community has to stick together at times like this. I really want to help if I can."

A nice sentiment but it made Clare cringe. She stiffened and looked at Gemma suspiciously. Was this genuine or was she up to something? Clare couldn't tell from her expression but for one fleeting moment she wondered if Gemma was enjoying seeing her pain. Maybe she considered it payback for flirting with her husband.

Gemma smiled. "If you need any help, feel free to call on me. I mean it, Clare. I want to help, to be a friend."

"That's good of you, Gemma, I'll bear it in mind."

CHAPTER FIVE

The police's visit was fleeting. There was blood, so the CSI officers would have to follow it up, though to call it an investigation was pushing it. They'd arrive, look over the bank and take samples. Eventually it would prove to be Callum's blood, but the wait could run to days, weeks even.

She'd chosen well. Callum had a past that offered rich pickings where suspects were concerned. If they did their work properly, the local police could find plenty to investigate. It would dredge up trouble for the family, which would serve them right. She'd no time for Clare, and Dave was nothing but a slob. It was a shame that people like them could afford to buy into the retreat.

The police had Callum down as missing. No further action would be taken because he was an adult, which wasn't the outcome she wanted. She was impatient to get this over with. She'd posted the tweet earlier today. Usually, this would guarantee she got the right interest, but this time there'd been nothing. She looked at her phone. Both internet access and the phone signal were so bad here that the tweet had failed. It was her own fault, she should have checked.

She felt a slight shiver of trepidation, unusual for her. This was important, it had to work. She wanted her life back, for this whole thing to end once and for all. It had gone on far too long, and now she was tired. She'd cross swords with her old enemy one final time, and on this occasion only one of them would walk away.

She stared out over Oak Lake. No one was fishing today. Pity, the conditions were perfect. Suddenly she felt a tap on her shoulder. It was Neil Lewis.

"I know what happened to Callum," he said.

She looked at him, trying to read the expression on his face. "Come on then, don't keep me in suspense."

"You know very well," he said. "I saw you. I watched you dragging him into the boathouse."

"You're mistaken."

"No, I know what I saw. We need to have a chat. I'm sure there's a way round this." He stared at her.

He was talking blackmail. She couldn't allow that to happen. She'd done her research and knew a great deal about everyone who owned a lodge at Still Waters. Neil and his wife hadn't been married long. He was quite a bit older than her. They had money, had to, to afford the fully furnished three- bedroom lodge they'd recently bought. He drove a top-of-the-range sports car and she wore jewellery that made the other women drool. Did they have their own business? High powered jobs? Not a bit of it. Neil was a retired teaching assistant, Gemma a part-time office worker. Everyone who knew them at the retreat wondered where the money came from.

She smiled. Neil Lewis had dangerous enemies — a couple of calls and his association with them would muddy the investigation nicely. He'd brought this on himself. "Okay, meet me here in an hour and we'll have that talk. I'm a reasonable woman. I'm sure we can come to an agreeable arrangement." The stupid man should have kept his mouth shut. Now he'd just made sure he'd be her next victim.

* * *

Clare Hilton cooked a meal that evening and watched Dave wolf his down while she pushed her food around the plate.

"This isn't doing me any good," she complained, wiping tears from her eyes. "I can't do waiting, not knowing what's going on. I can't eat or sleep. Where is he, Dave? Why hasn't our Cal come back?"

"He will, you'll see."

He spoke without even looking up. Clare shook her head. It made no sense for Cal to disappear, so why would he suddenly come back?

Dave mopped up the last of his gravy with a slice of bread. "He'll have gone off on a bender with a mate we don't know about. He finds this place claustrophobic, especially not having anywhere to go at nights."

"There's the pub," Clare said.

"Yes, but it's full of folk our age, not his." He patted her hand. "Don't stress, love. It'll work out, you'll see."

"What about the blood on the bank at Ash Lake?" she said.

"It might not even be Cal's. And if it is, he probably had a bit of an accident. There'll be a reasonable explanation, trust me."

"You did pay off those people who were chasing him?"

"Every penny," he said, and made a face. "Believe me, Clare, his disappearance isn't down to them. He only owed a couple of thousand, a paltry amount to those thugs."

"I can't stop thinking about what might have happened, different possibilities go round and round in my head. This just isn't like him. And why doesn't his mobile work?"

"You know what the signal's like here. Maybe the battery's gone, there could be any number of reasons. Look, love, you have to stop this. Just try and eat something."

Clare wanted to believe Dave. He was clearly doing his best to reassure her, doubtless he was worried too. "If Cal doesn't come back, I doubt I'll ever sleep again."

Someone banged loudly on the door and called out her name.

"That's Liz," Clare said, getting to her feet.

"She might know something," Dave suggested. "She's been out searching again with some of the others."

Clare opened the door to Liz who was deathly white and shaking. She took her arm and drew her inside. "Whatever's the matter? It's not Cal, is it?"

"Neil Lewis has been murdered," Liz whispered.

Clare stared at her in disbelief.

"Murdered, Clare. He was found with his head bashed in. Why him? I don't understand. It must have happened in broad daylight but no one saw a thing."

Clare shook her head, any questions she might have had sticking in her throat. Like Liz, she couldn't understand why anyone would want to kill Neil. She'd liked him, they got on, had a laugh. "I'm scared, Liz. What does this mean for Callum? Has he met the same fate?"

Dave appeared from the bedroom. "Is that Neil you're talking about, Gemma's husband? What happened to him?"

"We found him an hour ago, floating face down in Oak Lake with his head bashed in."

Clare gasped. "Surely it was an accident? Has to be. Who'd want to murder Neil? He was just an ordinary bloke."

"When we spotted him, one of the men thought perhaps he'd had a heart attack — he was a funny colour — but when we got closer you could see the wound on the back of his head."

Liz was holding something back, not wanting to say too much, Clare could tell. Liz knew she was worried sick about Cal and obviously didn't want to worry her unnecessarily. But if Neil had been murdered, the prospect for Cal didn't look good.

Liz swallowed. "We had to wait for the police. Some of the men tried to get him out. It was awful, gruesome. Poor Neil. He'd been beaten about the face and his hands were badly swollen as if someone had stamped on them. They called a doctor and he confirmed the blow to his head was what killed him. He said they'd done it with something metal like a hammer. Clare, his skull was split wide open." At this, she broke down in tears.

CHAPTER SIX

Monday

"What is this place?" DS Jason Hawkes asked as they drove through the main gates of Still Waters. "Some sort of holiday camp, d'you reckon?"

"It's no holiday camp, Jace, just look at the place," his colleague, DC Sadie Fox, said. "Those flower beds, the well-kept grass. That's the work of an expert gardener. It's a country retreat to give it its proper title, and an upmarket one at that. These lodges cost a bloody fortune to buy. If you want one next to a lake, you can add thousands."

"I'd no idea this place was even here. What do they get up to all day?" he asked, seemingly unimpressed.

"Fishing and golf mostly, but there's also the walking. We're only a stone's throw from the Pennine Way."

Jason Hawkes neither fished nor played golf, and as for walking, a stroll through the local park was about as far as he went. He didn't have the time or inclination. Life away from work was taken up with Beth, his wife, and their new baby daughter. Any spare time was given over to sleep not exercise. "What d'you reckon happened to our victim? He must have upset that crew from the farm pretty bad to end up like he did."

They'd had a complaint about a car driving erratically and far too fast around the retreat the previous day. A group of men were shouting at passers-by and throwing rubbish from the windows into the lakes. "Those farm workers have caused trouble all over the area. They get hired, do some work and move on. And they're tanked up most of the time. Neil Lewis must have tackled them at some point so they went for him mob-handed," Sadie Fox said.

"Pity one of the hooligans had that hammer handy. He might have stood a chance otherwise. We'll have to speak to the family," Hawkes said. "They'll want to know the progress we've made."

Sadie Fox looked at the notes she'd been given. "The victim's wife, Gemma, is a good few years younger than he was. No kids and they live in Stockport."

Hawkes nodded. "What did he do for a living?"

"He was a retired teaching assistant at the local college, and she works in an office in Manchester." Sadie Fox pulled a face. "Neither of those says money to me. Wonder if they went into debt to buy the lodge?"

"We're here," Hawkes said. "Number thirty." He stared at the wooden structure in front of him. It was large with a tiled roof, double glazed windows, and a decent-sized veranda with flower beds all around. "Looks nice, well-kept like the rest of the site. Pricy patio set too, I know because me and Beth have been looking. We've decided it'll have to be stuff for the inside of the house first."

Sadie grinned at the pained expression on his young face. "Oh dear. Sergeant's wage biting already, is it?"

Ignoring her comment, Hawkes got out of the car and knocked on the door. "Mrs Lewis? You in?"

It was Clare Hilton who came out to greet them. She'd been sitting with Gemma, trying to console her. "Police? We're in here."

"I want my friend to stay with me," Gemma said at once. "I don't think I can do this on my own."

"It's just a chat, Mrs Lewis, nothing heavy," Hawkes assured her. "Before we start, both me and my colleague here are sorry for your loss."

That brought on another flood of tears.

"I'd like to go over with you the events of yesterday," Hawkes said, gently. "Are you up to doing that?"

Gemma gulped. "I was out with Clare and the others most of the morning, asking folk if they'd seen her missing son, Callum."

Here, Clare interrupted. "Can I just say, it's taken you long enough to get round to speaking to us. Neil was killed yesterday afternoon, and a day later there's still no sign of any investigation or forensics. With the rain we had overnight, won't any evidence be useless by now?"

"The forensic people know what they're doing," Hawkes said. "And it's a straightforward enough case. We've already arrested four men who've been working at a farm a couple of miles away."

It was good news. Clare took Gemma's hand. "Are you sure it's them who killed Neil?"

"Yes. We found the, er, weapon they used in the boot of a car belonging to one of them. We know they were here yesterday — they were seen racing around the site in the afternoon and we received a complaint," Hawkes said.

"They're locked up?" Gemma asked.

Jason Hawkes nodded. "And they'll stay that way until the trial."

"Quick work, you've done well," Clare said approvingly.

"You said you were speaking to people about a Callum. Who's he?" Hawkes asked.

"My son," Clare replied. "He's disappeared without trace. After what's happened to Neil, I can't help worrying that something dreadful has happened to him too — you know, that the incidents might be connected."

"You reported it?" Hawkes asked.

"Yes, but nothing's been done."

Sadie Fox cleared her throat. "I doubt they are connected. No attempt was made to hide the victim yesterday, so if your son had been attacked it's probable he'd have been found by now. Are you sure he hasn't simply gone home?"

"He wouldn't do that without telling me," Clare insisted. "Despite what you say, Neil's murder has me worried that something has happened to Callum. He could be lying injured somewhere."

"Aren't we getting ahead of ourselves?" Sadie Fox said. "Most likely he'll turn up soon."

"Even so, surely you'll look more closely at Callum's disappearance now?" Clare asked hopefully.

"With respect, we have nothing to suggest that anything untoward has happened to your son," Hawkes said. "Mr Lewis was murdered. We've interviewed his killers and they've said nothing about your son. We have no reason to think that any harm has come to him."

Clare raised her eyes to the ceiling. In her opinion this was the police doing what they did best, wriggling out of spending money on a full scale investigation. "I hope for your sakes you're right. Because if there's the slightest hint that you're wrong, I'll sue."

"You're upset," Sadie Fox said. "Try all your son's contacts, his workplace and anywhere else you think he might have gone. If you get nowhere after that, we'll look at the case again."

"I've already done all that," Clare said. "We've also spoken to everyone on the retreat. No one saw Callum the night he disappeared except Bert Hodges. We're not experts, we don't have your facilities, but after what's happened to Neil I don't consider simply listing him as missing enough."

"We will look into it but it'll take time and the murder has to take precedence," Hawkes said.

"Shouldn't there be a DI or someone in charge of Neil's murder investigation?" Gemma asked.

"There is," Hawkes said. "DI Hopwood, but he's busy in court today. He'll come up here and speak to you when he can."

Clare was shocked. "When he can? What sort of an answer is that? Gemma's husband is dead, my son is missing. Don't you see that there could be a connection? I'm no detective but even I can see that it needs investigating."

"They are two very different cases, Mrs Hilton," Hawkes said.

Gemma burst into tears again. Clare put an arm around her and glared at the detectives. "Go. Go on, get out of here. You're just making things worse. With regard to my son, when you get back to your station, tell your superior from me that I'm not happy."

Hawkes got to his feet. "There will be a police presence on the site for the time being. If anything occurs, or you hear anything about your son, you can speak to them."

Clare showed the pair out, disappointed and upset. They were from CID, she'd expected more. She was beginning to think that Callum's disappearance would never be explained.

* * *

The people from CID didn't stay long and looked relieved to be leaving. That would be the Clare effect. At the very least, they should look around, ask questions, get on everyone's nerves and create a general atmosphere of suspicion. That's what police did. She supposed that as far as they were concerned they'd caught the killers and that was that. But what about a motive? Had one even been considered? Was it robbery? Someone out for revenge? She knew what she'd ask. But according to Clare, they hadn't asked much at all. Their ineptness amused her. If they'd spoken to the right people, thought about it instead of grabbing at the obvious, they could have worked it out. But that was asking too much. A souped up car, lads making a first-class nuisance of themselves, finding the murder weapon in the boot of their vehicle and the case was solved. So much for the local CID.

Seeing the lads racing around the narrow lanes of the site yesterday had given her an idea. She knew they were local and drank in the village pub every night. Once Neil Lewis had been despatched, she'd taken the hammer used to kill him and put it in the boot of their car while they were getting bladdered.

Simple and effective. Unable to stay out of trouble, they got into a fight in the pub, which meant the landlord calling the station. The constable who attended found drugs on one of them, which led to a search of their vehicle and bingo, the weapon was found. The police had their killers.

Now it was night, the site was quiet. After what had happened no one ventured out of their lodges after dark. The fishing and golf had all but stopped. As far as the local force was concerned, Callum had done a runner from his parents and Neil Lewis's killers were safe behind bars. Even so, the place was rife with gossip and everyone was scared of their own shadow.

The trap was set. It was time to up the game, play her trump card. A second post on Twitter, a few choice words under the familiar hashtag and she'd soon be doing battle with her old nemesis again.

CHAPTER SEVEN

Tuesday

A piercing scream — sharp, desperate, the cry of a man hurtling to his death. Seconds later it was over. The sound lingered for a while, reverberating against the walls, until there was nothing but silence.

Alice Rossi's eyes snapped open. Common sense told her it was a dream, but for a moment she was lost, as if she was wandering in thick fog and struggling to know which way to go. *It's not real,* she told herself. *I've buried it.* But still the old horror refused to leave her, occupying her waking thoughts and troubling her rest.

It took only seconds for Alice to realise she'd been saved from the nightmare by the ring of her mobile. She eased herself up in bed and looked at the screen. The caller was Superintendent Osbourne.

"Sir?"

"She's back."

Two short words. Alice immediately knew what they meant, and her stomach lurched.

"Two hours ago a DC on social media observation spotted a tweet. To quote, '*Come out and play one last time, Alice. Still*

Waters run deep.' She used the usual hashtag, 'Mad Hatter' and signed off 'see you soon.'"

Alice's heart was racing. *Why now*? It had been almost two years and she had begun to hope that 'Mad Hatter' was no more, that she'd taken on someone who'd finally got the better of her and met a grisly end. *Wishful thinking*. "I had no idea we still had people looking out for her, sir."

"We have no choice. There are outstanding cases, murders with her name on them. I'm sorry to dump this on you at such short notice, Alice, but you know I have no choice."

And that was what made dealing with Mad Hatter all the scarier. "Do we have anything other than the one tweet?"

"No, but a trace has been actioned. It looks like she used a mobile that pinged a mast in Tameside — Hyde to be exact — but what's the betting that phone is no more."

"Do we have any idea what she's done, if she's killed someone this time?"

"No, and there's nothing in the tweet to tell us what she's up to. I hate to say it, Alice, but if you're not appointed senior investigating officer she'll disappear with no guarantee that she'll turn up again and we'll have missed our chance."

Alice closed her eyes and laid her head back on the pillow. This wasn't how she'd planned to spend the last months of her career.

"I wish I could give you an explanation, Alice, tell you why she's back and playing her sick game with you once again, but I can't."

Alice could. She knew exactly why it had to be her, but it wasn't something she could share, not even with Osbourne.

"If we stand any chance at all of bringing her to justice, then we have to do things her way," he said.

"Can we narrow her location down, sir? Hyde is a sizeable area," Alice said.

"Not yet, and she might not be operating in Hyde. We need to decipher what the tweet means and fast. I'll meet you at the station in central Manchester in an hour. Wherever she is, whatever she's up to, we have to stop her this time, Alice."

Easier said than done, but then he didn't know the half of it.

* * *

Since her husband's death six years ago, Alice Rossi had lived alone in the house they'd shared. The large three-storey Edwardian terrace in Openshaw on the outskirts of Manchester had been left to her by her parents many years ago. The town had had its heyday back in the time when cotton was king. Today it was traffic-ridden with its fair share of problems. Not that any of that bothered Alice. Apart from the nightmares, her home was her haven from the harsh reality of her job, and the only place she got any peace.

She heard someone call up the stairs, "The larder needs a top up. Want me to do a shop?"

"Dilys, what're you doing here at this time? It's barely light," Alice shouted back.

"I want to finish by lunchtime and I've got you and Mrs Kenyon to see to today. After that, I'm off to my book club."

Dilys cleaned for Alice, and also did the shopping and anything else that needed doing. She had worked for Alice since the death of her husband, Paul, and was a real godsend. "Get the usual stuff, will you? And don't stint on the wine. I've got a tricky case on."

"Sitting in this huge house every night drinking on your own isn't good for you, you know. You need a man to keep you company."

No, she didn't. Alice had no wish to tread that path again. "Don't you worry. Me and this house do just fine."

Alice put her work clothes on the bed and went for a shower. Dilys meant well but she didn't know the ins and outs of Alice's life. She thought the wine was a problem — how would she react if she knew Alice had a murdering psychopath on her tail?

Fifteen minutes later, showered and dressed in a plain dark suit and white shirt, Alice stared at her reflection in the dressing table mirror. She was showing her age. There were lines under her eyes and her skin looked sallow from lack of fresh air. She'd meant to get her hair cut, have it reshaped into the short bob that suited her. That would have to wait. For the foreseeable there would be no time for visits to the hairdressers. The Mad Hatter case would take up every waking hour. She pulled a brush through the straight damp locks and wished she'd been blessed with thicker hair that she could actually do something with. A face that didn't look odd in make-up would be handy too. Other women her age managed to pull off the fresh out of the beauty parlour look but apply a little lipstick and blusher to her face and Alice's make-up looked like it'd been done by a five-year-old.

Alice was fifty, with over twenty-nine years in the service behind her, during which she'd risen to DCI. She worked in the Greater Manchester Serious Crime Squad. It was a large area to cover and crime didn't get any easier, but a few more months and she'd be able to retire. That should be a cheery thought but it wasn't. It contrasted with her belief that for her, life without her job was no life at all.

Since Paul's death, work had become the support Alice relied on. Not because she'd lost Paul and missed him, because she didn't. It was work that stopped the dark thoughts and memories from driving her mad.

Shortly before Paul's death, Alice had been at breaking point, seriously doubting that she could take much more. The truth of what went on between them was still able to terrify her, it was part of the horror that haunted her sleep. Memories of her husband's violence those last few days of their marriage. Add to that Mad Hatter's hatred and it was a heady mix. Not that she could discuss any of this with Osbourne, or anyone else.

Paul had been an abusive partner, which was one of the reasons she was now more at peace than she had been in years. At the first opportunity she'd reverted back to her maiden name of Rossi and tried to forget she ever was Mrs Paul Hunter. It was something her son, Michael, found hard to come to terms with. She'd never discussed his father's behaviour with him, or her true feelings. How could she? Michael had idolised his father.

Osbourne rarely asked about her private life or Paul's death, which suited her just fine, though she knew he was intensely curious about Mad Hatter. Why had the killer fixated on Alice? Why her and not somebody else? He had come to the conclusion that Alice had been seen making an appeal on the television at some time, or been observed in court.

Only Alice knew the truth.

CHAPTER EIGHT

GMP Serious Crime Squad was based in a nondescript-looking building in Ardwick, just a stone's throw from the city centre. Alice left her car in the underground car park and took the lift to the third floor. Superintendent Frank Osbourne was waiting for her. A man several years older than herself, his shock of untidy grey hair appeared more ruffled than ever — he looked shattered. The poor man must have been up half the night.

He pointed to a large screen on the far wall of the main office. "What d'you make of it?"

It was the tweet Mad Hatter had sent. "Usual opening, asking for me and the same hashtag as always, but the second bit is interesting and that's where the clue is. Still Waters?" Alice folded her arms and moved closer, studying the words on the screen. "Two words and both start with a capital letter. It's a name," she said. "A place perhaps, a village or a business. Has anyone done a search?"

"There's a restaurant in Glasgow, by the River Clyde," a young PC said.

"Too far," Alice said. "Mad Hatter usually keeps things relatively local, and the tweet was sent from somewhere in Hyde."

She turned to Osbourne. "Until we know exactly where she is, there's not much we can do. What about the tweet? Have we got anything else on that?"

"One last time, Alice, what d'you reckon she means by it?" Osbourne said.

"She's tired of the game, just like me."

"I've had communications on it, ma'am, and the report has just come through. Not much use I'm afraid, nothing we don't already know," PC Wallis said.

"Is the phone still active?" Alice asked, knowing the answer.

"No."

"Hyde. Not too far away." Alice nodded. She turned to the PC. "Restrict your search to both 'Still Waters' and any ongoing murder investigations in the greater Manchester area, particularly Tameside and Hyde, and see what turns up."

"We'll have to decide on a team," Osbourne said. "Any preference?"

Over the years, Alice had worked with many officers. Some she'd liked, got on with, and some she'd found hard work. Her last partner was a DI Angela Hardy. The two had been constantly at loggerheads until, to Alice's relief, Hardy had transferred out to Leeds. That left her with no one at the moment.

"I'd prefer to wait and see what comes out of the PC's search," she told Osbourne. "If this has already started, and I'd be surprised if it hasn't, then there'll be an officer already on the case. If you have no objections, I'll use them."

Osbourne nodded. "Good call, Alice. I'll leave the choice to you but keep me informed."

"What about the Robbie Barrett case, sir?"

"I'll assign another officer." He shrugged. "We have no choice, do we?"

Robbie Barrett was a Manchester villain they suspected of being responsible for a shooting in a city club. Alice had been on the case but wasn't getting anywhere. No one who'd been in the club that night would talk, and there was no sign of the gun. Fortunately the victim, one Barry Holden, was still alive, just, and he'd pointed the finger at Barrett. But without corroborative evidence, it was just the victim's word against Barrett's.

Osbourne picked up his briefcase ready to leave. "Whoever takes over, they'll find everything they need on the system. I'll get back to my own office. I've got a report to prepare for my meeting with the ACC later today."

* * *

It took PC Roger Wallis less than fifteen minutes to find DS Jason Hawkes's report on the murder at Still Waters. With a beaming smile on his face, he passed the printed sheet of information to Alice, who was sitting at a spare desk in the main office.

"Good work," she said, and skimmed through the report. One DI Hopwood was officially in charge but it had been a DS Jason Hawkes who'd made the arrests and spoken to the family. Four young males drinking in a local pub caused a fracas and the landlord called the police. The four became argumentative and lashed out at the PC. They were all arrested, searched and drugs were found on one of them. That led to a search of their vehicle and the discovery of the murder weapon in the boot.

Knowing no different, DS Hawkes must have thought he'd done a good job. Solving the murder had been quick, efficient, good for the statistics but totally wrong. Mad Hatter had played them all. She must be laughing her socks off at the police. Alice knew how she operated. Mad Hatter saw this as a game, one she must win. DS Hawkes had proved he was easy to fool. He offered no competition but how could he? He'd no idea what he was up against.

Alice didn't know how long she could continue to do this. To her colleagues it must look like just another murder case, and there had been plenty of them over the years.

Murderers came in all shapes and sizes — drug dealers, gang members, even people close to the police, but Mad Hatter was different. She was unlike any killer Alice had ever encountered. She killed only to tempt Alice to enter the fray, to taunt her. She'd threatened more than once that the deadly game would only continue for so long. Then, when the time came, Alice herself would become her final victim.

Was this her last outing? Was Mad Hatter finally calling time?

CHAPTER NINE

Alice was seated at DS Hawkes's desk in the Tameside station re-reading the report he'd written, while waiting for him to return from lunch. As he came through the door another officer gave her the nod. She watched Hawkes chat to his colleagues, and joke his way to her side. Alice put him at no more than thirty. He was tall and gangly with fair hair cut very short, dressed smartly in a dark suit, white shirt and tie.

"My desk," he said with a grin.

"DCI Alice Rossi, serious crime squad," she parried, showing him her badge. "Tell me about Still Waters."

He smiled, self-satisfied. "Bit of a coup that one." The grin got wider. "Fell into my lap — killers, weapon, the lot."

He had a lot to learn. "No, Sergeant, it was *thrown* into your lap, like chucking a bone to a dog. You got it wrong, all of it. You've been manipulated by an expert."

"No way," he said, turning red.

"No way, *ma'am*. Believe me, Sergeant Hawkes, there's a far brighter mind than yours at work here."

"How can you know that? It was me who worked the case. I spoke to the suspects, brought them in." He almost stamped his foot.

This one liked to argue the toss. He wasn't for giving up his arrest easily, hopefully he'd learn. "I've come across this killer before. I know how she works, her style, the messages she sends and how much she enjoys winding me up."

"Her? Messages? What messages?" Now he looked confused. "Why hasn't anyone passed them over to me?"

Alice passed him a printed copy of the tweet. He read it, his look of confusion deepening.

"What does it mean? Who's this Alice?"

"Alice is me." She smiled. "Mad Hatter is the killer. We don't know her real name, she's never used it."

"Like in the book, *Alice in Wonderland*."

"Exactly. Though I certainly wouldn't call it Wonderland. Her world is no fairy tale, believe me."

"You said 'she'. How d'you know that? And if you know who killed that man, Neil Lewis, why haven't you brought her in yourself?" Hawkes asked.

"It's not that simple. We don't know her name and we've never met. All I know for sure is that she's a woman in her early forties. I only know that because of a snippet of CCTV I got my hands on. As for being able to identify her, there's no way. The film wasn't that good."

Hawkes was silent for a while, digesting this, his expression slowly changing as it dawned on him what this meant. He looked so thoroughly deflated that for a moment, Alice felt sorry for him. She'd turned up out of the blue, rubbished his detective skills and stolen his desk. She'd be pretty pissed off too.

"Still Waters. What sort of a place is it?"

"A rural retreat," he said. "Whatever one of those is. It's up in the hills, off the beaten track along the old Woodhead Road at the back of the reservoirs above Glossop. The people who go there are mostly retired. They own the lodges — very nice they are too — fish the three lakes, play golf and generally doss about."

Alice had a map of the area up on the computer screen. "Show me its exact location."

"Here's the Greater Manchester/Derbyshire border. Still Waters is there." He pointed. "Lovely countryside if you like that sort of thing, but it is a bit out of the way."

Alice logged off the system and stood up. "Right then, let's take a look, shall we?"

He looked surprised. "You want me to come with you?"

"Yes, Sergeant. You can talk me through what you know about the killing on the way."

"I'm working with you then?" he asked.

"On the Still Waters case, yes. I had a word with your DI Hopwood before you returned from lunch and he's happy to release you for the duration."

"You told him your theory, about the arrests?"

She sighed. "It's not a theory, Sergeant. I've also arranged for the hammer to be sent to the forensic lab at Manchester Central, my own station. Despite arresting the wrong killer, I suspect you got the right weapon. Mad Hatter has used a hammer before."

"Will the farm workers be released?"

"I imagine so. It was a flimsy case anyway." She smiled.

"How d'you make that out? Ma'am."

"The hammer was found in the boot of an unlocked car. The legal people would have driven a bus through that one."

"Hopwood seemed happy enough."

Alice gave him an unimpressed look. "You need to consider your career and ask yourself if people like Hopwood are doing it any good."

"I've never thought about it like that, ma'am."

"I can see you haven't." She smiled again. "Now, this retreat. You've spoken to the family of the murdered man?"

"His wife. She was in bits, could barely tell me anything at all. She had a gobby friend with her, did nothing but criticise the investigation."

"Had a point, didn't she?"

"This friend, Clare Hilton, told me her son is missing. He went fishing on one of the lakes and never returned. The mother has asked everyone but no one has seen him and he's not answering his phone."

Alice's heart sank. She knew what that meant. "He's very likely another victim," she said. "It's a pattern I'm familiar with. At least one victim is left in the open to be found. She posts the tweet to get my attention but almost every time I've been on a Mad Hatter case there have been others, brutally killed, sometimes dismembered, and hidden away. She likes to make us work."

"You sure about this? That this missing bloke is dead?"

"Yes, Sergeant, I think he is, but not a word to the family until we know for certain."

"You reckon we're chasing some psychopath who likes to bludgeon people to death?" he said.

"Yes, I do. Me and this killer have done battle before. I know her methods and what buttons she likes to press."

CHAPTER TEN

"What do you think?" DCI Alice Rossi looked out at the expanse of lake and shivered. She cast her eyes skywards. Needle Crag, the highest of the hills surrounding the lakes, loomed above them. It was a place she knew well and she hated it with every fibre of her being.

"Who knows, he could be down there but it'll cost to find out."

She turned on her heel and strode off, back to the main path. There would be other expenses too — they wouldn't catch Mad Hatter on the cheap. "Sort it," she called back. "Get the divers in and let's see what they find."

"Will your boss go for it?"

"The wording in that tweet — *Still Waters run deep,* remember? We have no choice but to check it out." Though Alice doubted it was that simple. The wording, the choice of location, was it one huge bluff? She looked up at the peaks again and shuddered. The last time she'd been on Needle Crag, she'd vowed never to return. Did Mad Hatter know that? In that case this was no bluff, the location had been carefully chosen. Just the thought of it scared her witless.

Hawkes followed her to the path. "It seems she's a crafty one, this Mad Hatter. Just thinking about her gives me the creeps."

"Now you know how I feel."

"D'you reckon she's here? She could be staying in one of the lodges. They've got three that are let to holidaymakers on a weekly basis."

A scary thought indeed. She had no idea what the woman even looked like, but it was likely Mad Hatter would recognise her. As far as Alice was aware, they'd never met face to face, but being a high ranking police officer, her photo had occasionally been in the papers.

"Her usual routine is to absent herself from the crime scene once the killing spree is over," she said. "I don't get invited to the game until she's long gone. But this time it feels different. It'll depend on what happens next."

"If there's another killing, you mean?"

Alice nodded. "One last time — remember the wording. That alone tells me this time it'll be different. If she kills during the investigation it will be a huge deviation from her routine."

Alice stopped walking and took a deep breath of the cool fresh air. "D'you trust your instincts, Hawkes?" The young DS nodded. "Well, mine tell me you're right. She wants this to be the last time, so I think she's here, watching us. More than that, this time she'll try to steer the investigation a certain way."

"You say you've never met, but you appear to know a lot about her."

A fair point. "I've been after this one for a long time. I've worked on all her killings, seen what she did to her victims. Despite never meeting her, I do feel as if I know her well."

"And the tech boys couldn't clean up the CCTV footage you got?" Hawkes asked.

"No, it was dark and the camera that took it had a cracked lens," she said.

"Why doesn't she like you? Why go to all this trouble to get you on the case?"

Alice shrugged. "I've no idea, Sergeant." It was a blatant lie, she knew the reason very well. "Habit, perhaps."

"Weird though, isn't it? Becoming fixated like this and going to the extreme of killing to get your attention."

Alice shivered. "She's a psychopath. Does there have to be a reason for what they do?"

"I suppose not, but this one is a first for me. What's next, ma'am?"

"We speak to people. The parents of Callum Hilton and the widow of the victim, Neil Lewis. Once we've got statements from them, we'll speak to everyone else here."

Jason Hawkes whistled. "That's a lot of interviews."

"I know, but it can't be helped."

They were on the narrow roadway that ran through the site. Most of the lodges were situated off this but there were some larger ones on the banks of Oak and Birch lakes.

Hawkes pointed to one of those. "That one belongs to the Hiltons. You should speak to them, it's their son that's missing."

Alice nodded. "You take a walk round. Remember, we're interested in women around forty years of age. Without arousing suspicion, try and get the names of anyone matching that description, and which lodge they are staying in."

* * *

Clare Hilton stood at the door of her lodge, arms folded. "You're with that detective who spoke to Gemma yesterday. He was no use at all, so what makes you any different?"

Straight and to the point. "I'm DCI Alice Rossi and I've been appointed senior officer in the murder of Mr Lewis and the disappearance of your son."

That got more enthusiasm. Clare's eyes lit up. She was a woman in her sixties with blonde hair cut to chin length. "You're taking it seriously then? You believe that Callum's missing and he hasn't just gone off somewhere? Thank God for that. Come in, I'll tell you what I know."

Alice followed her inside and sat on the sofa. Clare turned to her husband. "Put the kettle on, Dave, make the detective a cup of tea." She handed Alice a sheet of paper. "I've made a timeline, listed all the things Callum did that day, what he told us, that sort of thing. He'd gone fishing with instructions not to be late — we were having people round and I wanted him here. To be honest, we all had a bit to drink and I didn't notice how late it was, or that Callum hadn't come home. It was only the next morning that Dave saw he hadn't slept in his bed."

Alice scanned the sheet and put it in her folder of notes. "Callum wasn't upset about anything, was he? He didn't tell you he might be off somewhere for a few days?"

"No, he was fine staying here."

"Your husband told my colleague that Callum had been victimised by people he owed money to," Alice said.

"Dave paid the debt, so there's no reason for them to be interested in Callum anymore."

Alice nodded. "Even so, it'd help to know who they are. Any investigations will be discreet."

Clare looked doubtful but returning from the kitchen, Dave nodded. "I'll give you their names, but I want no come-backs. They're a bad lot and I don't want them on our tails."

Alice nodded. "I understand. Rest assured that I'll do everything in my power to find out what's happened to your son, but you have to be honest with me. Don't hold anything back."

"What happened to Neil Lewis was dreadful, it shocked us all. I'm terrified something similar has happened to my Callum," Clare said.

She was looking for reassurance that Alice couldn't give her. "We can't say anything until we've done more work. Hopefully we'll know more soon."

"D'you think he's dead?" Having said the words aloud, Clare immediately went pale with shock.

"We can't be sure of anything until we've investigated further. Has your son ever been in trouble with the police?" Alice asked.

"No, of course not, he's always been a good lad. Why d'you ask?"

"If he had, his DNA would be on record," Alice explained. "Have you got something of Callum's I could take away, a toothbrush perhaps?"

Clare went off to the bathroom, returning with a toothbrush. "Here," she said. "I know what this is for, I'm not daft. Your forensic people will check for Callum's blood on that hammer you lot found. While you're at it, have a look at the blood on the bank by Ash Lake. I saw it for myself when I was out with Liz looking for him. I told the uniformed officer that came here but he just asked Minty — she's the manager — to cover it up."

"I'll check it out," Alice said, putting the brush into an evidence bag.

Clare began to sob. "You won't say it out loud, but you think he's dead, like Neil. I could feel in my bones that he wasn't coming back. A mother knows these things." She looked Alice up and down. "D'you have kids?"

"One, a son, and he's only a couple of years older than Callum."

"Live close by, does he?"

"No, he went to university in Edinburgh and has lived up there ever since. Now he's an accountant and married with a son of his own," Alice said.

"You're a granny, you're lucky. If Callum's dead, that puts an end to grandchildren for me and Dave. He's an only child, you see."

"Are you sure there is nowhere Callum could be? A girlfriend's, perhaps?" Alice asked.

Clare shook her head. "I've spoken to his friends — those I know of — but if he had plans, he'd have told us. I keep praying he'll just come walking through that door with some daft excuse, but he won't, will he?" she wailed.

Alice got to her feet. This was hard on the emotions. "Do you intend to stay at the retreat a bit longer?"

"We're here all summer, love," Clare said. "The place cost us enough, so we make the most of it."

"I'll appoint an officer to act as family liaison for both you and Mrs Lewis. I'll make sure you're kept in the loop at all stages of the investigation. Let me have that list of names as soon as you can, Mr Hilton." She looked at each of them. "We will find out what happened to your son, trust me."

"You haven't had your tea," Clare said.

"Sorry, work to do," Alice said gently. "I'll see myself out."

CHAPTER ELEVEN

Outside the Hiltons' lodge, Alice checked her notes. Gemma Lewis lived three lodges up. She'd have a word, introduce herself and then call it a day, returning tomorrow for a more in-depth interview. Looking at the details, she read that Gemma was forty-two. Despite being the wife of a victim, she did fit the Mad Hatter profile. Something to bear in mind.

The woman who opened the door eyed Alice with some hostility. She was tall and willowy with long dark hair that had streaks of blonde through it. She was younger than most of the others with lodges on the retreat by some twenty years or more. "Frankly, I've had enough of you lot. You got it all wrong last time. The other one was certain it was down to those lads from the farm."

"That was unfortunate but it wasn't his fault. DS Hawkes was following up on evidence and that's where it led him."

"So, what now?"

"I'd like to know who you're friendly with on the retreat, the people you and your husband mix with. Did he have any enemies here or back home?"

Gemma's face contorted with anger. "It wasn't one of our friends who killed him, and certainly no one else here either. They're a great bunch, the folk on the retreat."

"May I come in? We can't really discuss this on the doorstep," Alice said.

Gemma led the way into the sitting room. This lodge was far more spacious than the Hiltons' — top of the range, and so were the furnishings. Alice had checked their background, and on paper at least, no way could they afford this on their earnings. She wondered about an inheritance, and made a note to investigate.

A woman was seated on the sofa. Gemma introduced her as Erica, "a friend of mine. She's staying with me for a few days."

Alice nodded. Another woman in her forties. "D'you have a lodge here?"

"Yes, I share it with my sister, Emily, but I couldn't leave Gemma on her own, she's much too shocked and upset."

"Do you fish?" Alice asked.

"No, we come for the golf — well, Emily does. I just like the peace and quiet. Emily took early retirement, so we spend most of our time here."

Turning back to Gemma, Alice asked, "Have you owned your lodge for long?"

She glared at her. "Why the questions? I didn't kill Neil, he was my husband — or are you lot so desperate you'll pin his death on anyone you come across?"

Erica sank back into the cushions and fixed her gaze on Alice. The intensity of the dislike in her dark eyes made Alice shiver. She cleared her throat. "Are you aware of anyone in your husband's life away from the retreat who'd want to harm him?"

"No, I'm not. We're just ordinary folk who live in an ordinary house on a quiet street."

Alice smiled at her. "I've looked at the notes we have. Neil had a fairly mundane job, as do you. How did you manage to afford this place?"

Gemma gave her a filthy look. "We're careful, that's how. Neil saved all his bonuses from work."

Alice whistled. "Must be some bonus. Did you get a loan to buy the lodge?"

"We might have done, I can't remember. Neil saw to all that, and anyway, what's it got to do with his murder? For God's sake, just find who killed him instead of sticking your nose into my business."

"Sorry, Mrs Lewis, but it's my job." Alice could see she wasn't going to get a straight answer today, besides, the woman had just lost her husband. She decided to leave it for now. "There will be an officer here you can talk to should you recall anything." She smiled again. "Rest assured, Mrs Lewis, we'll do everything in our power to catch the person responsible for your husband's death."

* * *

Alice made her way to the office at the entrance to the retreat, intending to ask about vacant lodges. If the team wanted to know what made this place tick, they needed to really know both the place and the people. One way to do this was to move into a lodge for the duration, provided one was free. Certainly the FLO should be based here, and possibly herself for some of the time.

She met Hawkes on the path. "There's a lot of people here. Some are happy to talk, some not. I've started to make that list of women in their forties," he said.

"I'm thinking of staying over some nights," Alice said, "save on the travel. What about you? Fancy sharing a lodge? It's a long way to come every day."

"For you perhaps, but I only live a few miles away in Ashton. Besides, the wife would go bananas. We've got a new baby, and she likes me home nights to share the pain."

"Poor you, I can just about remember what that was like." She smiled. "If the manager can find us one, I'll text you the number and we'll meet there in the morning."

Leaving Hawkes at the office door, Alice went inside.

A small, thin woman in her fifties greeted her with a smile. "I'm Minty, the manager. You're that new detective from Manchester, aren't you? Can I help?"

Alice nodded. "DCI Rossi, and that's my problem — being from Manchester, I mean. It'd be a great help if I could stay here occasionally, and apart from me there will be an officer based here all the time until the case is resolved. Are there any lodges empty? The force will pay the going rent."

"Number thirty-five is empty," Minty said. "It's one of three we let to holidaymakers. Three bedrooms and all mod cons — that do you?"

"Thanks," Alice said, and Minty handed her the keys. "How does it work, the retreat? Is it open all year round?"

"Ten months, we're closed December and January. Our residents buy the lodges and pay ground rent each year. They're free to come and go as often as they choose when we're open. A lot of them are retired and they tend to spend a lot of their time here."

"Who owns the site?" Alice asked.

"Maxine Hamilton," Minty said. "She lives in that large stone farmhouse you'll have seen on the other side of the road as you came through the main gates. Mrs Hamilton owns this piece of land and the area surrounding her home. Work has already started on setting up Still Waters Two over there. Mind you, she's rarely here. She's got a place in Spain and spends most of her time there with her bloke."

"Make money does it, a business like this?"

Minty nodded. "For a start, the lodge owners pay several thousand pounds ground rent each year."

"Lucrative then — that is if you own the land. D'you have Wi-Fi up here?"

Minty shook her head. "It's not guaranteed, I'm afraid. Some of the residents get a signal on their phones and there's a hotspot if you don't mind slumming it outside."

Alice nodded. "Don't worry, I'll sort something. How long have you worked here?"

"These last ten years."

"In that case, you'll know all the lodge owners. I've had my sergeant out this afternoon compiling a list of women in their forties who have a lodge here or any connection to the place, but I doubt it'll be complete."

"Can I ask why you want it?" Minty said curiously.

"It's simply part of our investigation," Alice replied.

"I can print you off a list of all the owners and regular visitors. I'll go through it and put their age. It won't be exact, but to be honest there aren't that many people under sixty who own lodges here."

"Thanks, Minty. You should know that we're sending divers into each of the lakes tomorrow. Fishing will have to go on hold for the duration, I'm afraid."

"No problem, I'll let everyone know and I'll ring Mrs Hamilton later."

"I'll be back in the morning with my stuff."

* * *

Mad Hatter was pleased. Alice was a worthy opponent, she always put up a good fight and never ceased to surprise her. This battle, however, would be different, this time the tables would be turned and Alice would get her own fair share of surprises.

Starting with Neil Lewis. Alice should know how he really earned his money and who he worked for. If riled, his old employers could cause no end of trouble. One phone call was all it would take. The resulting fallout would tie up resources and take the heat off her.

The second surprise was more personal, really pressing the worry button. It'd do no harm to mix it up a little, get what little family Alice had involved in her work and the danger.

CHAPTER TWELVE

Alice was relieved to be back in the familiar territory of Openshaw. The wildness of the hills, particularly in that part of the Pennines, freaked her out. She couldn't look at the landscape without thinking of Paul.

Paul Hunter had been an avid walker and potholer. He knew several stretches of the Pennines in the Manchester area like the back of his hand. The walks were okay, Alice had no problem with donning her hiking boots and tramping along with him, but she wasn't comfortable with potholing. She had only ever gone with him to keep the peace — confined spaces, damp, fetid air and slimy rocks really weren't her thing. Now that Paul was dead, she was more than happy to remain a city girl.

Alice sat on the hearthrug in front of the open fireplace in her sitting room and studied the notes on the investigation so far. There wasn't much. Osbourne had rung earlier, the divers were scheduled for tomorrow. They'd scour all three lakes. If Callum Hilton's body was lurking in the depths of any one of them, they'd find it.

The trill of her mobile disturbed the silence. It was her son, Michael. "Everything all right?" she began. He wasn't a frequent caller, once a fortnight at the most. When his father, Paul, had died he'd kept his distance from Alice for several months. She knew why. For the first time in years she'd been happy. It showed, and Michael didn't understand. Paul had been a bully — coping with his moods, his temper, was hard, they'd argued continually. Michael wasn't privy to any of it, he'd been at university and afterwards worked in Edinburgh. When she'd tried to explain, he refused to believe that his father, the man he'd loved and idolised, was the way his mother described him.

"We're all fine, Mum, how about you?"

He sounded different, tense. There was an edge to his voice. "I'm the same as usual, son. Working hard, getting immersed in the new case we've landed, but you know I love the job."

"But does the job love you?"

An odd thing to say. Michael never questioned her work or how it affected her.

"You sure you're not taking on too much, Mum? Have you thought of taking it easy, perhaps going for a desk job for the next few years?"

Alice was both surprised and curious. This was out of the blue, so where had it come from? "I'm perfectly okay. Why the concern? I'm not that old, you know."

"It's got nothing to do with your age. I'm just worried about you overdoing it. I got a text today from a friend of yours, someone you've not seen in a while. She reckons you're working yourself into the ground, says you look strained and tired."

That caught her attention. "What friend? Who are you talking about?"

"She didn't give her name, reckoned you'd know. The text said she'd seen you at a place called Still Waters and was shocked at how much you'd aged since the last time you'd met."

Alice felt sick. It was Mad Hatter, had to be, but this wasn't the way she usually acted. Never before had she contacted a member of Alice's family. Alice went over in her mind all the women she'd spoken to today at the retreat. One of them had to be Mad Hatter. Or was this just another wind-up?

And why now? There were several reasons and they all terrified her. "Michael, send me the number the text came from."

"Sorry mum, can't, it was withheld."

"Okay, do something for me. Take your mobile into the station in Edinburgh. I'll have a word and tell them you're coming. I want that text analysing. I need all the info we can get from it."

"What's happening, Mum?"

"That text wasn't from any friend of mine. It was sent by the psychopath I'm chasing in my current case. She likes to play games."

"Are you in danger?" he asked.

"No," she said. "I'm not working alone, there's plenty of people around to watch my back. Promise you'll do that for me first thing tomorrow?"

"I'll take it in on my way to work."

Call over, Alice poured herself a generous glass of red. For the first time since Paul's death she felt uneasy in her own home. But at least she had her answer. Mad Hatter was at Still Waters, watching her from the sidelines.

Alice needed to firm up her team, make sure they were committed to catching the killer. She turned to the report of the initial arrests in the Neil Lewis killing, the farm workers. Hawkes had worked the case with a DC Sadie Fox. Alice didn't know her, but given she'd visited the retreat, she decided to earmark the DC for the FLO role. She'd speak to both her and Hawkes in the morning.

Half a bottle of wine later, Alice was ready for bed — hopefully not to dream. What with the recurring nightmare and now Mad Hatter, her subconscious was a scary place.

She made her way up the elegant staircase, musing once more on the fact that this house was way too big for one person who was hardly ever here. But could she bring herself to sell it? Some of the happiest days of her life had been spent in these rooms, but that had been back when her parents were alive. Her time spent here with Paul had not been so much fun.

CHAPTER THIRTEEN

Wednesday

Gemma Lewis was woken by a loud bang on her lodge door. She checked her phone for the time, it was early, too early for it to be a social call. "Erica!" she called to her friend in the next bedroom. "Someone's here."

She got out of bed, donned a dressing gown and peeped through the blinds. She half expected to see the detectives who were investigating Neil's murder, but it wasn't them. There were three men on the veranda and one of them was about to smash the doors open with an axe.

"Stop it!" she called out. "What the hell d'you think you're doing?"

"Let us in, Gemma, or we'll make firewood of this place."

"Who are you?"

"Friends of Neil's."

"No, you're not. My Neil never knew anyone like you."

The men laughed. "Come on, open the door. It's all right, we don't want to hurt you."

Gemma was terrified. These men meant business. She'd no idea what was going on but it had to be some mistake.

She whispered to Erica to ring someone — Minty, the police, anyone she could get hold of.

"What can Minty do?" Erica hissed.

"Ring Dave then, tell him to round up some of the others and get here quick."

"Gemma! We're losing patience. We've come a long way and we're not going back empty handed."

"What d'you want?" she called back.

"Let us in and I'll tell you."

Gemma looked at Erica. "What do I do?"

"Don't open that door. The one with the axe is a mean-looking bugger."

Erica was right, but she had to do something or they'd use that axe and get in anyway. Gemma took a deep breath and went back to the locked door. "Tell me what you want and I'll think about it."

"We're not after trouble, love, we just want what's ours. Robbie gave Neil an item to look after and now he wants it back."

Gemma had no idea what he was talking about. "Robbie? Neil never knew anyone called Robbie."

"Oh, he did, believe me. The pair of them did a lot of business together. How d'you think he got the money to buy this place?"

Erica gave Gemma a nudge. "I don't like the sound of that. It's what that detective asked last night. Was Neil up to something?"

"Of course not," Gemma said angrily. "What they're saying is nonsense. Neil wasn't bent, every penny of what he spent was earned legitimately. His savings paid for the lodge."

The men outside heard this exchange and laughed. "Neil told a good story, I'll say that for him. Give the item back, Gemma, and we'll be on our way."

"I've no idea what you're talking about. Neil never said anything to me about having anything for this Robbie."

The two women heard more voices, another group of men were approaching the lodge. It must be the other residents coming to help them.

"Okay, Gemma, have it your way, but we'll be back. You'd better find what Robbie wants or next time we'll tear the place apart."

Gemma watched the three men disappear towards a black car parked in the lane. She snatched Erica's mobile from her hand and took a photo of the registration number. "They're going," she whispered.

"What d'you reckon that was about?" Erica asked.

"He's made a mistake, must have. Neil didn't know any Robbie, he'd have told me."

"You'll have to tell the police, Gem. It might be that lot who murdered Neil."

Gemma sat on the sofa and began to cry. "I know, but I'm worried, Erica. What did he do to get on the wrong side of that crew? Neil didn't like trouble, he was always one for the quiet life. This sort of thing has never happened before."

"That man said Neil was looking after something for them, d'you know anything about that?"

Gemma shook her head. "Whatever it is, he never told me."

There was another knock on the door, this time it was Dave Hilton. Gemma let him in, Martin Webb following in his wake.

"What's going on?" Dave asked. "Got me out of my pit that call. She sounded as if the world was about to end." He nodded at Erica.

"Three men tried to knock the door down with an axe. They said my Neil was keeping something for one of them and they wanted it back. They terrified me, Dave," Gemma said breathlessly.

Dave looked at Erica for confirmation and she nodded. "I got the car registration for the police."

"Did you know these men?" he asked Gemma.

"No, and I don't know what they were talking about either."

"You know what this means?" Martin Webb said thoughtfully.

"Yes," Gemma snapped. "When that detective shows her face I'll tell her. I'll be asking for protection too and complaining to management. Those men just drove into Still Waters and no one stopped them. Why weren't the front gates locked?"

"Minty must have been expecting a delivery at the shop. We'll tell her, make sure she puts something in place," Martin said.

What was the use? For anyone approaching on foot there were numerous ways to get in, a public footpath ran along the perimeter of the site.

CHAPTER FOURTEEN

"I might be gone a few nights," Alice told Dilys the following morning. "I'll bag up some of the groceries you bought, I doubt there's many shops where I'm going."

"Somewhere nice?"

"I'm not sure what to make of the place, anyway it's work not a jolly. I'm off to a rural retreat up in the hills in Derbyshire above Glossop, not my thing but I have to go where the case takes me."

"Still Waters?"

"You know it?" Dilys had surprised her.

Dilys laughed. "No, I've never been, it's way out of my price range. I was sent a brochure about the place a few weeks back."

Coincidence? Alice didn't think so. "Had you asked for one?"

"No, it came with the other post, like most advertising stuff."

Alice made a mental note to ask Minty if this sort of advertising was a regular practice. "Keep an eye on the house, will you?" she asked Dilys. She had a bad feeling. Mad Hatter had gone to a lot of trouble, hadn't followed her usual pattern. Ordinarily Alice didn't worry when she worked away from home, but this case made her uneasy. She couldn't shift the notion that Mad Hatter had been planning and putting things in place for a while in order to get to her. The house would be empty, possibly for several days, and the last thing Alice wanted was the killer coming here and getting up to mischief.

"Yes, love, I'll pop in every day and check on things. Any problems and I'll give you a ring."

Reassuring, but Dilys was only one woman. It would do no harm to mention her fears to Osbourne. He was next on her list of things to do. Alice needed to speak to him to make sure the divers were organised for today.

"They'll arrive about ten," he said when she called him. "Let me know straight away if anything is found."

"Certainly. Perhaps you'd do something for me. Get a uniformed officer to check my home on a regular basis while I'm away at the retreat. My gut is telling me to be wary and I can't shift it."

"Don't worry, I'm on it. You concentrate on the job in hand, keep me posted and I'll have uniform watch your home."

The job in hand this morning was the prospect of finding Callum Hilton's body in one of the three lakes. Should that happen, his mother would fall apart. She hoped DC Sadie Fox was up to the role of FLO.

Alice said nothing to Osbourne about her son's call last night or the brochure sent to Dilys. She decided it was all a bit tenuous, she needed more evidence before pointing the finger at Mad Hatter.

* * *

An hour later, Alice arrived at the entrance to the retreat. The man on the gate handed her a key card. "Minty said to give you this. Just tap it against the barcode when you want in or out."

Alice knew which of the lodges was theirs, she'd identified it on her way out the night before. She parked up outside and rang DS Hawkes. "We're in thirty-five. DC Fox turned up yet?"

"Yes, she's with Gemma Lewis. Apparently, she had some visitors first thing this morning. Three blokes threatening violence and brandishing an axe. Her and Clare Hilton are convinced it was them who killed her husband."

Was that a possibility? Given the Mad Hatter involvement, Alice doubted it but they'd have to investigate anyway. "Do we know who they were? Have you spoken to her?"

"They were after something Neil Lewis was keeping for a Robbie or someone. At least, that was the tale."

Now Alice was curious. "Robbie? No surname?"

"Didn't give one. Why? Is it important?"

"Could be." Alice had been working a case featuring a Robbie Barrett before coming here. Was this something else Mad Hatter had set up to confuse the issue? But how could she know about that particular case, and even if she did, how was Neil Lewis involved?

"The divers are here," Hawkes told her. "Minty's busy showing them around, currently they're at Ash Lake."

"Good enough place to start, I'll be right with you."

Alice unlocked the lodge and went inside. It was pleasant, comfortably furnished and well kitted out. Minty had left a map of the site for her, so she had no excuse for getting lost, not in daylight anyway. She changed into a pair of walking boots, donned a waterproof and went to find out what was going on at Ash Lake.

* * *

Despite being early summer it had rained continually all morning and the route up to the lake was slippery. Alice climbed up the slope towards the open water, clinging on to the shrubbery for support. Once at the top, she looked down on an expanse of water that loomed grey and misty in front of her. A team of four divers were standing around at the lake's edge talking to Hawkes. She looked up at the surrounding hills. One of them, a fair distance away with a rocky outcrop near the top, made her shudder: 'Needle Crag,' an infamous peak full of hidden openings that led down into the very guts of the Pennines. It was windy and the mist was gradually clearing from the hilltops. Alice spotted a group of climbers making their slow way to the summit of the crag. She shuddered, and said to no one in particular, "Why would anyone want to go up there?"

Hawkes heard her. "I'm with you, ma'am, not fond of all that climbing stuff myself. Far too dangerous, particularly on that one up there. That's the highest peak around and it's claimed several lives over the years."

"Yes, I know."

"Why 'Needle?'" he asked. "I've never understood that."

Alice raised her eyebrows. How could he live just a few miles away and not know how the landmark got its name? "The tale is that those rocky outcrops you see at the summit are needles used by a female giant called Allegra who lived inside the peak. During a row with a rival, she threw them at her and that's where they landed. Halfway up that crag is the entrance to an equally infamous pothole, 'Allegra's Cauldron.' Heard of that?"

Hawkes shook his head. "No, it's all a bit fanciful for me, like kids' stories."

"It's folklore, Sergeant, and anyway, you did ask."

"Quaint story but that hillside is still a dangerous place," he muttered.

As well she knew. Her partner, Paul, had been a keen potholer. A long time ago she'd been up there with him and had stood quaking with fear while he'd poked fun and called her a coward. She was more certain than ever now that Mad Hatter's choice of this place was no accident. She'd deliberately settled on a venue that would play on all Alice's fears.

"Are they ready?" she asked.

Hawkes nodded. "The senior diver, Malcolm here, says they should get going. It's a large lake and will take a while to search."

Alice sighed. She had a bad feeling. Whether they found Callum Hilton or not, either outcome would be unhappy for his parents. After what had happened to Neil Lewis and those men with their threats this morning, they'd be expecting the worst.

She gave Malcolm a nod and watched the group climb into their boat and row out into the water. She shuddered. "It looks so cold and dark. Not a job I could do."

"Me neither. I'm not much of a swimmer to be honest. Have you seen Gemma Lewis?"

"Not yet," Alice said, "I'm saving her for later. I want to see what happens here first."

"Odd though, don't you think? They turn up, threaten violence if she doesn't hand over something of theirs. What d'you reckon it could be?" he asked.

Alice sighed. "If you're asking me for a best guess, I'd say it was a gun. If I'm right, I can also tell you the last time it was used and who it killed."

Jason Hawkes looked at her, surprised and impressed. "Want to elaborate, ma'am?"

"Not really, but it adds up to Mad Hatter still being one step ahead and testament to her ability to get under my skin." At that moment she spotted Minty on the bank above her. "That reminds me, I need a quick word."

Alice clambered up towards the site manager. "Question. Does the company advertise the retreat — you know, produce a brochure on the benefits of owning a lodge here?"

Minty nodded. "Yes, it's printed on an annual basis and interested parties can get one from the show lodge."

"You don't send brochures out in the post?"

Minty laughed at that. "People see our adverts on social media, they ask questions and then we send them a brochure. They're too expensive to send out to all and sundry. Given the nature of this place, that wouldn't be cost effective anyway. Mrs Hamilton isn't one for wasting money. I've done that list for you by the way. Pop into the office on your way back."

Alice thanked her and went back down to the lake. Dilys hadn't received that brochure by chance. It was yet another piece of the Mad Hatter puzzle.

"They've got something, ma'am!" Hawkes shouted. "They're bringing it to the surface now."

CHAPTER FIFTEEN

The lead diver, Malcolm, and one of the others struggled out of the lake carrying a black plastic bag between them. Even from this distance, Alice could see it was heavy. It was tied at the top with vivid yellow rope.

She donned nitrile gloves and went to meet them. "Stay back," she warned Hawkes. "If this is Hilton, every shred of forensic evidence must be preserved."

Malcolm brandished a Stanley knife. "Want me to do the honours?"

Alice shook her head. "No, let me." She took the knife from him and slit the bag from top to bottom. One of Callum's arms rolled out. It was minus the hand. The police officers watching stepped back, gasping. Unperturbed, Alice knelt down and moved the flap of black plastic back to take a closer look. She saw at once that the body was incomplete. "Don't touch anything else," she called back. "I'll get a pathologist and CSI up here."

"Want me to ring, ma'am?"

"No, Hawkes, I want people I know on this. You stay here, get a tent over the body and keep prying eyes away." She turned to Malcolm. "Get your people back in the water, there's still more of him to find."

Someone called out from the bank, several metres away. It was Clare Hilton and her friend, Liz.

"Is that my Callum?" she shouted. "It is, isn't it?"

Alice walked towards her. "You shouldn't be here," she said kindly. "It's too early to say anything about what's been found, but rest assured if this is connected to Callum's disappearance you'll be told."

"You're lying, I can see it on your face. Tell me," Clare insisted.

"I can't say anything yet. You're better off going back to your lodge. As soon as I know something, I'll come and tell you."

Liz Webb took her friend's arm and started to lead her away. "I'll look after her," she called back.

"There's a patch of blood on the grass over there." Clare pointed. "You should test it, see if it's Callum's."

Alice looked at an area that'd been covered with a small tarpaulin. "Yes, I'll get our CSI people on it when they come." She walked away, mobile in hand. Out of Clare's earshot, she rang the lab. Dr Jack Nevin, the senior forensic scientist, answered.

"Alice," Nevin began. "Osbourne said to expect a call. What've you got for us?"

"Body parts, Jack, and they've been in water for a few days. I've had a quick look and there isn't anything that will easily identify him, no hands or head, but I suspect it's Callum Hilton, a young man who's currently missing. I had his toothbrush sent in to you. Have it checked for a DNA match. Also the hammer that killed Neil Lewis, there might be tissue belonging to Hilton on that too."

"Where are you?"

"Still Waters Rural Retreat, Derbyshire. Know it?"

"Oddly enough, yes. I was sent one of their brochures only last week."

More of Mad Hatter's doing. She'd worked it out perfectly, right down to the team Alice would choose to work with.

"D'you want Dolly as pathologist on this?"

"Naturally. The old team is fine by me."

"It'll be good to see you again, Alice, and I know Dolly will be pleased too. Be with you in about an hour."

Alice made her way across to the boathouse. It was the only building around and she wanted a look before going back to the lodge. All it took was a hefty shove with her shoulder to get the door open. Inside, Alice was immediately assailed by the smell of bleach, a sure sign that someone had tried to obliterate forensic evidence. She went to the door and called Hawkes over.

"I think this is where he was brought and carved up," she told him quietly.

"Want me to take a quick look, ma'am?"

"No, you watch the door and don't let anyone in." Alice moved to the back of the building and an area of the stone floor where the boat was kept. She lifted the tarpaulin but there was nothing to see but freshly swilled flagstones. Had Callum been brought here? Had he been conscious? She could picture the scene, like something from a horror movie — Mad Hatter kneeling on the ground, instruments in hand, methodically taking Callum Hilton apart bit by bit. "Get the building sealed off. I want no one in here until Dr Nevin has taken a look."

The stench of bleach inside the building turned her stomach. Out in the open air, Alice inhaled deeply. She'd leave the experts to unravel the horrors of that place. Meanwhile, she'd tell Minty that the lakes, and now the boathouse too, were off limits, and ask her to have a word with the owner of the retreat, Maxine Hamilton.

Malcolm waved to her. His team had retrieved something else from the lake. At first, Alice thought it might be more of Callum, but it was his fishing trolley. The diver dragged it up the embankment, all Callum's gear still on it. Fortunately, Clare Hilton had left.

* * *

At Minty's office, Alice explained that the three lakes and boathouse would have to remain off limits for the foreseeable. She didn't go into detail, just said that they'd found something significant.

"Callum?" Minty asked.

Alice wasn't about to commit. "We're waiting on our forensic people. Meanwhile, we don't want anyone near the lakes until I give the clearance. Would you contact Mrs Hamilton, the owner, and tell her I need a word?"

Minty handed Alice a business card. "With all this going on, she's delayed her impending flight back to Spain. She's at a meeting in Birmingham today and will be returning tomorrow. I suggest you ring her mobile, she'll take off back to her villa the minute things calm down."

"Thanks, Minty."

"Here's that list you asked for," Minty said.

There were a dozen or so names, more than she'd expected. "Regular visitors, are they?"

Minty nodded. "This place is too expensive not to make good use of it."

Alice put the paper in her pocket and left the office. Outside, she rang Maxine Hamilton.

"You are aware of why we're here?" she said after the introductions. "We have found something in Ash Lake. I'm awaiting a report from the pathologist before I say any more, but it's not looking good."

"Minty rang and told me about Neil Lewis," Maxine said. "Now you're telling me that another lodge owner has been murdered? Nothing like this has ever happened before. The publicity could ruin me. How long will you lot take to wind this up?"

Not much sympathy there. "Our investigations are ongoing, and until they're complete there's not a lot I can tell you."

"You have a job to do, I understand that, but I want this over and you and your colleagues out of there as quickly as possible. Still Waters must return to normal or the residents will leave in droves. I'll instruct Minty to help in any way she can. Once I'm back, I'll ring you and arrange a meeting."

"At this point we have no idea where the investigation is going or how long it'll take to find the person we're looking for. It will take time, Mrs Hamilton, there is nothing I can do about that."

"But you have a suspect, or suspects? You're not working blind here?"

"It's a tricky case, and that's all I can tell you for now."

Maxine Hamilton hadn't shown a lot of compassion for the bereaved. It seemed that as far as she was concerned, her business was everything. Alice returned to her lodge. She put the list in her folder and flipped through the brochure that had been left on the coffee table. Had Mad Hatter sent them to everyone she thought would be involved in this case? And if so, why? What was so important about them? Probably nothing, more than likely it was a case of Mad Hatter attempting to tie up her time and resources on yet another wild goose chase.

Alice threw the thing back onto the table. She'd give it a closer look later. She should get back to the lake, help Hawkes keep the curious away. Suddenly there was a loud bang on the door. It was Gemma Lewis.

She pushed in through the door. "I was threatened this morning, with a bloody axe. You want to know who killed my husband, that's your answer. It was some Manchester villain he got involved with who sent his bully boys to my door to do their worst."

"You're all right? They didn't hurt you?"

"Only because they took flight when Dave and some of the others turned up, but they could well come back. I'm a sitting duck in that lodge."

"Does this villain have a name?" Alice asked.

"The other detective asked me that. I was too stunned by what had happened at the time and couldn't think clearly, but I've since been able to go over it in my mind."

That was a lie. Alice could tell from the look on her face that Gemma had known all along.

"One of those thugs mentioned the name Robbie. I'd forgotten but Neil was going about with a Robbie Barrett a while back. He owns a club in town that he was fond of," Gemma said.

"So, what did these men want?"

"Something Neil was keeping for Robbie." Gemma handed Alice a piece of paper. "Here, I got the registration number of the car they took off in."

"I'll follow it up," Alice promised, ushering Gemma towards the door. "Don't worry, there will be a police presence on the site for a while, so I doubt they'll be back."

Gemma stopped and turned to Alice. "It's obvious to me that this Robbie and his gang killed Neil. I don't know why you're holding back. I want that villain arrested."

"We will certainly be speaking to Mr Barrett, never fear. Has the FLO, DC Sadie Fox, made herself known to you?"

"I sent her away." Gemma grimaced. "I don't want police cluttering up the lodge and scaring off my friends."

"DC Fox is there to help you, answer your questions, provide reassurance. Anything untoward happens, you contact her. That's what she's here for."

"Pity she wasn't with me first thing then, isn't it?"

There was just no getting through to some people. When Gemma had finally left, Alice locked up and made her way back to the lake. The pathologist and her team were due anytime.

CHAPTER SIXTEEN

The pathologist was Dr Dolly Parkes, a consummate professional and an old friend of Alice's. With Hawkes beside her, she was bent over the body parts. At Alice's approach, she stood up, lowered her mask and smiled.

"Hi, stranger, long time no see."

"You know how it is, work, stress, general life stuff."

"I certainly do," Dolly said, nodding at the remains. "Mad Hatter at her worst. It didn't take long for the divers to find him either. I'll get him back to the morgue and have a proper look tomorrow. The bag was left in deep water about ten metres out. She didn't make it difficult, that's for sure."

Alice nodded. "Wanted him found. That boathouse back there, I reckon that's where our victim was cut up."

"Jack's sent a team, he'll be on the job himself tomorrow," Dolly said. "Meanwhile, keep everyone out. If anyone goes in there, contaminates the scene, Jack won't like it. You know what a stickler he is."

"No worries. I'll have a uniformed officer stand guard all night," Alice said.

After the remains had been carefully stowed in the morgue vehicle, Dolly joined Alice, who was staring out over the lake.

"There's still half of him out there," Alice said. "What sort of monster would do that?"

Dolly made a face. "After all we've seen of this killer, do I really have to answer that?"

One of the divers searching towards the far bank of the lake suddenly surfaced and stuck his hand up.

"Another find," Alice said. "Let's hope it's the rest of Callum."

But she was wrong. The divers brought out what looked like a complete body wrapped in a torn, dirty sheet that had once been white. It had plastic wrapping around it and was sealed with gaffer tape. Dolly and Alice walked around to meet them.

"That's not what we were hoping for," Dolly said.

"As far as I'm aware, there hasn't been another killing here," Alice told her.

"Well, the Mad Hatter case is several years old, and we've always suspected that not all the bodies have been recovered. Whoever this is could be from any of the historical cases." Dolly bent over the bundle and started to cut through the plastic. Her blade pierced both plastic and sheet and, gingerly, she moved the materials away to get a glimpse at what was inside. She looked up at Alice and shook her head. "Bones, and not much else. As I thought, this has to be one of the old ones."

Alice cast her mind back over all the cases she'd investigated involving Mad Hatter. "There is an old case where we never found the victim. Celia West, remember her?"

"I recall the name but you were never certain if she was a victim or had simply done a runner. Wasn't she the one with a difficult family life?" Dolly said.

"Yes, she lived with her sister and they were constantly at loggerheads. Celia complained to the local station about her many times, said she was afraid for her life. We were given a detailed description of what she was wearing the night she disappeared, as well as photos, but we never found any trace of her," Alice said. "But her DNA, medical records and other details about her are on file, so if it is her, we should soon know."

Dolly had the remains put in a second vehicle and got ready to leave. "We'll have that long overdue chat tomorrow after the post-mortems. I'll text you a time."

Alice waited until the vehicles had pulled away. DS Hawkes, with Sadie, had left for the lodge a good ten minutes ago, and apart from the uniformed officers left on watch, Alice was on her own. She looked at the scene around her. The lake was quiet now, the waters flat, as if nothing had ever happened here. One last glimpse and she turned to make her way back.

Darkness had fallen like a black curtain, obscuring the path in front of her. Alice could see lights twinkling in the trees ahead — fairy lights, and not much use to someone who'd lost her way. Only the main route through the site had proper lighting but it was nowhere to be seen. It'd got cold too. Alice fastened up her coat and quickened her pace. The way up here had seemed straightforward enough, but she hadn't given it a lot of thought. She hadn't even brought the map with her. She took a right turn onto a narrow path, but several metres along realised it wasn't the one she wanted. There were no more lights now, just tall trees casting shadows on the ground in front of her.

Her mobile rang, with a number she didn't recognise. "Hello?"

"Alice, how nice to speak to you. It's been a long time."

She stopped in her tracks. It was a woman but her voice was obviously disguised, and it was difficult to make out the words. Even so, Alice guessed immediately who it was. "What d'you want?"

"Just a chat, Alice. You must have known I'd contact you at some point. How could I not? We're old friends."

Mad Hatter. There was no doubt in her mind. Alice's legs turned to jelly, she wanted to run, reach the safety of her colleagues and the lodge, but she'd no idea where she was. What Mad Hatter said next terrified her and confirmed her worst fears. Not only was the woman here at Still Waters but she had to be close by, watching her.

"You need to turn round, go back the way you came. At the junction, go straight on past the clump of three leylandii trees. Your lodge is several metres along there."

Alice wasn't usually afraid of the dark but her surroundings suddenly felt sinister, threatening. After the discovery of two bodies this was a nightmare she could do without. "Where are you?"

"Very close, and that's all I'm telling you. Don't fret, Alice, we'll get together soon, have a proper catch up, talk about old times."

"We've nothing to catch up on. I don't know you, except that you're a psychopath who's killed people. All I want is to bring you to justice." Alice tried hard to keep her voice from shaking, knowing she was doing a bad job of it.

The woman laughed. "Oh, Alice, you crack me up, you really do. You're already terrified and we're only talking on the phone. You must realise that you'll never catch me. I'll complete my work here and neither you nor your colleagues can stop me. And when I'm done having my fun, I'll finally get even with you for what you did."

"What're you talking about? I've done nothing."

"I'm surprised at you, Alice, and a little disappointed. You know very well what you did. Perhaps I should remind you?"

"You're raving," Alice hissed into the phone.

"Tut-tut, no need to lose it. You caused me immense heartache back then and I'm still in emotional pain today. I can't forgive that. All that distress has to be paid for. You've got away with what you did for far too long and now it's time for retribution. Have you discussed our relationship with your colleagues, told them about me and the secret we share?"

"You're insane," Alice said.

"You're fooling yourself, Alice. Pretending it didn't happen won't do you any good. I bet I feature in your dreams.

I do, don't I?" She laughed. "And don't think I'll just slip away out of your life either. I have a task to complete and I will see it through."

"More people to kill." Alice spat the words out.

"This time the focus is on you, Alice. You see, I want you dead, out of my head for good. Sorry to be such a spoil-sport but I'm calling time on our little game." The line went dead.

Despite being terrified out of her wits, almost without thinking Alice had taken Mad Hatter's advice, turned around and was back at the junction. Her heart was pounding, blind panic setting in. The notion that her arch enemy was watching her every move was horrific. She quickened her pace and within minutes saw the familiar row of lodges.

* * *

"DCI Rossi?"

Alice stared at the young woman who'd addressed her. After her conversation with Mad Hatter she was too dazed to even make out the words. Her mind was still full of what the killer had just said to her.

The young woman asked again, "DCI Rossi?"

Shaking herself, Alice nodded at the DC. "And you're Sadie Fox."

"Yes, ma'am. I've done us some food. I hope spag bol is okay for you."

The warmth of the lodge and the presence of another person had a calming effect. Alice managed a smile, she was grateful for the company. "Thanks, that'll do fine but not too much for me." The thought of food turned her stomach. Going into the kitchen she reached for one of the bottles of red she'd brought with her and poured herself a generous glassful. "Have you spoken to the families?"

"I tried but they're not easy, Gemma Lewis being a prime example. She's rude and doesn't want to say much.

She knows I'm here to help, offer support, but she's wary. She keeps walking off into another room or outside to talk on her mobile. I just know she has information that she's not sharing with us."

"That might be so but she's had a shock," Alice said soothingly, "so we'll give her time. If those body parts turn out to belong to Callum Hilton, it'll be his parents who'll need the support. They'll be devastated, particularly when they learn what was done to him. But we don't say a word until we know for definite."

"What're your thoughts on Gemma Lewis?" Sadie asked.

Alice had already noted that Gemma Lewis fitted the Mad Hatter profile, as did Minty, Erica Cross and her sister Emily. Minty seemed only too pleased to help but that could be a cover. Alice had found the other two sullen and obstructive. Gemma she could understand up to a point, she'd just lost her husband, but the look Erica Cross had given her at their first meeting had been venomous. The killing of Neil Lewis would be investigated thoroughly to exclude or otherwise any involvement by Robbie Barrett. If his death was down to Barrett, it would only add to the possibility of Gemma being Mad Hatter.

"I'm still working her out," Alice said. "We need to find out more about those men who visited her first." Alice could see from the stack of notes on the table that Sadie had been reading through the Barrett file. "If they are working for Robbie Barrett, he'll be interviewed, never fear."

Sadie dished out the meal and the pair sat down at the table to eat. Alice picked at the food, pushing it around the plate. Finally, she took a mouthful and was pleasantly surprised. "It's good. All your own work?"

"Yes, but don't get carried away, ma'am, it's all I can do." Sadie laughed.

"Don't worry, I'll do my bit," Alice said.

"Hopefully, we won't be here too long. I don't know about you, but after dark the place gives me the creeps," Sadie said. “It’s the quiet and darkness plus that cold wind that blows off the hills. I don’t understand why people would part with thousands to buy lodges out here. Give me a caravan by the sea and a busy clubhouse any day.”

Alice nodded. What she wouldn’t give for the safety and comfort of her own home right now.

CHAPTER SEVENTEEN

Clare Hilton closed the blinds and turned to her husband. "Those detectives have finished for the day, Dave. I went up to Ash Lake earlier. They wouldn't tell me anything but I know they found something. Those divers were pulling a black plastic bag out of the water."

"Then there's probably nothing to tell," he said, turning the sound up on the TV.

Clare was fast losing patience with her husband. She was worried sick and he didn't seem bothered at all. "Our Cal has been missing a while now, what does it take to get your interest?"

Dave reached for his can of beer. "They'll find him, you'll see. He'll come back and wonder what all the fuss's been about. Look, I'm trying to watch the football here."

Clare grabbed the remote and switched the TV off. "What about that black bag, Dave? The lot of them were dead cagey, wouldn't let anyone near."

"I'm getting sick of this. Cal is fine, he'll come back and you'll realise how stupid all this is. Now turn that set back on."

"And the bag?"

"It'll be rubbish someone's dumped, don't stress, woman."

Clare had had enough. "I don't understand you sometimes. You just don't get it, do you? Cal might be dead but heaven forbid you miss your bloody football."

Outburst over, she grabbed her coat and went next door to talk to her friend. At least Liz appreciated what she was going through.

Liz Webb ushered her inside, where Minty was sitting on the sofa. "I'm pumping her for information," Liz said, handing Clare a glass of wine.

"I don't know much," Minty said. "But that bigwig woman detective was seriously put out by whatever was in the bag they pulled from the lake. Their forensic people went over the boathouse too."

"You spoke to her? I want to know what they found," Clare said. "What did she say? I was up there too but she wouldn't tell me anything."

"She didn't say much to me either," Minty said, "but whatever they found, it was significant. I saw them drag your Cal's fishing gear out too."

Clare was shocked. "They found his gear? Well, that proves it then. It'll be my Cal they dragged out, I just know it. But why won't they tell me? I can't stand not knowing." Clare began to cry.

Minty cleared her throat. "The bag wasn't that big. Your Cal's tall, it can't have been him, not unless someone did him some serious damage."

There was a wild look on Clare's face as the possible horrors went through her mind. Then the penny dropped. She looked at the two other women, wide-eyed. "That's why they won't say, why I can't see him. He's damaged and they're checking to confirm his identity." Clare was shaking. She clutched her throat, gasping for air, close to having a full-blown panic attack. "I can't do this, Liz. I've got to go, talk to Dave, make the lump listen for once."

Clare was on her feet being consoled by Liz when Liz's husband Martin appeared, having been out walking their pet dog.

"It's quiet out there tonight," he said. "The police are still up at the lake keeping watch, but there's not a lot going on. You all right, Clare?"

"D'you know what those divers dragged out today?" Clare asked him.

Martin shook his head. "They were giving nothing away, so I reckon it has to be something significant."

"My Cal?"

He gave her a look full of sympathy. "No, Clare, your Cal will turn up. And when he does, be sure to give him hell for putting you through this."

"I might believe that if it wasn't for Neil's murder," Clare said.

"Neil's death was down to those morons who came after him. I spoke to Gemma earlier, not that she made much sense, but she did say they were gangsters from Manchester. What would they want with your Cal?"

"Gangsters?" Clare didn't understand. Neil was just an ordinary man, a former teaching assistant. They'd got on, had things in common, so how come he'd been mixing with people like that?

"Gemma told me they were after something when they banged on her door. Something Neil was keeping for them, apparently. She's no idea what it was but thinks they must have been here the day before, killed Neil when he wouldn't hand it over and returned to get it."

"And no mention of my Cal?"

"No, Clare, so relax."

Martin made it all sound so straightforward, but it wasn't. Something awful had happened to Cal, she just knew it.

But at least Martin had given her a glimmer of hope. Feeling a little better, Clare left her friends to it. They could speculate about Cal's fate all night but it wouldn't get them anywhere. When she got back to her own lodge, Dave was still on the sofa, watching TV.

"Turn that off. I need a word," she said.

"Look, woman, you need to stop this, you'll make yourself ill."

Clare had had enough. She picked up a cushion from the chair and began to bash him around the head. Dave rolled onto the carpet, bringing half the sofa with him.

"Watch my back!" he yelled. "Twist it and I won't walk for a week."

"You're a disgrace," she shouted. "Our son has disappeared and you don't give a toss."

But Dave wasn't listening. The sofa cushions were all over the floor, leaving the base exposed. Tucked down deep between the base and the back cushions was something wrapped in plastic. He bent over and picked it up. He knew instantly what it was.

"Dave, what've you got there?"

Dave Hilton was shocked. "Well, it's not mine," he said, holding it at arms' length and staring at it. "What use do I have for a damn gun?"

A gun? Clare couldn't believe her ears. "How did it get there? Could it be Cal's?"

"He'd never be that daft. Anyway, if it was his, he'd have hidden it somewhere safe, not shoved it down the back of the sofa."

"What do we do?" she asked.

"We give it to the police of course, let them deal with it," he said.

"I don't understand how it got there," Clare said.

"I reckon I do. Think about it. It'll be down to Neil. I bet he brought it here Friday night when we had folk round. You and him spent the best part of the night on our sofa. Bet he was just looking for somewhere to stash the thing. He probably intended to return and pick it up but got murdered instead."

Clare gingerly took the package from his hands and made for the door. "This is what those thugs must have been after when they threatened Gemma," she said. Dave was right, this had nothing to do with Cal. It was all down to

Neil Lewis. "The light's still on in that detective woman's lodge. I'll take it to her now."

* * *

As soon as Sadie Fox opened the door, Clare Hilton thrust the package containing the gun at her. "Here, you take it. Just thinking about it makes me nervous. And before you get clever, know this, it has nothing to do with me and Dave. We've just found that thing shoved down the back of our sofa. Dave thinks it could have been Neil's."

Sadie took the package from her and called to Alice. "Ma'am, Mrs Hilton has found something."

Alice took one look and knew immediately what Sadie was holding. In all likelihood this was Robbie Barrett's gun.

CHAPTER EIGHTEEN

Thursday

Alice was up early the following morning. She and DS Hawkes had a date with Dolly Parkes and Jack Nevin at the morgue in central Manchester. First, she rang Osbourne and told him about the gun. Sadie Fox would get a statement from Clare and it was agreed that Alice would give the gun to Jack Nevin to examine as he had been involved in the forensics on the Barrett case.

Alice was looking forward to seeing Dolly and having a proper chat. The two of them were the same age and had often worked together. Dolly was the only person Alice had been tempted to confide in about her husband Paul and his behaviour, but the opportunity had never arisen.

Dr Jack Nevin was ten years their senior and was one of the best forensic scientists Alice had met in all her years in the job. If Mad Hatter had left any trace of herself on either of the bodies or at the locations, he would find it.

Jason Hawkes arrived just as Alice was about to leave. She met him at the door of the lodge, a piece of toast still in her mouth. "She's not a bad cook, your mate."

Hawkes said nothing. He looked worn out. Parenthood in the raw, Alice decided.

"Come on, cheer up. The morning will be bad enough without you pulling a moody."

"Post-mortems. Can't be doing with them, I'm too squeamish," he admitted.

"Don't worry, Sergeant, so am I. In all my years in the job, I've never got used to them." She sat in the passenger seat of his car. "You drive, it's some distance and I want to read through the file again."

"Where are we going, ma'am?"

"The new annex building next to the Royal in Manchester."

Hawkes headed for the exit and out onto the steep winding road that led down to the nearest village several miles away. "Any idea who she is yet?"

He was referring to Mad Hatter. "No, but she rang me last night and given what she said, I'm certain she's either staying at Still Waters or working there, and is taking a close interest in what we're doing. I want Gemma, Erica Cross and Minty watching carefully, and any others that fit the bill."

He glanced at her. "That must have been one scary call."

"And then some. By the time she'd finished, I was a nervous wreck."

"Any particular reason you've picked out those three, ma'am?"

"Instinct, Sergeant. Apart from Minty, neither of the others has been particularly helpful or pleasant but more importantly they all fit the profile, and given recent events we can't exclude Gemma." She told him about the Hiltons finding the gun. "It's possibly the gun Robbie Barrett used to shoot someone in Manchester. We'll know once Nevin gets his hands on it."

"Want me to get some background on the three women?" he asked.

"The team in Manchester are already on it. Those three, and the others on the list I sent them last night. I also sent them a few dates and places. I want to know where everyone on that list was on those dates."

"Important, are they?"

"They're the dates of killings — well, those that we know of. I've been chasing Mad Hatter these last six years. The first time I encountered her was a suspected killing in the village of Chinley, and I missed her by a matter of hours. The victim was one Celia West — at least, we think it was."

"Chinley. That's Whalley Bridge way."

"That's right, and we never found Celia's body nor any trace of her. There was a lot of blood at the house. Her sister told us some tale about a robbery and Celia being badly cut on the arm. But Mad Hatter was involved all right — there was the usual tweet. The problem is, Celia hasn't been seen since. I want to know if anyone on the list was in that area and we'll go from there. I've asked them to look at Penistone and Mottram too."

"You do realise that Chinley isn't that far away, ma'am? It's a drive of thirty minutes or so from Still Waters. The other places are fairly close too."

Alice was well aware of that. She had spotted a pattern while going through the Mad Hatter file. "Still Waters is central to them all. I have a sneaking suspicion that the retreat is her base and has been for some time."

"The second body pulled from the lake yesterday, you think it could be the Chinley woman?" Hawkes said.

"If it is, it'll give her family — well, her sister — some chance of closure."

Before the retreat had featured in the current Mad Hatter case, Alice had had no reason to notice it. Now it made perfect sense. It was handy for all the places she had committed murder and stood in the shadow of Needle Crag. For reasons Alice didn't want to dwell on, that peak was significant to both her and Mad Hatter. "I think the fact she's lured me here is no accident. In the call last night, she said this would be our last encounter."

"She plans to stop killing?" Hawkes asked.

"I don't know, Sergeant, but the other thing she told me is that I'm to be one of her victims."

Hawkes gave a low whistle. "D'you reckon she means it?"

"Yes, I do. Like me, she's tired of the battle and wants it to end. Not that I'll make it easy for her." Alice smiled. "She wants a fight, she'll get one."

She gazed out of the window at the scenery. She'd always thought this a beautiful part of the world. If it hadn't been for Paul's obsession with potholes and caves, she would probably have enjoyed their many visits. Now she knew of its existence, she wondered why he'd never suggested a holiday at Still Waters. It was exactly the sort of place he would have liked, and it was situated close to his favourite climbs.

"You said battle, ma'am. Why does she call it that? I don't get what she has against you."

How to answer that one? "Who knows, Sergeant? What goes on inside the head of a psychopath is a mystery to me."

"D'you think you might know her? Perhaps she's some-one from your past."

Hmm. This one was quite perceptive, time to change the subject. "I doubt it," she said. "She'll have seen me at some time, perhaps in the papers or in court, and become fixated."

"Seems a bit strange to me. Killers usually have a more substantial reason for the choices they make," he mused.

"We used to come climbing near here," Alice said, swiftly changing the subject. "We always stayed at a little bed and breakfast near Glossop. I'd no idea there was anywhere like Still Waters here."

"Shame, it's a nice place and it's been here a long time. Did you come climbing with your husband?"

Alice nodded. "Not that I did much climbing. But it's a while ago now. He died six years back, after an accident."

"Car crash?" Hawkes asked.

"No, Sergeant, and if you don't mind I'd rather we left it there." The conversation was straying into realms Alice preferred not to visit. "How long before we get there?"

"Half an hour or so if the traffic's kind," he said.

* * *

Dolly Parkes greeted Alice with a hug. "Apart from that hasty meet by the lake yesterday, it's been a while."

"Sorry I never rang. That night out we promised ourselves, I should have made more of an effort. Work has a habit of getting in the way, and I do nothing to stop it," Alice said.

"I'm just as bad," Dolly agreed. "We've been as busy as hell here, and now this." She nodded at the body on the slab. "I can't say I've missed the workload she gives us."

Dolly had worked on Mad Hatter's previous victims and knew her methods. "The bad news is that she's as forensically aware as always." She grimaced. "We've found very little to help, but there is something."

Alice gave her a questioning look. This was unusual. In all the Mad Hatter cases they'd worked on, she'd never left a single trace, no prints, no DNA. "You sure? What sort of something?"

"Neil Lewis tried hard to defend himself. He's got three broken fingers and extensive bruising to his right hand but the significant thing is what's under his fingernails. I think he must have made a grab for his attacker and scratched her. Jack is confident we'll get a DNA match."

Alice took a moment to think. Would Mad Hatter make such an error? If she had, it was a first.

"This is a result, Alice," Dolly said excitedly. "We're rushing the tests through and we'll soon have a DNA profile."

"But there's every chance that she's not been in trouble before and won't be on the database," Alice said.

"With a profile, we can test everyone at Still Waters if we have to, ma'am," Hawkes pointed out.

The pair of them made it sound so easy, but was it? Was this really the breakthrough she'd waited so long for?

Alice didn't want to get too excited. It could just as easily be a deliberate act on Mad Hatter's part to fulfil some aspect of her overall plan. More likely she was still calling the shots and sending them off on some wild goose chase.

Alice looked at Dolly. "You know what I'm thinking. You know how she operates. I'd like to see this as the potential breakthrough you suggest, but I know her of old. She would never make things so easy for us."

"Clever psychopath she might be, but she's still only human," Dolly said.

CHAPTER NINETEEN

Dolly had Neil Lewis's body laid out on the slab. Even from the viewing gallery, the sight was chilling. Seeing Mad Hatter's work in all its horrific detail made Alice shiver with fear. This was the work of an adversary like no other, and Lewis was testament to what she was capable of. He'd been a tall man and well built but she'd got the upper hand, beaten him black and blue before caving in his skull.

"The blow to the head is what killed him. He suffered a catastrophic cerebral haemorrhage," Dolly said. She'd already opened the skull and removed the brain. She pointed to a section of it. "He was hit twice, and the damage here was caused by a second blow which is what caused his death."

"Why twice?" Alice asked.

"We can't know for sure, but he has several injuries to his hands and limbs." She pointed these out. "He took some beating. From the shape of the bruises and the fact that I've found fragments of wood in the wounds, I'd say she used a wooden bat. His kneecaps are shattered too. Once he hit the ground he wouldn't have been able to get up again."

Alice winced.

"A man that size, how would she manage it?" Hawkes asked.

"I reckon that's what the first blow to the head was for," Dolly said. "There's a bruise on his temple here. She hits him, he falls to the ground, perhaps semi-conscious, and she gets to work."

Alice looked at her friend. "She really put him through it. What I don't understand is why."

"She wanted something?" Hawkes suggested.

Alice nodded. Hawkes could be right, but what was so important that Mad Hatter had to beat the man half to death to find it? There was nothing special about Lewis, apart from his association with Robbie Barrett. Given the subsequent visit to Gemma by those three heavies, that had to be it. Mad Hatter then used the information to confuse the investigation and send Barrett's people to Gemma's door, baying for blood.

"She's still playing games," Alice said. "It's possible that like everyone else at Still Waters, Mad Hatter wanted to know how the Lewises could afford to pay for the lodge when their earnings on paper didn't match up. He must have told her, and that led to the visit to Gemma's."

"She wanted to send us on a wild goose chase?"

"Something like that, Sergeant."

Dolly was now examining Lewis's heart. "His heart was in good condition, his coronary arteries too. The lungs are clear and the internal organs unremarkable." Dolly looked up at them and shook her head. "This man is healthy, he looked after himself. If he hadn't been murdered, he could have had many years ahead of him."

Jason Hawkes turned away. "Gross."

"Get a grip, Sergeant," Alice said. "We none of us like this part of the job, but it has to be done. Callum Hilton will be much worse, you know."

And indeed it was. In an adjoining room, Dolly had the body parts they believed belonged to Callum laid out on a slab.

"We've matched the blood found near Ash Lake to that of this victim," she began. "Tests are still ongoing to check the DNA against the blood traces found in the boathouse and the toothbrush you gave us."

"Are you able to tell us anything about how he was killed?" Alice asked.

Dolly shook her head. "I'm afraid not. Whoever cut him up didn't do a bad job. The wounds have been cleanly sliced as have the bones. It's probable that a power tool was used."

"Please tell me he was dead when she started," Hawkes said, now very pale.

"Yes," Dolly replied. "There is no bruising. Butcher a body while the victim is still alive and the blood loss would be catastrophic. The little blood found in the building was consistent with him being dead when he was taken apart."

"We have a team still looking for the rest of him," Alice said. "The problem is that Still Waters is a big site and our resources are limited, so it might take a while." Looking at the victim, laid out in front of them in bits, upset Alice. If this was Callum Hilton, it'd fall to her to tell his parents. Not a prospect she relished.

"The plastic bag he was found in had contained building rubble at some time. Despite having been in the water, we found traces of cement and brick dust," Dolly went on.

That might help. "There is building work going on at the retreat. I'll have one of the uniforms check on the bags being used," Alice said.

"I'm afraid that until we have the rest of the body I can't give you a cause of death," Dolly said.

Understandable. There wasn't much Dolly could do with the body parts, except wait until more were found, then she might be able to ascertain exactly what killed him.

"What about the second body in the lake?" Alice asked.

"Nothing but bones, I'm afraid, but on first examination I can confirm that it's possible that the body is that of Celia West. I had a look at her medical records. She had a pacemaker fitted and we found one in the chest cavity," Dolly said.

"Will you check the pacemaker out, make sure it's the one she was fitted with?" Alice asked.

"Once I know, I'll ring you."

Alice nodded. It would bring some small comfort to Celia's family to know that she'd been found at last and that they could finally lay her to rest.

Alice and Hawkes went down to the office, where Dr Jack Nevin was waiting. He handed Alice a report. "The murder weapon in the Lewis case was the hammer. It caused the fatal wound to his head and it had traces of both blood and flesh on it. The DNA matches the dismembered victim and the blood found in the grass. That means the same hammer was used on the man we believe to be Callum Hilton. Give me a little longer to analyse the DNA from the body parts and I'll be able to tell you if the victim is definitely Callum."

Alice glanced down at his findings. "Same weapon, both killings. That's straightforward enough."

"Not entirely. The fatal blow which caused Lewis's death was administered by the hammer but I doubt it caused the other bruises on his body. The bruised area on his torso is large, as if he was hit with something longer and most likely wooden. Dolly reckons a bat and I tend to agree," Jack said.

First she takes a bat to Neil Lewis, knocks him out and then finishes him off with the hammer. Why? The bat alone would have done the job.

"Did you find anything significant at the Hilton crime scene?" Alice asked.

"Footprints. We've taken casts, and we have evidence that the murderer must have watched the victim fishing for some time before they killed him."

"What d'you mean?" Alice asked.

"There are plenty of places where the killer could have waited to strike, but there's one particular patch of flattened grass behind a hedge overlooking Ash Lake. I found the same footprints there as on the bank."

Alice wasn't sure how that would help. So, Mad Hatter had watched Callum fish for a while before striking. "Is that significant?"

"I also found a stray cigarette end under a bush. It's been trodden into the mud but you never know." Jack smiled. "We'll do tests, see if we can get a saliva trace. We'll also run tests against the blood and gore found under Neil Lewis's nails. We might get a match."

Alice had her doubts about that. Again, it had been made far too easy. Mad Hatter would never make such a fundamental mistake. "Your people did a search. Did you find Callum's mobile?"

"No," Nevin replied. "The comms unit say the last time it was used was the morning he went missing and then it pinged a mast close to the retreat."

"What about the boathouse?" she asked.

"Someone made a reasonable job of covering their tracks but swabs have been taken and I will make sure it has my undivided attention after lunch today." He smiled again.

Alice rummaged in her bag and produced the evidence bag containing the gun. She handed it to Jack Nevin. "Here, you'd better have this. It was found in the Hiltons' lodge. They think Neil Lewis may have hidden it there."

"You're thinking the Holden shooting?"

"Exactly."

"If it is, it's a significant find," Jack said.

Alice turned to go, much to Hawkes's evident relief. "Thanks, both of you. Let me know when the results are in."

CHAPTER TWENTY

"Where to now, ma'am? Back to the retreat?"

"No, Hawkes, we'll visit the station first. The team might have some information for us and I want to remind Osbourne about the gun and to tell the team that it's been found."

While Hawkes drove, Alice rang her son, Michael. No answer, so she left him a message. She wanted to know if there had been more calls and what her colleagues in Edinburgh had said, if anything.

"You look worried," Hawkes said.

"Preoccupied, let's say. I've a lot to think about. It's a complex case and I'm keen we don't miss anything." She didn't mention Michael to Hawkes.

"Worried about your son?"

"He's a big lad. I'm sure he can look after himself." Said with a confidence she didn't feel.

"D'you think forensics will get anything?" he asked.

"I'm sure they'll try their best. They're good people and work hard, but they haven't yet been able to find any tangible proof against Mad Hatter. It's evaded them in every case so far. Evidence there might be, but there's no guarantee it's genuine and not deliberately planted to fool us. We still don't even know who Mad Hatter is, after all this time." Alice looked out of the window. "But we mustn't fail now, Sergeant. Though the odds are stacked against us, our investigation has to bear fruit."

It took half an hour to negotiate the city centre traffic, but finally Hawkes pulled into the station car park. They took the lift up to the third floor and went into the main office. Jason Hawkes looked impressed. "I've not been here before, ma'am. Working here must be something else. All the high profile cases and plenty of resources. The perfect place to get yourself noticed."

Ambitious, eh? Alice gave him an amused look. "That all depends on who does the noticing, Sergeant. It's no different here from other workplaces, just the same old hotbed of jealousies and office romance."

"None of that bothers me. I just want to get on," he said.

"And this is where you see yourself?"

"It certainly is. Tameside is a backwater. We don't get many cases you can get stuck into, but things are very different here. Look at the Carruthers case last year. He was another killer who'd evaded the law for years, and it was a team from this station who brought him down."

Alice smiled. She knew the case well, although another team in the station had worked it. "Don't get too carried away. The detectives here aren't that brilliant. What cracks a case is solid hard work, as you're finding out. The Simon Carruthers case was tricky and could easily have gone wrong. Two years the team worked it, so they deserved all the glory they got."

As they made their way through the office, Alice was aware of Hawkes's eyes darting to and fro, taking in every detail. It was a large open-plan room, whose large windows let in plenty of light. The desks were arranged in banks of four, and the place was busy. The far end had been partitioned off with glass. As they entered, Alice saw Hawkes's face break into a smile of recognition. The notes and images covering the huge whiteboard all related to the Mad Hatter case, every single piece of the puzzle had been included.

"I send in everything we get each day. It's all collated and put up on the board," Alice explained. "The team over there at the two banks of workstations do all the research my notes throw up. I'm hoping they've got something for us today."

"Alice. Any progress?" Frank Osbourne entered the room.

"A little, sir. There's a lot of processing and forensic work going on. We need confirmation that the body parts are in fact Callum Hilton, so it's important we find the rest of him. We also need to determine how he died and tie his death in with that of Lewis. Forensics are working on the DNA. We should get final confirmation any time. We've been given a comprehensive list of likely candidates for Mad Hatter who reside at Still Waters, and the team here are chasing up their backgrounds."

"Dr Nevin might get Mad Hatter's DNA from what was found under Lewis's fingernails," Hawkes said. "If he does, we can test all the women who match the profile."

Osbourne shook his head. "It won't be that simple, it never is with her. We've found possible DNA traces before, but they've all come to nothing."

"This woman isn't superhuman, sir," Hawkes said. "She will slip up and get caught."

Osbourne looked at Alice and raised an eyebrow. "I like his optimism. I hope for all our sakes it's justified, DS Hawkes."

"I've given Jack a gun found at the Hiltons' place," Alice said. "I suspect it's the one Robbie Barrett used to shoot Barry Holden. Neil Lewis made a poor attempt to hide it in a neighbour's lodge."

Osbourne nodded. "Good work. If it is, we'll soon know."

"I think it's what drew Barrett to Still Waters. He must have heard or been tipped off about Lewis and sent his men to look for the gun," she said.

"Let's hope forensics find prints or DNA on it. Nothing would please me more than to get Barrett banged to rights."

Report to Osbourne over, Alice handed a member of the team the car registration number Gemma had noted. "Pass that and the information we've gathered so far to whoever has taken over the Robbie Barrett case, will you? The details of the incident it was involved in are in my report."

* * *

Alice and Hawkes spent the next hour reading through the intelligence gathered by the team at Central. Mostly it was profiles of the women whose names Alice had sent through.

"They're all pretty solid, ma'am," a DC Smethurst told her. "They've got jobs, families and pretty ordinary lives." He handed Alice a handful of sheets of paper. "These profiles, however, are possibles. They all live within hailing distance, none has a settled employment history except for the manager of the retreat, and they have very few family members they see regularly."

Alice ran her eyes down the list. They were all there — Minty, Erica Cross and Gemma Lewis as well as a couple of others. "Gemma was married to one of the victims. What, in your opinion, makes her a suspect?"

"Her and Lewis had only been together for eighteen months, whirlwind romance and wed within weeks. I can't find out much about her before that. And Jessica Minto is a mystery too."

"In what way?"

"No family, no employment history prior to working at Still Waters, and very little life outside her work. It's as if she suddenly appeared out of nowhere."

"Check if she's changed her name, will you?"

"I can find no record of her legally doing so, ma'am, and she's never married either." Smethurst pointed to a map of the area on a nearby computer screen. "Still Waters is central to all the killings, slap bang in the middle of the different investigations. The retreat has to play a significant role in the case, ma'am, and she's well placed, given her job."

Alice looked at Hawkes. "Interesting, don't you think? Especially the bit about Minty and Gemma. Recently widowed or not, I reckon we should go and have a word with Mrs Lewis, and after her we'll tackle Minty."

"Minty has been working at the retreat for several years," Hawkes said. "She has her ear to the ground, knows the place well. I reckon she's a good bet."

Alice was about to reply when her mobile rang. It was her son, Michael. "There's not a lot to tell about that call," he began, "just that the phone number that rang me pinged a mast in Glossop. It's a pay-as-you-go and unregistered. Does that make sense?"

It was as expected. Alice jotted down the number he gave her, it was the one last night's call to her mobile had been made from. "Well, I suppose Glossop is far enough away from you and the family, but watch yourselves. The woman we're chasing doesn't like me much and is obviously trying to rattle me by contacting you."

"Don't worry, Mum, I've blocked the number. There'll be no more calls from there."

It was something at least. If the call had been made from somewhere local to Michael, it would have caused Alice no end of panic. She'd no sooner finished speaking to Michael than her mobile rang again. This time it was Minty from the retreat.

"The boathouse is on fire," she said, panic in her voice. "Your people here have done their best but there's not a lot of it left. I've no idea what happened but it's all gone up — building, boat, the lot."

That was a blow. They had been hoping to get more forensic evidence, fat chance of that now. "Okay, Minty, thanks for ringing me." Alice gave Hawkes the news.

"We don't know if there was much evidence left to be gathered, ma'am," he said. "I saw Dr Nevin collect some swabs on his first visit."

"Another sweep of the place might have been useful. Let's hope Jack got what he needed." She turned to a DC sitting at one of the computers. "Ring Dr Nevin, would you? Ask him to meet us at Still Waters."

"Back to the retreat, ma'am?"

Alice picked up the file on the likely suspects and tucked it under her arm. "Yes, but first I want to pick up some more stuff from my home in Openshaw. It won't take long, it's not far away."

CHAPTER TWENTY-ONE

Alice turned into her house, whose long driveway was overgrown with tall shrubs.

"You'd never think we were so close to the city centre," Hawkes remarked.

"The garden at the rear is large too, though there's a railway line running along the bottom of it." She smiled. "Not that it bothers me." Alice led the way inside and watched the young detective's eyes move around, noting the old-fashioned furniture, the lack of knick-knacks. "I'm going to get some stuff from upstairs, take a look around. The house is Edwardian, there's not many left along here. It's got three storeys, large rooms with high ceilings and still has many of the original features."

He nodded at the Art Nouveau fireplace in the sitting room. "Is that original?"

"Yes. Despite my husband's objections, there's no way I could ever remove it. He was all for ripping the place apart and modernising. A bone of contention that caused many arguments between us, but he was never going to get his own way."

Alice nipped up the stairs and into her bedroom, leaving Hawkes nosing around. A few minutes later, she reappeared with a small overnight bag. Hawkes was nowhere to be seen.

"Sergeant?" she called. "Where've you got to?"

The kitchen door leading into the attached workshop was open. Hawkes was staring wide-eyed at a sparkling white sports car. "You took the dust cover off," Alice said accusingly.

"Sorry. I was curious," he said. "What a little beauty. Yours?"

Alice shrugged. "I suppose it is now that Paul is dead. It was his pride and joy, but since his death it's not seen the light of day, hence its condition."

"A Lotus Elan, very nice. What I wouldn't give to own one of these."

Alice laughed. "Come up with the market value and you can have it. It's a 1969 model. Paul's dad bought it new."

"Doesn't he want it back?"

"He's dead and gone too. In fact, all Paul's family are except for Michael, our son. I suppose one day, if he shows an interest, he'll take it away and finally bite the bullet and flog it. It's not a car suitable for a growing family, that's why it's still here. And because Paul loved the thing so much, Michael's not keen to sell, hence I'm stuck with it."

"Lucky sod."

She smiled. "Watch it, Sergeant. Well, if we make headway with the case I might let you borrow it one weekend. You can take your wife for a ride, turn a few pairs of eyes."

"The missus would love that."

"Well, we'll see how everything goes. The damn car could do with a spin, it's not been anywhere in months. You ready for the off?"

Reluctantly, Hawkes pulled the workshop door shut and Alice locked it.

"What happened to your husband, ma'am? He was very young when he died."

"He had a potholing accident, fell off a ledge and it was a long way down to the bottom. And, yes, he was young, only forty-five."

This wasn't a subject Alice was comfortable talking about. What happened to Paul was a bad memory she didn't like to revisit. "I wonder what the story is behind the boathouse fire?" she asked to divert the sergeant's attention.

"I reckon it was down to Mad Hatter," Hawkes said. "She got scared, worried that she'd left something behind to incriminate herself."

"No, that's what we're supposed to think, Sergeant. This is typical of Mad Hatter, it's what she does." Alice climbed into the passenger seat. "You drive, I've got a couple more calls to make. First, I'd better have a word with Jack, see what he has to say about the fire."

Jack Nevin wasn't happy. "My team took samples from the entire building after the body parts were found. Hopefully, they'll be sufficient and tell their own story, but losing the boathouse is a blow. Given your theory about our killer being active at the retreat for some time, it's possible she butchered others in there — the woman in the Chinley case for example. I know we found the skeleton but on closer inspection, Dolly has spotted signs of partial dismemberment."

Jack had a point. Had Celia West been killed or rendered helpless elsewhere and brought to the boathouse? It was a possibility, Chinley wasn't that far away. "Do we know how the fire started?" Alice asked.

"An accelerant was used — petrol, according to one of the firemen. The place was dowsed in the stuff, with no attempt made to hide what was intended."

"Are you still up there?" she asked.

"Yes, I've just arrived. I'm trying to do what I can but all I've got to work with is the flagstones the thing was built on, and they're still roasting hot."

"We're on our way back. Give me an hour and we'll have a catch up."

"The divers are back on the job. They've finished searching Ash Lake and have moved onto Oak. Nothing else found so far," he said.

What Mad Hatter had done with the rest of the body was a puzzle Alice could do without. She'd expected the victim's further remains to be somewhere in Ash Lake. If, as Jack said, they weren't, where else could they be?

CHAPTER TWENTY-TWO

From the car park at Still Waters Alice could see the forensic vans up on the hill by Ash Lake. "We'd better get up there, see what they've got." She locked her briefcase and bag in the boot, changed into a pair of wellies and beckoned for Hawkes to join her.

A five-minute trek later, they were met by Jack. He was right, there was nothing left of the boathouse except for the ancient flagstones it'd been built on.

"A quick and amateurish job," he told them. "A can of petrol sloshed around the wooden structure and then set alight."

"Damn shame. I recall seeing cupboards and shelving in there I wouldn't have minded a look at," Alice said.

"Too late now."

"Jack! We've got something over here." It was one of Jack's colleagues. He'd thrown a bucket of water over one of the flagstones to get a better look at what had been carved on it. "It's a cross, if I'm not mistaken."

He was right. The flagstone looked for all the world like an old grave, but the cross carved on it was primitive, the effort of someone unaccustomed to working with stone. Looking at it made Alice shiver. "Who'd want to do that, and why?" she asked. "Is something buried there?"

"It could be nothing more than the resting place of a beloved pet. Almost everyone with a lodge here appears to have a dog." Jack smiled. "We'll lift it and take a look." He beckoned to a couple of his colleagues and they got to work.

Alice was on edge, and rightly so. This was Mad Hatter territory, she certainly didn't go for the buried pet theory. A good half hour later, the stone had been lifted and they'd dug down beneath it. Jack was all for giving up when his colleague struck something with his spade.

Alice had a bad feeling. She closed her eyes and inhaled deeply, hoping it would relax her. First a dismembered body, then a skeleton and now this. What further horrors did this killer have in store for them? Not the missing body parts, couldn't be, whatever was under that flagstone had been there for some time.

Within minutes Jack and his colleague had exposed a small white casket. They all stood and stared down at the thing. Finally, Jack broke the silence.

He wiped the sweat from his brow. "This would probably have been down there forever if it hadn't been for the fire."

Alice felt sick just thinking about what it might contain. She wanted to voice her fears but the words wouldn't come. All she could think was that for a man of sixty, it was just as well Jack was in such good shape.

She turned to Hawkes. "It's so . . . small," she stuttered.

One of the forensic crew brushed the earth away from the casket's surface, exposing a girl's name written across the lid in gold lettering. 'Ruby'.

"Jack's right, ma'am, it could contain the remains of a pet," Hawkes said without conviction.

Alice saw the fear in his eyes. He didn't believe that any more than she did. But she couldn't contradict him, couldn't say the words tearing at her very soul. Mad Hatter had killed a child.

Jack had wandered off to call Dolly. "Don't touch anything, mind," he called back.

Endless questions were spinning around inside Alice's head and none of them had any answers. "Sergeant, we'll have to find out if any of the residents here or people connected to them have reported any missing children." She hurried off towards Jack, who was standing by his car.

"Dolly is on her way," he said. "She's asked if we could wait until she arrives before we lift and open the casket."

"You're thinking what I'm thinking then."

"If you mean have we found something truly awful, and Mad Hatter is responsible for the death of a child, then yes. I'm going to take photos of everything along with samples of the soil."

"We've exhumed the body of a child," Alice said flatly. "Should we have done that?"

"This isn't a registered burial site, Alice," Jack said. "And when we get enough information to check, what's the betting the mite's birth and subsequent death isn't even registered?"

He was right. Alice was now close to tears and Jack had noticed.

"I'll give you a call when Dolly gets here. Meanwhile, go and get yourself a strong coffee."

She might as well. It'd take her friend at least an hour to make the journey. Alice walked off towards her lodge, glad of Jack's suggestion. She needed to be away from this place. On the way, she rang Osbourne and gave him the news. He was surprised. Like her, he saw it as a departure from Mad Hatter's usual way of operating.

"There are no children here, Frank," she said. "Those that do come are usually on a fleeting visit to see grandparents."

"Don't assume it is a child, Alice," he said gently. "Wait for Dolly."

"It's a small, white casket with gold edging and the name Ruby on it," she said, her voice shaking. "What else could it contain?"

Alice's emotional response was not very professional but she didn't care. Harm to children was the one aspect of the job she'd never been able to cope with.

"I also have some news," Osbourne said. "But I'm not sure I should burden you with it just now."

What was the difference? "Go on, tell me. It'll give me something different to think about."

"The DNA results are through from the lab. The body parts do belong to Callum Hilton," he said.

She'd expected this, but it meant she'd have to deal with his mother, not something Alice wanted to do right now. "I'll have to find a way to break the news. It'll be tricky, she'll want to see her son and we can't put her through that."

"You can't keep her in the dark. Tell her as much as you think she can take and say that the tests are still ongoing."

Clare Hilton was a strong-minded woman. She might accept the excuse, but equally she could dig her heels in and insist on viewing the body.

"There's more," Osbourne continued. "The debris found under Neil Lewis's fingernails is a match for one of the thugs in Robbie Barrett's gang, a Stuart Roper."

That made Alice stop in her tracks. "Barrett's gang killed Lewis, not Mad Hatter?"

"They certainly contributed to his death, but the fatal blow was caused by the hammer. Tests show that it has blood from both Lewis and Hilton on it."

"Hang on. What are you saying? Mad Hatter kills and dismembers Callum and then somehow stumbles on Lewis having been beaten up, decides to kill him too and caves his skull in?"

"That's how it would appear. Two members of Barrett's gang have been arrested and they insist they only wanted to scare Lewis into handing over the gun he was keeping for Robbie. Now that we have it, they've admitted to that one. They are adamant it was never their intention to kill him. When they left Lewis on the bank of Oak Lake, he was badly injured but a long way from being dead."

Alice was almost back at her lodge. She could see a group of residents gathered outside, Clare Hilton among them. "I'll have to go, sir. There's a welcome party waiting for me."

Call over, Alice forced a smile. "Want to see me?"

Erica Cross pushed forward. "We want to know what's going on. What are you lot doing up at the boathouse?"

"As you no doubt noticed, someone burned it down. Which is a shame because we still had a deal of evidence to gather. My colleagues are trying to determine who that someone was and why they'd be so stupid."

"There's a killer on the loose and you waste time with an old building. It was falling apart anyway and hardly ever used," Erica said.

"I'm told it housed the boat used to check the aerators on the lake," Alice replied calmly.

"The bloody boat could be kept anywhere, tethered to the bank for one. You're wasting time — unless the building is significant in some way."

"I've nothing to say at the moment." Alice raised her voice. The crowd was shouting out their questions and it was difficult to hear. Suddenly, in the middle of all the mayhem, Clare Hilton began to weep.

"It's where you found my Callum, isn't it?" she said. "Why won't you tell me what happened to him?"

Alice moved towards her with the intention of telling her they'd talk later. As she got closer, she detected an overwhelming smell of petrol emanating from Clare's clothing.

"Come into the lodge for a moment, Clare. I think we need to talk."

CHAPTER TWENTY-THREE

Clare Hilton remained standing just inside the door. "I can't stay. Stuff to do."

"Like setting more fires," Alice retorted. "What you did was extremely dangerous. Apart from the physical damage and jeopardising our investigation, you could have been seriously hurt."

"You're wrong! It wasn't me," she shouted.

"You stink of petrol, Clare. I'm not stupid. What I don't understand is why."

She scowled. "It's where my Callum was killed, lured into that boathouse and done to death."

She wasn't far off the truth, but where had this come from? "Who told you that?"

"Minty gave me the idea," she said. "No one saw or heard from Callum after Bert Hodges left the lake. It was dusk then, and there were folk about, walking dogs and the like, so Minty reckons whoever murdered Cal must have taken him somewhere."

"And you decided that that somewhere had to be the boathouse. Didn't you think that it would be more helpful to keep the place intact so we could still glean evidence from it?" Alice sighed. She'd have to tell Clare the truth, otherwise the rumours would run rife. "Come and sit down."

"You know something. What?"

Now Clare was shaking. "D'you want your husband here?" Alice asked.

"No, he's neither use nor ornament. He hasn't even helped me search for Cal."

Alice sat down opposite Clare. Her own nerves were shot after the discovery of the casket. The conversation she was about to have would be every bit as unpleasant. "I'm afraid I do have some bad news, Clare. Your instincts are right, they always have been. Your son, Callum, has been murdered." The words said, Alice's eyes drifted to the clock on the wall. She couldn't look at this mother's face, see the anguish there.

"You've found his body?" Clare began to sob.

"Yes."

"Can I see him? Please, I have to go to him."

"I'm sorry but that isn't possible yet," Alice said. "We need a little longer to complete our tests and process the results." As Alice had feared, Clare wasn't so easily fobbed off.

"Surely I can see him, your tests don't have to stop. I won't interfere."

"We need more time, Clare. That's all I can say. When our forensic people give us the nod, I'll arrange for you to see him."

Though still full of tears, Clare Hilton's eyes rested on Alice, suspicious. "There's something wrong, isn't there? It's written all over your face. You don't want me to see him because he's been disfigured in some way. You're doing tests to prove it's my Cal."

"It is your Cal, there is no mistake, and you'll see him soon. You'll just have to trust me, Clare. Believe me, this is for the best."

Clare hung her head. "For the best! You're keeping me in the dark, and it's not fair. I'm his mother and I want to see him."

"It won't be long, just be patient."

Clare Hilton still didn't look convinced but dropped the subject. "I'm sorry about the fire. I just wanted that building gone."

"I don't understand why. You have no proof that anything at all happened in there."

"He has to have met his end in that building, where else? I couldn't bear to look at it, watch those forensic people go in and out and not know what happened."

Alice had heard enough. It was time to get back. Dolly would arrive anytime. "You should go back to your own lodge and wash off that smell. I've got to get back to the boathouse now, see what my colleagues are up to."

"Will I be charged?" Clare said.

"I don't know. Let's wait a while and see what happens."

Clare Hilton gone, Alice made a quick mug of coffee and checked her mobile for calls. There was more noise outside followed by a knock on the door. An elegantly dressed woman she'd never seen before was standing on the veranda.

"What can I do for you?" Alice asked.

"My name is Maxine Hamilton," the woman replied. "I own Still Waters. I thought it was about time we met."

She was tall, with short, dark hair, an attractive woman in her early forties who'd looked after herself judging by her athletic build. She wasn't smiling. This was no social call.

"You've heard about the boathouse?" Alice began.

"Yes, but more importantly I've heard about the deaths. What is going on here and how d'you intend to stop it?"

"We're doing all we can, Mrs Hamilton."

"D'you know who's responsible? Surely by now you have someone in the frame for the murders?"

"We're still investigating, and right now we're waiting for the results of our forensic tests," Alice said.

"And the boathouse, what happened there?"

She didn't want to drop Clare in it while she was in such a fragile state. "My colleagues are up there now. When we know something, I'll be sure to tell you."

"When you do find out, I want to know immediately. Whoever did it will have to pay."

Alice's mobile rang. "Excuse me, I must get this," she said. It was Dolly, she was up by the lake. "I'm sorry, Mrs Hamilton, but I'll have to leave. I've got a pathologist waiting for me up at what's left of the boathouse."

Maxine Hamilton groaned. "Not another body. Is there no end to the upheaval here?" She stood closer to Alice and held her eyes in a dark, unreadable gaze. "I want my business back, Ms Rossi. I've got Still Waters Two almost ready to open and the lodges are up for sale. Who d'you reckon will want to buy one when the news gets out about this little lot?" With that, she turned on her heel.

"Mrs Hamilton," Alice called after her. "Have there ever been any children here, belonging either to staff or residents?"

The woman stopped and glanced coldly back at Alice. "The people who buy here are usually well past childbearing age."

CHAPTER TWENTY-FOUR

By the time Alice reached the charred remains of the boathouse the casket had been lifted out of the hole and placed on one of the flagstones beside it. The lid had been unscrewed and Dolly, suited and masked, was ready to find out what was inside.

Alice stood well away, her fingers crossed behind her back. She hoped with all her heart that Jack and Hawkes were right and this was nothing more than the body of someone's well-loved pet.

"Here we go." Dolly raised the lid.

For several long seconds, no one said a word. Dolly stared into the interior, cleared her throat, and moved away. Alice's stomach felt hollow and tears pricked her eyes. She told herself to get a grip. This could be murder and the child's parents, whoever they were, deserved answers.

"From the size of the bones, I'd say she was a newborn baby," Dolly said. She looked around at the people watching. "I say *she* because of the name on the lid. There are also remnants of clothing. The infant was wearing a white Babygro and a pink hand-knitted cardigan. There is a teddy bear and a necklace placed beside her."

Alice felt sick. Did this mean that the fiend she'd been after all these years was also capable of murdering babies? But if this was Mad Hatter's work, she'd not drawn attention to it as with the others. Alice stepped forward and took a closer look at the tiny skeleton with the items placed around her. If this was down to Mad Hatter it was very different from all her other killings. She had never taken this amount of care with any of her other victims. Her usual method was to dismember them, like she had Callum. Alice's doubts grew with each passing second. This child had been laid to rest with love and attention. Not Mad Hatter's style.

"How long has she been here, d'you reckon, Dolly?" she asked.

"We need to do some tests first, Alice. But the clothing and that toy look fairly new."

"The necklace must have been important to whoever buried her," Alice said.

Dolly picked it up and studied it. It was a chain with a round gold pendant that had a heart-shaped ruby set in the centre. "It's old, made of eighteen carat gold."

"Like her name," Alice said. "Ruby is the birthstone of people born in July."

"There's an inscription on the back. Since the pendant is so old it's illegible but we may know more once it's cleaned up," Dolly said.

"Can I take a photo with my mobile?" Alice asked.

Dolly placed the necklace on a flat surface and turned it over so Alice could photograph both sides.

"The objects could be significant," Jack agreed. "They might give a clue as to who she was. We'll take everything to the morgue and get to work."

"Any chance of DNA?" Hawkes asked.

"We'll try. The bones might yield something. I have contacts in Berlin who've been working on an exciting project to hasten the analysis of DNA extracted from bone."

"Find out if they can help us, Jack," Alice said. "It would be useful to know who her parents were. This is very different from all the other Mad Hatter killings, and that makes it significant. Ruling Ruby in or out of the current case is a priority."

"How is it different, ma'am?" Hawkes asked.

"For starters, I have never known her to harm a child," Alice said. "I doubt that this baby has anything to do with our current case. But Mad Hatter has committed other murders over the years, and this little one could be connected to one of her previous victims. I'll contact the team back in Manchester, get them to look through the files and find out if any of the victims had babies."

Alice had seen enough. There was nothing more she could do here. "I'm off to have a word with Minty, see if she can help. If there have been any children here, she'll know."

* * *

"You've had Mrs H on your back," Minty said as soon as she saw her. "She's livid about the boathouse. I can't think why, it was a ramshackle old place. We've only got the one boat and the leak in the roof is so bad it was always full of water."

"I think she's more concerned about the retreat's reputation, Minty. She's worried the bad publicity will put the buyers off," Alice said.

"Well, it has. We've had two people cancel their orders just today. Still Waters Two isn't as popular as she'd hoped. If that doesn't change soon, Mrs Hamilton will be on the warpath for months."

"Fierce, is she?"

"Can be. I wouldn't take her on. For a start, she's had to leave her place in Spain to come back here, and that won't please her."

"Is there a Mr Hamilton?" Alice asked.

"No. She divorced him years ago and there's been a succession of men since. The latest is some chap from the city she took up with a while ago."

"This one is serious then, is he?"

"I'm not sure Maxine does serious relationships. Despite having this regular bloke, I've seen her out with several others," Minty said and winked. "She lunches every Sunday at that posh place near the reservoir and has someone new on her arm nearly every week."

"Are you talking about the Needles Hotel?" Alice asked.

"That's the one."

Interesting as Maxine Hamilton might be, she wasn't what Alice was here about. "Has there ever been anyone with a lodge here who was pregnant or had a small infant?"

"Martin and Liz Webb have a daughter who used to come here when she was pregnant. I can't think of anyone else," Minty said.

"How long ago?"

"Five years perhaps? You should talk to them."

"No one else? You're sure about that?"

"It's not that sort of place," Minty said. "Still Waters attracts a certain type, retired fishermen and golfers mostly. And the lodges are damned expensive to buy."

"Thanks, Minty." Alice smiled at her. "I'd appreciate you keeping what I've asked you to yourself. I don't want the people here speculating about what we may have found or what's going on."

"What have you found?" Minty asked tentatively. "Can you tell me?"

"Not yet, we're still investigating, but the way gossip circulates here, I'm sure everyone will find out soon enough."

Alice left the office. Next on her list was a chat with the Webbs.

CHAPTER TWENTY-FIVE

Martin Webb and his wife Liz were both in when Alice knocked on the door of their lodge. Martin invited her in, asked her to sit down and offered her a glass of wine.

"Go on, have one. I bet your nerves are shot. There's a regular circus up at the boathouse, which tells me you found something nasty," he said. "First the fire and then a flock of forensic people. Another body?"

Alice gave him a faint smile. "We're still working on it so I can't discuss it just yet."

"Another body then." He nodded. "The fact you're not giving me a straight answer speaks volumes."

"Anything to do with Callum?" Liz asked.

"No," Alice said.

"Only, if you do want to talk about Callum then I should fetch Clare. Keeping her in the dark isn't on. She's upset enough without her imagination working overtime," Liz said.

"I've not come here about Callum and I don't want to upset anyone more than I have to either. Believe me, if I could give Clare more details, I would."

Martin Webb nodded as if he understood.

"I'm told your daughter used to come here," Alice said.

Martin nodded. "Kirsty. Yes, she did."

"Does she still?"

"Rarely. Back then she was going through a bad patch. She was going around with a lad from a dodgy estate back home and got pregnant and needed our help."

"In what way?" Alice asked.

"In every way." Martin chuckled. "Kirsty was only seventeen, and the lad did a runner the minute he learned about the baby. She spent most of her pregnancy here with us. We took care of her until she had the baby and sorted herself out."

"Where was the baby born?" Alice asked.

Liz Webb frowned at her husband. "What is this about? Why all the interest in little Amy?"

"It's just routine, nothing to stress about," Alice said soothingly.

From the look the pair gave each other, Alice knew they were hiding something. "Where are Kirsty and Amy now?"

"Look, we did nothing wrong, we rang for an ambulance but it took ages to come so we had no choice."

"What're you saying, Mrs Webb?"

"Kirsty went into labour a week early. It happened so fast there wasn't time to get her to a hospital. Me and Minty delivered Amy here in this very lodge. It was all over so quickly we couldn't have done anything else," Liz said.

"What happened? Was the infant okay?" Alice asked.

"Yes, of course. Minty did midwifery training back when she was in her twenties. We were lucky, there were no problems. Eventually, the ambulance arrived and took Kirsty and little Amy to hospital."

"And she was all right, perfectly healthy?" Alice persisted.

Liz rummaged in her handbag and pulled out her phone. "Here, take a look. This is the pair of them taken a fortnight ago."

The image showed a smiling young woman with a child of about six playing in the sand.

"Kirsty met Ken when Amy was six months old. They're married now and very happy. The only problem is that they live in Southern Ireland. Ken works there, you see."

Alice smiled. "You must miss them."

"We do, but we're just grateful that they're happy."

Alice put her empty glass on the coffee table and stood up. "Thanks. I'll leave you both in peace."

Outside the lodge she took a lungful of fresh air. It had been a hellish day and Alice didn't want to spend the night here. As far as she was concerned, this place was poison and she'd had enough of it. She made her mind up to go home and return tomorrow.

"Why the questions about Kirsty?" It was Martin Webb, he'd followed her out. "My guess is that you've found something up at the boathouse and you're fishing to find out who it might be."

"I can't discuss the boathouse, Mr Webb."

"But you are interested in babies who were born here. I wonder why?"

"It's a line of enquiry," she said smoothly.

"At the same time Kirsty was pregnant and staying here with us, for reasons I never understood, Maxine Hamilton took an interest in her. She invited her up to the house, took her shopping for baby stuff, bought her childcare books, that sort of thing."

Alice was surprised. It didn't sound at all like the Maxine Hamilton she'd just met. "Why would she do that?"

"I've no idea, but Kirsty told me and Liz that she thought Maxine was secretly pregnant too, and all the talk of morning sickness and the rest of it was because of her own condition."

"And was Maxine pregnant?" Alice asked, her mind racing.

"I really don't know. There was never a baby, and the bloke she was going about with at the time disappeared."

"Thank you, that could prove useful." Alice smiled at him.

She went to her lodge. Sadie Fox was back and was busy looking through the food cupboard.

"Food's a bit sparse, we might have to send out for something," she said.

"Not for me, Sadie. It's Friday tomorrow — not that it makes much difference to me, but I've decided to go home. It's been a long day and I've got a lot to mull over."

"I've been keeping an eye on the Hiltons for most of the day but Jase told me about the find. Horrific if you ask me. What sort of person could snuff out such a young life?"

"We don't know that's what happened. We'll have to let Dolly and Jack do their stuff before we try to piece together the circumstances of the baby's death."

Alice grabbed her work folders and left for home. Given the choice she'd never return, but that wasn't possible. She had to see this one through to the end.

CHAPTER TWENTY-SIX

It was a long and tiring drive home. The traffic was bad and by the time Alice reached her house, she was exhausted. She'd no sooner put the key in the door than her mobile rang. It was Jack Nevin.

"We've had a bit of luck with the pendant," he said. "I cleaned it up and found something. It's old and hallmarked which gives us the year of manufacture. The inscription reads, '*for Ruby on the occasion of her coming of age in the year 1932.*' That corresponds to the date letter on the rim of the pendant."

"Not bought specially for the infant then," Alice said.

"No. Initial research tells us that the teddy bear has only been in production these last seven years, so we have a timescale for the age of the bones. Perhaps the pendant is a family piece, possibly once owned by the infant's grandmother or great-grandmother. Most likely that's where the name 'Ruby' came from too."

It was another strand to investigate. A search through the antecedents of the possible suspects might throw up something. "Thanks, Jack, a little family history research is called for, I reckon."

"Yes, the Ruby who was originally given the pendant was twenty-one in 1932, making her birth year 1911."

Something to think about. Alice decided on a shower before she ate, and then, if she still had the energy, she'd have a look on the 'Ancestry' website. Finding the correct Ruby without a surname wouldn't be easy, but she'd have a look at the immediate families of her list of suspects first, that might give her a clue.

Not bothering to cook, Alice made a plate of sandwiches and coffee. She was about to tuck in when her doorbell rang. A quick peek through the front window blinds revealed the surprising sight of her son, Michael, standing on the doorstep.

"Mum." He smiled at Alice. "Sorry it's so late, but the damn train was held up."

For a moment Alice thought perhaps she'd forgotten he'd told her he was coming, but she could see from his mischievous smile that this was meant as a surprise. "Michael! It's lovely to see you. You should have phoned, I'd have sorted your room."

"No need. I'm a big boy now, I'll sort myself." He came into the hall, suitcase in hand.

"Are you down here on business?" she asked.

"No, I'm here to see you. I thought I'd better check in, make sure you're okay."

"As you can see, I'm fine." She smiled, ushering him through to the sitting room. "Still overworked, and with a right teaser of a case at the moment, but you know how it is."

"You can tell me all about it over some food."

"When was the last time you ate?" she asked.

"Not since breakfast," he said.

"Let me get you something. I could cook you a bit of a fry up."

"No, don't go to any bother, Mum. A sandwich, same as you, will do, or we could go out."

Alice shook her head. "Sorry, son, I need my bed. How long are you staying?"

"A few days."

"Okay, we'll go out tomorrow night."

"What's the case you're working on?" he asked.

"An old enemy back with a vengeance and giving us no end of trouble. We've got two murders currently, possibly a third. And one of the two bodies is incomplete."

Michael grimaced. "Not something I'd like to deal with."

"Very wise. You stick to accounting, it's safer." Alice disappeared into the kitchen with Michael at her heels.

"Neither me nor Dad ever understood why you do the job. Financially, there was no need for you to work at all — as Dad was constantly telling me."

Paul's attitude towards her work had always angered Alice, and even though he was dead, the idea that his influence had been passed on to their son was profoundly irritating. "If he'd had his way I'd have been permanently wearing a pinny and tied to the kitchen sink." She turned to look at her son. "I love my job, my independence, I always have. Your father found that difficult to accept." Alice was tempted to add that Paul was too possessive, jealous of her job, but she bit her tongue. It wouldn't go down well with Michael.

"It wasn't that you worked, it was the fact you were in the police that bothered him. He worried that you'd get hurt one day. It used to worry me too. When I was a kid, thinking about what you might be doing used to keep me awake at night."

Alice shook her head. "You should have spoken to me. I could have reassured you. As for your father, his problem with my work wasn't the possibility of me getting hurt, believe me. I valued my independence, but your father wasn't keen. He was possessive, controlling. You've no idea how difficult life with your father was in the last few years of our time together."

Michael's face fell. He found her criticism of his father hard to take. "It's not easy listening to this, but I've been told I should, that I ought to let you get it all out."

Alice smiled. "And whose bright idea was that?"

"Zandra's. She's always been on your side, you know. Whenever I talk about Dad, she tells me what a hard time he gave you."

Zandra was Michael's wife. Alice liked the young woman, but they hadn't spent a lot of time together. Though she and Michael had been married for six years, Alice was still getting to know her.

"Perhaps you should tell me your side of things," Michael said. "It might help you get rid of all that anger you carry around from those memories."

Alice looked at her son and wondered why this was coming up now. What had happened to bring him to her door and within minutes bring up the subject of Paul? Alice was tired. Perhaps she was reading too much into this. She changed the subject. "What d'you want in your sandwiches? I've got some nice ham, fresh and lean."

"That'll do fine," he said. "Is the car still here, the Lotus?"

Was that the real reason for his visit? It was the first time he'd asked about the car in years. "It's in the workshop, just as your father left it."

"You've never taken it out for a run?"

"No, son, I never liked the thing. It was too expensive and not fit for a family, but of course your father wasn't interested in a family car, was he?"

Alice bit her lip, wishing she'd not said that. She went to the fridge and got him a beer. Here they were after a gap of many months, and already they were close to bickering. Same old topic — Paul.

"Perhaps he bought it as an investment," Michael suggested.

"Investment!" Alice retorted. "Not the way Paul drove it." She could see from her son's face that the cogs were turning. "I could tell you many things about your dad, Michael, none of which you'd like, but that doesn't make me a liar. That car was bought for no other reason than for Paul to impress his lady friend."

Michael said nothing, and for several seconds Alice thought he might even turn around and leave, but then he said, "Zandra thinks the same. She's had the other woman theory for years. She brought it up again just the other day, and it got me thinking too."

Zandra was clever, she picked up on things. She'd obviously been working on Michael, trying to shift the scales from his eyes.

"I told her about the call I had from that supposed 'friend' of yours. She suggested I visit you and that we should talk. You know me, I just saw it as an opportunity to bring up the car. Zandra questioned whether that was a good idea, she said talk of the car would only stir up bad memories. I couldn't see it, and my initial reaction was to disregard what she said but then she got angry and we rowed. Zandra had a right go at me, said that where Dad was concerned I had blinkered vision. A proper shouting match it was. Just as well little Paul was away on a sleepover."

"What on earth did she say?" Alice asked in surprise.

"At first it upset me, but then I couldn't get it out of my head. It gave me a sleepless night."

Alice handed him his plate of sandwiches and another beer. "Poor you. Come on then, what little nugget of wisdom did she impart that had such an effect?"

"Zandra said that in the last few years of his life, Dad had been seeing another woman, and that was the reason he went missing so much. It was why he wasn't pleasant towards you and wanted a car like the Lotus to mince around in."

Alice smiled. "Your wife's a clever woman. What d'you think about her theory?"

Michael took a swig of his beer and shook his head. "I couldn't believe it, I wouldn't believe it, but then Zandra started to remind me of the early days, when you came to stay with us without him. You always said he was working, but he wasn't, was he?"

"No, Michael, he wasn't. That was back in the day when your dad's antics still had the power to hurt. I wanted to tell you the truth but I knew it would upset you and anyway, you wouldn't hear a word said against your dad back then. You idolised him, remember?"

"Can't have been much fun for you."

"It wasn't. I knew he was off somewhere with his bit on the side. Although by the time he died, I suspect she was a lot more than that."

"You should have said something, made me listen and told me what you were going through," he said.

"You know how you were about your dad. He could do no wrong in your eyes. Any ramblings on my part about him having another woman wouldn't have stood a chance."

"It must have been hard going through all that on your own. But in that case I don't understand why the pair of you simply didn't divorce."

How to tell him? "Your dad wouldn't hear of it. He had his reputation to uphold. He was a well-respected forensic scientist with a top job at the university. He and I had work colleagues in common, Jack Nevin being one of them. Paul didn't want to lose face, he was obsessed with his reputation. As far as the world was concerned, we had the perfect marriage. A divorce, particularly one where the wronged wife alleged domestic abuse and adultery, wouldn't have gone down well. Had he agreed, we could have split amicably, without any mud-slinging. But your dad didn't want any of it. In fact, he threatened to kill me if I so much as spoke to a solicitor." She nodded at her son. "You remember the conversations, how he went on and on about the perfect murder. Knowing what he did about forensics, Paul always reckoned that if anyone could pull it off, he could." Alice poured herself a generous glass of red. "And I believed him. He was the one person I was truly scared of."

Alice saw the doubt written all over her son's face. This wasn't just about Paul's adultery, it was a lot more than he'd bargained for. "Your father was a control freak, Michael. I had my career to consider, so I disregarded the threats and the taunts, but then he'd lash out and I'd have to suffer the bruises. At one point I had to take sick leave because he wouldn't let me leave the house." She saw the horror on his face at this. "You brought it up, or rather Zandra did. There's a lot more I could tell you, but it'll keep for another time. As far as I'm concerned, he's gone now and my life is a whole lot better for it."

Without a word, Michael put the plate on the table and walked out of the room. She knew this was hard for him to hear, but after all he'd come here to get the topic out into the open. Alice heard the workshop door open. He had gone for a look at the car.

"You can take it if you want," she said, following him in. "I've no use for it."

"It's a Lotus Elan, Mum, in pristine condition with only ten thousand miles on the clock. It's worth a lot of money."

"Sell it then, take Zandra and little Paul on holiday somewhere."

"Is it insured?" he asked.

"No. No point as I don't drive it."

"I'll sort it tomorrow and then if you still want rid of it, when I leave, I'll drive it home," Michael said.

Alice nodded. "Good, but remember it's not a family car. Sell it, Michael, and spend the money on something you can all enjoy."

That seemed to please him. Alice watched her son run his hand over the gleaming paintwork. She hoped she'd done the right thing. Selling the car and spending the money was what she wanted him to do, but the look on his face hinted that he had other ideas.

"Sorry I wasn't there for you, Mum," he said, turning to look at her, "that I was so blinkered. Dad always made out that things were fine between you, so did you if you were ever asked. I had no reason to believe otherwise."

"You have to turn over a few stones, look underneath and see what's hidden. Your father was a bully, an adulterer, and an expert at covering his tracks. As far as I'm concerned, he deserved everything he got."

"You never told me exactly what happened that day."

Alice felt the cold shiver slip the length of her spine. She really didn't want to revisit that terrible day, but the look on her son's face told her she had no alternative.

"We climbed Needle Crag together. I didn't want to. I fought against it, made every excuse I could think of but Paul insisted, he wore me down until arguing with him was pointless. I didn't know it but his intention was to explore the pothole known as 'Allegra's Cauldron.' That bloody pothole had always held a fascination for him. He knew every inch of it. He even knew about the hidden narrow path that led down from near the entrance to the bottom of the crag. It's not easy to find or navigate but it brings you out on the other side of the hill. Your dad found it listed on a map of the Cauldron dating back to the nineteenth century."

"Did you go in with him?"

"No. There I drew the line. He could threaten me with whatever he liked but no way would I venture in there again. I'd been inside once, thanks to your father's bullying, but this time I dug my heels in. I huddled down in the rocks to wait for him, since I doubted I could make it down the crag on my own. There was a gale blowing, and driving rain."

"How did you know he was in trouble?" Michael asked.

Alice looked at her son. Her hands were trembling. "I was so cold, Michael, and hours had passed with no sight of him. Finally I had no choice but to go inside and shout down to him. I hate confined spaces and I was terrified. I shouted and shouted but got no response. I flashed my torch around the cave but couldn't see anything. At first I thought he'd taken the secret path, that he was trying to scare me and make me believe he was in trouble. I genuinely thought that's what he was up to, and then I heard a scream. Paul hadn't done a runner and left me clinging to the crag, he was in trouble but was in far too deep for me to help him. By this time the rain was lashing, running like a torrent down the sides of the pothole. I knew from what Paul had told me in the past that it would be several metres deep at the bottom, and if he got stuck down there he wouldn't make it back up."

"Couldn't you call for help?" Michael asked.

"I wanted to, but look where I was. There was no mobile signal and visibility was so bad I couldn't see more than a few inches ahead of me. But I knew I had to try, so I started to inch my way down the crag. About halfway, I met another group of climbers and told them what had happened. One of them took me off the peak and the others organised a rescue party."

"But despite all their efforts, he wasn't found."

"No. That took three more years and even then it was only by accident."

The two of them fell silent. Alice's gaze rested on Michael's face, trying to read his thoughts. "Your father's disappearance made headline news. Many attempts were made to find him but they came to nothing. Eventually the accident got forgotten and the pothole became popular again. It was a group from France who found his body. They'd strayed into a remote part, way off to the right. Paul was lying on a ledge near the bottom. The day he'd fallen, the spot where he landed would have been several metres under water. The PM showed that he had a broken femur and a bash to the head."

"You were never in any doubt that it was him?"

"The body was badly decomposed, nothing but bone, but blood on his clothing and on the rocks surrounding where he was found proved conclusively to be Paul's."

"What about dental records?" he asked.

"No use. When he fell, Paul landed heavily on his face and his teeth were smashed to bits. His belongings were all still on him, his mobile phone and his wallet, although what he'd need money for down there I don't know, plus the watch his father gave him, the one with the inscription. If you still have doubts, Michael, read the coroner's report, it's all there. Your father died from catastrophic injuries as the result of an accidental fall."

CHAPTER TWENTY-SEVEN

Friday

Alice had a fitful night's sleep. She put it down to the talk she'd had with her son. Thinking about what happened to Paul never did her any good and talking about it was even worse. But at least now Michael understood that the rift between his parents was down to his father. That alone would allow him and Alice to mend their own shaky relationship and move on. Alice was grateful to Zandra for the part she'd played. She owed her daughter-in-law huge thanks for putting Michael straight.

Alice rose early and made them both breakfast. "I'm afraid I'll be out most of the day on this case. You happy to amuse yourself?"

"Yes, I'll sort some insurance on the car and book us a table for tonight. Don't be any later than seven now, got it?"

Alice nodded. "There's an Indian place down the road. The food is great and I've been there several times. It's my favourite take-out too. Their card is on the dresser in the hall."

"Okay, I'll give them a ring."

"You sure you're okay with this, staying, I mean? Zandra won't be missing you?"

"Yes, it's fine, and Zandra understands. Anyway, it's coming to something if I can't spend some time with my mum."

"I'll be an absent mum for most of the time," she said, and laughed ruefully.

"It'd be good if you could free up time tomorrow. I would appreciate it."

Alice nodded. She could do with a day off. "I'll cook us lunch or we could go out somewhere. I'll tell the team we'll resume on Monday."

"I'm not Dad, you know. I do understand about your work." Michael poured himself another cup of tea from the pot. "Our chat last night got me thinking, especially about his other woman. I didn't twig at the time, but I think I may have met her."

Alice stopped eating and stared at her son. "You think? Or you're sure?"

"Remember that weekend me and Zandra spent in the Needles Hotel near Ladybower Reservoir? It was just after little Paul was born, and Zandra's mum looked after him for us so we could get a rest."

"The one where you met up with your dad and I wasn't invited," she said with a look.

"That's the one. And it wasn't deliberate on our part. Me and Zandra just assumed you'd be there, we didn't even know you weren't coming. When it was just Dad who met us, I put it down to your work and thought nothing more of it. It was Zandra who suspected that something wasn't right. It caused a lot of bad feeling between us that night. Now I see it was down to me. I wouldn't listen. She said at the time that Dad was acting odd, but I took no notice. There was a twenties-themed cocktail party on the last night we were there. Everyone was dressed up, drinking heavily — you know the type of thing. Well, Dad met us in the bar and he had a woman with him. He said she was a colleague from work, another forensic bod, and I didn't question it, but Zandra reckoned there was more to it than that. Don't ask me how she picked up on it, that's just what she's like. We argued, and I stormed off to drown my sorrows at the bar, but Zandra followed Dad and the woman back to his room and lurked in the corridor to watch. They went inside together. Zandra waited a good twenty minutes but the woman didn't leave. Zandra was really upset at his behaviour. She did try to tell me, but by that time I'd drunk too much and was fast asleep."

"And you didn't think to tell me?"

"You and Dad were already at each other's throats. I saw no point in making things worse."

Alice leaned back in the chair, folded her arms, and looked her son in the eye. "So, you took his side as always."

"Yes, and Zandra has never let me forget it. The next day at breakfast she got talking to the woman, who said the hotel was a regular haunt of hers and that she lived close by. Apparently, they do a brilliant Sunday lunch."

"I like Zandra more and more with every sentence you utter. What did she look like, this woman?" Alice said.

"Difficult to say. When I'd seen her the night before she was done up in twenties gear and probably looked very different from normal. The following morning I was nursing the mother of all hangovers, didn't go down to breakfast and so missed her. At the do she had a black wig on for starters, in a twenties bob. She was younger than Dad — a looker, no doubt about it. Zandra went after them but left her bag with me, she kicked herself later that she didn't have her phone and hadn't been able to get a photo."

"That's a shame, I'd have liked to know what I was up against."

"I can't see why. If it was me I'd want to forget all about her," Michael said.

"Well, you're not me. After that woman came into your dad's life he became even more violent than before. He resented me, wanted me out of his life, but wouldn't do it the legal way, he still wasn't up for divorce. I kept having to take days off work and I was taking pills for depression. The day he dragged me up Needle Crag I was in no fit state to do any potholing, believe me."

"I can't believe he was violent," Michael said.

"Well, he was, Michael, but I don't want to talk about it."

"The woman wrote to me, you know, after Dad's body was found. She said some dreadful things about you. She even suggested that you'd had a hand in his accident."

"What a thing to say," Alice exclaimed. "True, I was there but I never even went inside Allegra's Cauldron. I left that to the rescue party, I wasn't brave enough."

Alice had had enough. She went to get her stuff ready for work. Any more discussion about what had happened that day and she'd be a nervous wreck. She was trying to calm down by sorting through her files when her mobile rang. It was Jason Hawkes.

"There's a possibility that the rest of Callum Hilton has turned up, ma'am."

News she'd been expecting sooner or later, just a shame it had to be today. "At the retreat?"

"No, a landfill site near Glossop."

"Is it bad?" she asked.

"An amount of decomposition has occurred to the body parts and the gulls have been at him, but the head isn't too damaged so he should be identifiable. He was stuffed in a rubble bag like the one found in the lake."

"I'll join you there. Are Dolly and Jack on site?" she asked.

"On their way."

At least now they'd be able to determine how Callum died and whether the same weapon was used to kill both him and Neil Lewis.

"Michael, I'm off," Alice called to her son.

"Look, I never believed a word in that letter. She was simply stirring up trouble. Both me and Zandra saw that."

"What happened to that letter?"

"Zandra burned it. Said it was a load of rubbish and we should take no notice."

"Shame, I would have been interested to see exactly what she wrote."

"You're not planning to go after the woman, are you, Mum?"

Alice smiled. "What for? Your dad's been dead six years. I'm curious, that's all. I'd just like to know a bit more about the woman who helped make my life a misery all that time."

Michael nodded, he appeared to accept her explanation. Which was just as well, because no way could she tell him the truth.

CHAPTER TWENTY-EIGHT

The smell of the landfill site was horrendous, the noise was almost as bad, the air filled with the screeching of hundreds of gulls circling above their heads and diving after any morsel they could eat. A number of white-suited forensic people were knee-deep in rubbish, while Hawkes, Dolly and Jack examined something laid out to one side.

"The black bag must have been put in one of the skips dotted around Still Waters," Hawkes said. "It's the same as the bag pulled out of Ash Lake. They are brought here and emptied once a week."

"Any chance we can find out which skip it was?"

"I doubt it," he said gloomily.

Dolly Parkes beckoned her over. "Problem is the bags are tipped out of the trucks on arrival, they roll and the contents get scattered. His top half was dismembered too, so finding all of him will be tricky. We're still missing a hand, hence the search going on over there. I just hope to God a gull hasn't had it."

Alice stared at the face of Callum Hilton and shuddered. His eyes were open and had a grey misty sheen to them. Alice had a strong urge to close them. His skin was a yellowish white, streaked with dirt and punctured with holes made by the beaks of gulls. There was no way his mother could view him while he looked like this.

As if reading her thoughts, Dolly said, "Don't worry, there's a lot we can do, you know. His family won't see the extent of the damage. I will suggest that Mrs Hilton is shown the body from the viewing window and doesn't actually get up close."

"Good idea, she wouldn't want to see that he's been hacked to bits," Alice said, turning away.

"We'll get him back to the morgue and make a start. He has a wound on the top of his head, it shattered his skull and bled a lot. The mark it left is similar to that on Neil Lewis. I'll confirm if it was caused by the same weapon later."

That was all very well, and if it was the same weapon it would tell them that Callum had been the first to die. But that was only part of it. "What I really want, Dolly, is evidence against Mad Hatter. Solid, forensic proof that'll get her convicted for what she's done. We need to bring this woman to justice, we owe it to the families of her victims."

"I feel the same as you, Alice, and I'm equally puzzled as to why we can't find any. But as you are only too aware, this one knows her stuff. Our Mad Hatter is quite the expert."

With a sigh, Alice turned to watch the uniformed officers sifting through the heaps of rubbish for Callum's hand. "She's been doing this for several years now. I just can't believe that she hasn't slipped up. Surely, there must be something amid all the stuff we've collected." The words were out before she realised what she'd said, and now she felt bad for criticising her friend's skills.

Dolly looked hurt. "We do our best. Jack Nevin is one of the top forensic scientists in the country. If she's left anything at all, the merest trace, he's the one to find it. But so far, there's been nothing, and that frustrates us every bit as much as it does you."

Dolly bent down to examine Callum's chest more closely. "He has a tattoo here, and there's a bit of it missing. It's difficult to tell what caused the wound but it was definitely no gull. The edges are straight, as if a patch of skin has been cut out."

"We thought she'd done something like this before, one of the victims in a case three years ago, remember. He had a tattoo as well, but the body was too far gone to be sure. Will you look at Neil Lewis again, see if you find anything similar?"

"It's a small patch of skin, easy to miss when a body has been beaten or is decomposed. When I get back I'll check, I'll go over my post-mortem photos from the other cases too."

"Thanks, Dolly. I don't mean to criticise, I'm just frustrated, sick and tired of her orchestrating everything so perfectly. There's been a sizeable body count over the years, and we're still no further ahead. That worries the hell out of me. I know the team work hard but we need that break." Alice looked down at Callum again. "If she did take that piece of skin, what on earth would she want it for?"

"A trophy, perhaps?"

"Won't keep though, will it? Unless she's got it in the freezer." Alice wandered off to join Hawkes, who was talking to one of the uniforms.

"Tricky not being able to find the hand," he said. "It's his right one too. What do we tell his mother? She might want to hold it."

"We put her off. Dolly will sort it, have Clare view him through the window. But sooner or later the truth will come out. Sorry, Sergeant, I'm off back to the station to get some coffee and speak to the team."

"Want me to come with you?" he said.

Alice had had enough of getting nowhere. "I'm no sort of company just now, so best you stay here and keep me updated on events by phone."

* * *

One of the tasks Alice wanted the team to do was search for the Ruby born in 1911. If the infant was connected to the

Mad Hatter case, the information might lead somewhere. A starting point might be to look at children with that name born in the Still Waters area.

Thirty minutes later, she pulled into the station car park. Frank Osbourne was in his office as usual, time to tell him about finding the rest of Callum Hilton.

"The half of him with all the identifying features was dumped in a skip on the retreat, which then went on to landfill. Mad Hatter must have realised he'd be found and identified relatively quickly," she said.

"At least now forensics can get to work, confirm exactly how he died and you can give the parents closure," he replied.

Alice nodded but doubted that any parent could ever come back from what had happened to Callum Hilton.

"You don't look happy, Alice."

"I'm not, sir. The deeper into this case we get, the more complex it becomes. We have two bodies and now that of an infant as well. I'm desperate for forensic evidence but there just isn't any. The woman doesn't have special powers, she must make mistakes like the rest of us. How does she manage to keep one step ahead?"

"She must work hard and plan carefully. Any closer to finding out her name?" he said.

"I have another avenue of research. I get anything, you'll be the first to know."

"Are you talking about the baby?" he asked.

"Yes, though she may have nothing to do with this case. Jack Nevin has a colleague in Germany who's working on extracting DNA from a sample of bone."

"You hope to find her parents from that?"

"Providing either of them are in the national database. If not, we're back to square one," she said.

"How's Hawkes doing?"

"He's fitting in nicely, sir. Enjoying the challenge, I reckon."

CHAPTER TWENTY-NINE

Alice sat at a computer with PC Roger Wallis and gave him the information about Ruby. "I realise there are no guarantees, there will be thousands of babies with that name, but concentrate on the month of June, the year, and stick to this area." She circled her finger over a map on the screen.

"You into this stuff, ma'am?" he asked.

"Not really. All I know is tracing a family tree and getting it right can be a slog." She gave him a wry smile.

PC Wallis made a start and within minutes had a screenful of names. "There are a further twenty pages like this," he said.

"All born in the same area?"

"Greater Manchester, ma'am. If I stick to Glossop there's nothing."

Alice groaned. She'd hoped it would be easier. But the truth was, Ruby could have been born anywhere and moved into the area. People were just as mobile back then as they were today, they had to be if they wanted to find work.

"I'll see what forensics can give us. Don't waste time on this until I get more details."

Alice left him to it and went to her own office, a small room with a large window looking out over the street. She picked up the phone and rang the forensics lab. She'd spent so little time here these last weeks that a plant she kept on the filing cabinet was dying from lack of attention. While she waited for someone to answer her call, she tipped what was left in her water bottle over it. Eventually, someone picked up. "DCI Rossi here, have you got anything more on the pendant yet? We've been given the inscription but a maker's mark would be good."

"We've done more work on it and although it's not that clear, it looks like it was designed by a jeweller called Overton."

"D'you know if they were local?"

"No idea, ma'am, that's as far as we've got."

"Thanks, I'll take it from there."

A quick internet search and Alice found the jeweller. Overton used to have a shop in Sheffield but sold out to a large chain forty years ago. She didn't reckon much to the chances of them still having records from 1911.

"I'm off for a walk, clear my head," she told PC Wallis, who was still intent on his computer screen. "Your time would be better spent doing something else."

The young PC shook his head and smiled at her. "I think I've got something, ma'am. I extended the search for records to towns the other side of Still Waters."

Bright lad, Alice realised. "Sheffield, by any chance?"

"Yes, and I've found something. A Ruby Phillips was born there in the right month and year. She's the only one, so it has to be her."

"Excellent work, move your research forward and if any of the names we're interested in turn up, let me know." The young DC had used his initiative and it'd paid off, Alice liked that.

* * *

It was late afternoon so there wasn't time to return to the retreat and then get home for her dinner date with Michael.

An early finish it was, and given the hectic pace of her work life currently, very welcome.

It took only fifteen minutes to get from the station to her home in Openshaw. Entering the front door, she heard her son whistling in the workshop.

"Hope you don't mind but I gave the Lotus a tidy up and a polish. There were lots of bits and pieces in the glove compartment and on the floor. I've put everything on the kitchen table for you."

An unimpressive collection of small change and other items sat in a dish. She pushed them around with a pencil and caught sight of a large, diamond ring. "This looks interesting, what d'you think?" She held it out for her son to see.

He shrugged. "Can't be real, surely? A stone that size? The thing would have cost a fortune."

Alice studied the band. "It is, you know, it's stamped platinum."

"Well, it can't have been Dad's."

"I haven't seen it before — he could have bought it for someone," she said.

"What? And then just lost it in the car?" He sounded dubious. "It's a large ring, the chances are it slipped off the owner's finger and they didn't notice."

She examined the beautiful ring and noticed that one of the prongs holding the diamond in place had been bent at some time and snapped off, forming a sharp point. "I think this is blood," Alice said. "Someone's had a go at cleaning it, but look."

"I found it under the passenger seat. Could be anything and we've no idea how long it's been lying on the floor of the Lotus," Michael replied.

Alice popped the ring into an evidence bag. It had no direct bearing on the case, but she'd get Jack to look at it nonetheless. "Was there anything else?"

"Yes, but I'm not sure if I should show you."

"Something to do with your father? Don't worry, Michael, I'm well and truly over him, so just tell me what you found."

Michael passed her a photo. It showed Paul in front of a hotel. He was sitting on the bonnet of the Lotus and smiling broadly at the camera. He looked relaxed, nothing like how he was around her.

For a moment or two, Alice was taken aback. She'd never seen Paul look so well, so alive and happy. "No doubt another of your father's weekends away with his woman. Shame she's not in the picture."

"It was probably her taking the shot. I saw the look on your face. I regret showing you now. I thought you'd be interested."

Alice looked at her son. "Oh, I'm interested all right. This could prove useful."

"You're not angry then?"

"Hard as it is for you to hear, Michael, nothing about your father upsets me. I'm beyond getting angry." She looked at the photo again. "I wonder how long before he dragged me up Needle Crag this was. Makes you think, doesn't it? If it'd been me that didn't return, his life would have been very different. He might have been happy."

"We don't know he wished you any harm, Mum."

"He wanted me out of the way and he wouldn't consider divorce. What other way is there?" To his evident surprise, she suddenly said, "Can I keep this?"

"Can't think what you want it for, but sure, if you must."

"That building — it's the Needles Hotel, isn't it?" she said.

"Yes, it is. That's where the weekend do that we went to was held."

"Interesting place, and to think I've never been there."

CHAPTER THIRTY

Saturday

Alice slept well, which she put down to having Michael in the house. So well, in fact, that she was still in her dressing gown at lunchtime the next day. "This isn't what I'm usually like, so don't run away with the idea that I'm some sort of slob. I can't recall the last time I had a weekend off."

"You work too hard," he said.

"Can't be helped, and given I love my job, I wouldn't have it any other way."

"Look, I don't want you slaving over a hot stove all day just to feed me. Let's go out, eat somewhere nice in the country," Michael said.

Having given it some thought Alice decided she had no intention of cooking. Eating out was exactly what she wanted, and she had the perfect place in mind. She smiled. "You just want to drive the Lotus."

"I've insured it, so why not drive the thing? Where d'you fancy going? A ride out over the tops, find a nice pub Holmfirth way?"

Alice pulled a face. "I have a better idea. What I really fancy is a visit to the Needles Hotel. I want to give the place the once over, see what I've been missing all these years." A chat with the staff might prove useful. There could still be someone working there who recalled Paul and his lady friend.

"It's a long way to go," he said. "Are you sure you wouldn't prefer somewhere closer, and not filled with all those awful memories?"

"No, my mind's made up. I want to visit the place, see what the attraction is."

"Okay, the Needles Hotel it is then. If you can put up with knowing how fond Dad and his woman were of the place, so can I, I suppose."

"You're forgetting, Michael, I've no memories good or bad associated with the place. Your dad never took me there."

Alice went upstairs to have a shower and get organised for the days ahead. She'd need clean clothes and more food. She was hoping for a forensic breakthrough any day and if it came, it would be a long, hard week.

Dressed in a smart trouser suit, she joined Michael downstairs. "It's the weekend and the Needles is posh, so you'd better wear a tie," she said.

"Didn't bring one."

"Try your father's wardrobe in the spare room, take what you want."

Minutes later, Michael reappeared wearing a tie, grabbed the keys for the Lotus and told his mother to wait for him in the drive. "I've booked us a table." He winked at her. "I'll get the Lotus out of the workshop."

"Make sure you lock up after you," Alice called.

* * *

The Needles Hotel was an imposing stone building from the Victorian era. Set in landscaped gardens, it was obviously not a venue for a cheap weekend away. Paul must have spent a fortune bringing his woman here. Alice sat in the Lotus, looking at it for several minutes. "How close are we to Still Waters?" she asked her son.

"Can't be far. A couple of miles that way." He pointed.

Alice nodded. It was what she'd been thinking. "Try taking it slower on the way home," she said. "My heart was in my mouth on those bends back there."

"Relax, you're quite safe. It's a good little drive, Zandra will love it."

"I've told you, sell it. The money will give you a lift up the housing ladder. You can buy somewhere bigger, more room for your family."

"Even so, we might want to keep it. Look, I'll leave the decision up to Zandra. She says sell, then that's what we'll do."

"There's no room for little Paul or another baby should one come along." She turned and looked at him. "I don't like this car much, Michael. It's bad luck — for me anyway. This car and that hotel there have caused chaos in my life over the years. Don't get sucked in." She turned to look at her son. He looked good in his dark suit and with his dark hair properly combed. He was tall like his dad and had his angular features but thankfully that's where the resemblance stopped. It was only then she spotted the tie he'd chosen. She gave it a flick. "Why that one?"

He shrugged. "I liked the colours. It's some sort of club tie, I think."

"Still Waters golf club. It tells me a lot — that your father was familiar with the retreat for starters. Makes me wonder who he knew there."

"You think Dad's other woman was connected to that place?"

"Possibly," she said. "It would explain why he never took me there — or brought me here for that matter." She saw the hurt on Michael's face. Learning all this about his father's past was killing him. "Let's go and eat. We can continue this inside."

They strolled through the foyer and on into the restaurant. The place was busy. Alice looked around the room, wondering what sort of people came here, and her eyes settled on someone seated by the window. Maxine Hamilton was alone, her gaze fastened on her mobile. Minty had told Alice that the woman often came here at the weekend. Alice caught her eye and nodded, but Maxine chose to ignore her. She nudged Michael. "See her over there? That's Maxine Hamilton who owns Still Waters. It seems there's no getting away from that place or the people connected to it." Finally Maxine looked her way. Alice smiled again, but all she got in response was an icy glare. "She's there on her own but the table is set for two. Wonder who she's with?"

"Stop being so nosey," Michael said.

"Who're you to criticise? You're staring too. I've got an excuse for my curiosity, it goes with the job, and it might be important."

Alice saw Maxine Hamilton put her mobile to her ear and speak to someone. Then she got up and left by the French doors that led into the garden. "That woman is up to something. I bet she's just rung whoever she was supposed to be meeting and warned them off. Seeing me here must have made her nervous."

"Forget it, Mum. This is your day off."

"Order for me, Michael, I'll have the beef. I just want a quick word with reception."

Alice walked out through the main entrance and then doubled back towards the garden at the rear. She wanted to get a look at whoever Maxine was trying to hide. She'd no idea what to expect, but it certainly wasn't Liam Purvis, the odd job man from the retreat. Hand in hand, Maxine and he walked quickly across the car park and got in a car.

Back in reception, Alice showed the woman at the desk her warrant card and asked her to check the booking.

"Mrs Hamilton is a regular customer. She eats here at least once a week, and I believe she's been coming here for years," the woman told her.

"Has she been here with that young man before?"

"A number of times in the last few months."

Alice fished in her bag and took out the photo of his dad Michael had found in the Lotus. "What about this man? Have you ever seen him here?"

The woman shook her head. "I've only been here six months, but Mandy might know, she's been here years." The woman beckoned her colleague over.

"I wonder if you've ever seen this man here," Alice asked.

Mandy took the photo and smiled. "That's Mr Johnson. There was a time when he was a regular, but he hasn't come for a good few years now."

"You said Mr Johnson? You're sure that was his name?" Alice asked.

"Yes, Mark Johnson."

"Did he used to meet anyone here — a woman for instance?"

Mandy looked worried. "Look, I don't want to make trouble for anyone, but I know Mr Johnson was married and the woman he was seeing didn't want his wife finding out."

"How d'you know that?" Alice asked.

"He always gave me a hefty tip in return for my discretion."

"Given he no longer comes here, surely you can tell me who the woman was?"

"He was always in a group, six of them at least. They used to go potholing up there." She nodded at the hills. "At first I couldn't work out who he was with, but finally the penny dropped. It was Mrs Hamilton. She was devastated after the accident. The poor man died up there, alone, and his body wasn't found for ages."

Alice's stomach flipped. She managed to give the woman a fleeting smile and turned away. The woman spoke the words casually. To her they had no real meaning, didn't impinge on her life, but to Alice they were everything. This was it, finally the guesswork was over. This was the missing piece of the Mad Hatter puzzle. She finally knew the killer's identity.

Alice should have been surprised, but she wasn't. Maxine Hamilton fitted the profile for Mad Hatter exactly. But the fact that Paul had used a false identity to cover his tracks came as a revelation. It was something Alice had never considered, and she should have done. Back at the beginning, when Mad Hatter had first started her campaign, after the first barrage of taunts, Alice had tried to find out who Paul had been seeing but got nowhere. Now she knew why. She looked out of one of the huge front windows in reception and nodded at the crag. "You're talking about the accident up there?"

"Yes. It's been a number of years, but I don't think Mrs Hamilton has ever got over it."

'Mark Johnson' needed more investigation. How entrenched was Paul in the identity, and why did he think he needed it? They'd never spoken openly about his other woman but it was understood between them that there was someone. Alice had often accused him of adultery and he'd never denied it.

That after all this time she had a name for her arch enemy made Alice feel slightly unreal. She returned to her table and sat down. "She's with a young man ten years her junior who's one of her employees. I've just seen them together."

"Surely she can go out with whoever she likes," Michael said.

"Interesting though. Young Liam was pally with our first victim," Alice said.

"Forget it. Rest day, remember?" He poured her a glass of wine. "You never do switch off, do you, Mum?"

Alice shook her head and gave him a smile. "Can't afford to. It's a complex case, a bit like doing a tricky jigsaw. Lose a piece and you'll never solve it."

"That Hamilton woman, is she a piece of this jigsaw?"

Alice met his eyes. What to tell him? Not the truth, not yet. "Oh yes, very much so. She has an edge to her and I don't think she likes me very much. I certainly don't trust her either. Plus, she does fit the profile for our killer."

Michael's face fell. "I was hoping this would be a work-free lunch but you're still at it. Look, relax, will you? A couple of days and I go home, I'd prefer not to spend all our time together talking work."

Alice sighed. How was she supposed to do that? This was huge. Alice had always believed that the other woman in Paul's life was Mad Hatter, nothing else made sense. She was convinced that Mad Hatter's murderous game was geared to ruin her professional reputation as revenge for Paul's death. She was the detective who failed to solve the most vicious killings despite there being so many of them. It was down to Osbourne's belief in her that Alice had survived in her role for so long. Now she knew Mad Hatter's identity, what she needed was proof. But Michael was right, this wasn't fair on him. She shook herself and smiled. "You're right. That's enough of work, let's eat. Tomorrow we'll take another drive out but this time Cheshire way. We'll have a wander round Quarry Bank Mill, remember that?" she smiled. "You loved the place when you were a little boy. When we're done there, we'll have afternoon tea somewhere posh in Prestbury village."

CHAPTER THIRTY-ONE

Monday

Sunday had been the kind of day memories were made of. Both Alice and Michael thoroughly enjoyed their time spent together. There'd been no talk of work and no harping on about the past. But it couldn't last. First thing Monday morning, the moment she opened her eyes, there she was looming large in her mind, Maxine Hamilton.

She'd owned Still Waters for a long time, and given that Paul had one of the retreat's golf club ties in his wardrobe he must have been a regular.

Was that why her husband had kept well away from both Still Waters and the Needles Hotel when she went walking with him? Why they'd always stayed at anonymous bed and breakfast places? Maxine Hamilton was the other woman in Paul's life and the implications of what that meant were only too clear. She had to be Mad Hatter.

"Eat your breakfast, Mum. The toast will be cold. You've been away with the fairies again. The case?"

"I'm afraid so, it's a puzzler and no mistake." She tried on a smile but could see it didn't fool Michael.

"Whatever's bothering you, my advice is to let it lie," he said. "You can do without the aggro."

Alice rolled her eyes. "Investigations don't work like that, son. Anyway, you mustn't worry about me, I'm fine. How will you spend the day?"

"I intend to give the Lotus an oil change and fill her up, ready for the trip back tomorrow."

"I don't know when I'll be home tonight," she said.

"Any time before nine and we'll go to your Indian place again. A last celebration before I leave."

Alice nodded. "Sounds great. I'll give you a ring, let you know what I'm up to."

Alice went to gather her files ready for the off. Her intention was to go to the station and see if the team had anything for her before driving up to Still Waters. She was about to set off when her mobile rang. It was Jason Hawkes.

"Problem, ma'am. We've got another body."

Not again. Alice felt mild panic setting in. "Where? The retreat?"

"No, about five miles away in a lay-by off the Woodhead Road."

"Do we know who it is?" she asked.

"Liam Purvis. He works at Still Waters."

Liam! The breath caught in her throat. On Saturday he'd been lunching with Maxine. Today, he was dead. The woman had some nerve. "I know who he is. How did he die?"

"Same as the others, fatal blow to the head."

More of Mad Hatter's handiwork, had to be. The question was, why? "Make sure the lay-by is taped off and call Dolly. I should be with you within the hour."

* * *

PC Roger Wallis had a problem and he wasn't sure what to do about it. He was hoping DCI Rossi would be in this morning so he could discuss it with her, but she was a no show. He picked up the wadge of papers from his desk and read the top sheet one more time, hoping he'd made some huge mistake. He hadn't.

He rang Alice's mobile. "You in today, ma'am?"

"I did intend to go to Still Waters, but I'm on my way to Glossop. Why? Is it important?"

"I think it might be. I've found something and I'm not sure what to make of it."

"Sorry, you're breaking up," she said. "If it's that important have a word with the super. He's up to speed and will advise you."

The signal was so poor up in the hills that Wallis heard only part of what she said. He wanted to explain exactly what he'd found but they were cut off mid-sentence. However, it was important and he knew it shouldn't wait. Osbourne it was then. Picking up the paperwork, he hurried along the corridor to his office.

"DCI Rossi isn't here, sir, and I think someone should see this."

Osbourne looked up from his computer, saw Wallis and his eyes narrowed with irritation. "Are you sure you can't wait, have DCI Rossi deal with it?"

"The truth is, I don't know what to do with what I've found. It's my research into the name on the pendant found up at the retreat."

"Is it really so important it won't wait?"

"I think it is, sir."

"Okay, I'll take a look."

Wallis heaved a sigh, suddenly reluctant to give up the papers in his hands. He wasn't sure what his finding meant but was concerned that it would have implications for DCI Rossi. But he had no choice, so reluctantly he placed his research in the super's hands. "What I've found makes little sense to me."

"Want me to read your notes? No, better still perhaps you should just explain," Osbourne said.

"DCI Rossi was with me when I found an entry in the registers for Ruby Phillips. We suspect the infant in the casket was named after her. What the inspector is unaware of yet is what my extended research turned up. Ruby married in 1938, her husband was Edward Hunter, they had a son, William, born in 1945. I'm presuming the gap is down to the war. Twenty-five years later in 1970, William married. William Hunter was Paul Hunter's father, sir. The deceased husband of DCI Rossi."

CHAPTER THIRTY-TWO

One lane of the Woodend Road had been closed while the forensic team did their work. The stream of traffic in the other lane was bumper to bumper and slow, meaning there were plenty of curious eyes.

"He's been dead since Saturday night," Dolly confirmed.

"How d'you know that?" Alice asked.

Dolly bent down and lifted Liam's arm and showed Alice his broken wrist watch. "It shows both the date and time. I reckon it got smashed during the altercation that finished him. Apart from that the state of the body and the temperature are consistent with him being dead between twenty-four and thirty-six hours."

Saturday night, only a few hours after she'd seen him with Hamilton.

"No attempt was made to hide the body. A lorry driver spotted him first thing this morning after it was light and rang it in."

Alice looked down at the twisted body splattered with mud, his face staring skyward, his eyes empty. It was Liam all right, the young man who'd worked at the retreat and been friendly with Callum. "How old, d'you reckon?" she asked Dolly.

"He's thirty-three. No attempt was made to hide his identity, his driving licence is in his wallet," she said. "But there's no mobile, keys, or anything else."

"Was he killed here?" Alice asked.

"No, there are deep abrasions on his face and body but no blood. I think he was killed elsewhere and thrown here from a car or van. I suspect the abrasions are from bouncing off the tarmac along here."

"Dumped then."

Dolly nodded.

"Mad Hatter?"

"It has all the hallmarks. He has a wound on his head that looks like it was made by a hammer. I'll do his PM along with Callum Hilton's tomorrow morning and we'll run the usual tests."

Alice was frustrated. Tests were all well and good but what she needed above all was the elusive evidence that would nail this woman. "Let me know when you're doing the PM."

She went off to find Hawkes. "I'll be at Still Waters if anyone wants me. You find out where Liam lived and who his family are. One of us will need to have a word and organise for a family member to formally identify him. Also see if there's any CCTV along here. If so, get someone on it."

"It's a back road, ma'am, so I doubt there's any. But in any case, we've no idea what we're looking for."

"Use your initiative, Sergeant," she retorted. This had gone on long enough and it was annoying the hell out of her.

Alice was on her way back to her car when Jack Nevin called her over.

"Bad news, I'm afraid. We've got nothing from the cigarette stub we found near Ash Lake. It was too degraded, sorry. We took casts of the footprints but we've nothing to match them with. Find me the right footwear and we might get somewhere."

"What about the pendant?" she asked. "Could that belong to Mad Hatter, or is that just wishful thinking on my part?"

"We're still doing tests but the DNA on the pendant belongs to a male."

They were getting nowhere with the proof that was so badly needed. "Will you run tests against the DNA of Liam Purvis, our victim over there? See if it matches anything we've got so far as well as that on the pendant."

"But he's a victim, so you must have a theory," Jack said.

"Something like that."

Alice said nothing to him or the others about seeing Liam at the Needles Hotel the day before yesterday. She needed to discuss it with Osbourne before telling the team. But first, Alice wanted to pin Maxine down, have a word with her about Liam before the woman disappeared.

Alice was out of luck. She rang the number she had for Maxine and got no reply. Minty in the office wasn't much help either.

"She was meeting with the building contractors in Birmingham early doors. There's a problem, apparently. Mrs Hamilton's not best pleased, I can tell you."

"Is she expected back?"

"She did have plans for this week but given the problems with Still Waters Two, I reckon they'll have changed," Minty said.

"When she returns or checks in with you, would you ring me?" Alice asked.

* * *

Alice left the forensic team at the lay-by and went back to her lodge. She wanted to catch up with Sadie Fox. The young woman was the FLO to Callum's parents and Gemma Lewis. Where the Hiltons were concerned, things had changed now that the rest of their son had been found.

"Dolly will do a PM on the most recent remains of Callum in the morning. After that, they'll be able to see him."

"Do they know?" Sadie asked.

"Not yet. I want you to tell them, liaise with the morgue and arrange a time to accompany them to the viewing. It's not a formal identification, we already know the body is Callum, but his mother is anxious to see her son."

"What if she asks questions?" Sadie asked.

"He was murdered. That's all you tell her for now."

"I understand, ma'am."

Alice's mobile rang. It was Osbourne.

"Would you come in, Alice? There's something we need to discuss."

"I'm at Still Waters, sir, hoping to catch Maxine Hamilton. We have another body — Liam Purvis. He works here and I saw them having lunch together at the Needles Hotel."

"Is Hamilton there?" Osbourne asked.

"No, not until later today."

"Well, what I have to say is important and won't keep."

CHAPTER THIRTY-THREE

Alice arrived at Central and went straight to Osbourne's office. She'd no idea what he wanted but his tone when he'd called had sounded a little 'off,' which, given their longstanding friendship, was odd.

He got straight to the point. "Are you aware of the information PC Wallis's research has thrown up?"

"No, sir. But he's a bright lad and I guessed he'd find something."

"Oh, he has, and that *something* has given me a problem."

Alice had no idea what he was talking about.

He cleared his throat. "It looks highly likely that the pendant found in the child's casket belonged to one of your husband's forebears. Given that the infant has only been buried for seven years or less, I'm forced to wonder who put it there."

Alice was stunned. This revelation had come totally out of the blue. "But I've never seen the thing before. I don't get it. What could Paul possibly have to do with Ruby?"

"I was hoping you might be able to tell me. Currently the inscription, along with PC Wallis's research, point to your husband being heavily involved in whatever happened to that infant. There is also DNA, I believe. Jack Nevin will see if there's a match between what's on the pendant and Paul."

Alice knew that wouldn't take long. Paul's DNA was on the database. "The blood on his clothing when his body was found was matched to an item of his I handed over to the forensic team at the time," she said.

Alice was frantically trying to work it out. Was it possible that Paul was the father of that mite in the casket? Osbourne wanted answers, and she didn't have any — well, apart from telling him about Maxine Hamilton being Mad Hatter, that was. But did she dare? It would mean an end to her involvement in the case. Realistically, she had no choice, Osbourne had to know what was going on. It was only a matter of time before he pieced it together anyway.

"I believe Paul was having an affair with Maxine Hamilton, the owner of Still Waters," she said finally. "I don't have actual proof but it's highly likely that I'm right."

"An affair? I'm sorry, Alice, but neither you nor Paul ever gave any hint that there was anything wrong with your marriage. Why would you think that now?"

"It's difficult to explain," she began. "Some of it is personal stuff that I've only ever spoken to my son about."

"I can be discreet, Alice."

"You can't promise that. Like it or not, you might have to make it official. Paul's involvement has already compromised me." She saw Osbourne's expression change from one of curiosity to concern. "Me and my son lunched at the Needles Hotel at the weekend and we saw Maxine Hamilton there. She was with Liam Purvis, one of her staff, and within hours he became our latest Mad Hatter victim."

Now Osbourne looked alarmed. "Are you suggesting that Hamilton is Mad Hatter?"

Alice had to tell him. Lie, and he'd see right through her. "Yes, I do. I spoke to one of the hotel receptionists and she remembers them together."

"So she knew Paul." He shrugged. "Even if they were having an affair, what makes you think Hamilton is Mad

Hatter? That's one huge leap, and a rather wild accusation if you don't have the evidence to back it up."

"Something I've never told anyone is that she's been playing games with me for years. You know that when she kills she ensures it's me who investigates. I've never spoken about the personal stuff though, or added it to the case notes. The taunts, the phone calls I've had, the accusations she's made. From what she's said over the years it's become obvious that the woman we know as Mad Hatter was close to my husband. She's made it plain that she has this vendetta against me because she blames me for Paul's death in that pothole. She maintains that I should have saved him, could have done much more to get him out, but that instead I left him to die."

Osbourne shook his head. "She has said this to you? In as many words?"

Alice nodded. "Over the years she's hurled many insults and accusations my way. I've suspected Mad Hatter was Paul's lover for a long time. I just didn't know who she was until now."

"I read the report," he said, "attended the inquest with you and heard what the coroner had to say. So, I know that any accusation of your involvement in his death is utter nonsense, there was nothing you could have done. I'm sorry, Alice, but the man was a fool to even attempt what he did in such foul weather."

"I have no proof but I think that climb was more about putting me in danger than him. But whatever plans Paul had backfired and he ended up dead. And his lover, who for the last six years I've believed to be Mad Hatter, has been punishing me for it."

"You should have told me this. It could have opened an entirely new avenue of investigation. We could have looked at Paul's life — who he knew and where he went," Osbourne said. "Like the Needles Hotel."

Alice shook her head. "I've been doing some clandestine investigations of my own during the last six years and got nowhere. Until this case, I had no idea Still Waters even existed, or that Paul and Maxine Hamilton frequented the Needles Hotel. He was careful, left no clues. Eventually, I gave up, realising that it wasn't getting me anywhere."

Osbourne didn't look convinced. "You're a good detective. I find that hard to believe."

"As I said, I asked the receptionist at the Needles Hotel about Hamilton and I showed her a photo of Paul. She recognised him but said his name was Mark Johnson. I'll check it out, but I bet the identity stands up. Paul's thing was forensics, and in the course of his work he'd met some dodgy people. If anyone was capable of creating a foolproof alter ego, it was him."

"Do we have any solid evidence that links Maxine Hamilton to Mad Hatter?" Osbourne asked.

"Solid evidence?" Alice shook her head. "Only my say so."

"But you're sure Hamilton is the woman who had an affair with your husband?"

"I believe so — well, according to the staff at the hotel, she is. I also know now that Paul was familiar enough with Still Waters to have been a member of the golf club there."

"To summarise, you do not have proof positive that Hamilton is Mad Hatter. All you have is a theory, the word of a hotel worker and some dubious phone calls." He looked her in the eye. "Are you even sure it was Hamilton who made them?"

"Well, no — she disguised her voice."

Frank Osbourne rolled his eyes. "I don't doubt for one minute that you're right, Alice, your instincts are, more often than not, correct. But until we have solid evidence that Hamilton is Mad Hatter we can't act on what you've said." He gave her a smile. "I don't want you off this case, Alice. If what you've told me turns out to be correct, I'll have no choice, but until then, you are still the SIO."

Alice knew he was bending the rules. "I'm grateful, Frank. I want this woman brought to justice and I want to be there when it happens."

"Good. So we understand each other. PC Wallis has worked hard," he said. "The lad has ambitions to join CID, and when this is over we might consider him."

"He knows about Paul's involvement?" she asked.

Osbourne shook his head. "Your husband is dead and his affair ended six years ago. Where Hamilton is concerned, the absence of proof of her guilt means that everything you've said is still only conjecture. You saw Hamilton with the latest victim the day before yesterday, so you should interview her as a matter of course and thoroughly check what she tells you."

Alice relaxed. He'd taken this well. The outcome of their discussion was a great deal better than she'd feared.

"Is there anything else you're keeping from me?" Osbourne said. "I want you to stay on the case, and I think that is still possible. Given that your husband is no longer with us, he can't influence you, neither can you tell him anything that may come out of our investigations. I'll have a word with Wallis and tell him to discuss the matter with you and me only. The official line is that Mad Hatter is unknown to us and is still out there."

"There is nothing else, sir — well, apart from wondering what to do about Clare Hilton. She set fire to the boathouse."

"Do we have evidence of that?"

"She told me herself, sir."

"Have you taken a statement from her?" he asked.

"Not yet, there's been other more important stuff to see to."

"The woman's been through enough. Let's just drop it, shall we?"

She nodded. Osbourne was a good sort. "I'll watch Hamilton like a hawk. As we all keep saying, she's only human. She has to slip up sometime."

"Watch her by all means, but don't put yourself in danger, Alice. The woman is ruthless and she's after your blood. When you interview her, make sure you're not alone. Take Hawkes with you."

Alice nodded. "Thank you, sir. Well, I'd better get back to Still Waters and make sure she doesn't try to get away."

CHAPTER THIRTY-FOUR

Alice returned to Still Waters, stopping at Minty's office before she went on to her lodge. She found Minty talking to a group of residents who all fell silent as soon as she walked in the door.

"Is Mrs Hamilton back yet?" Alice asked.

"I haven't seen her," Minty said. "D'you know what's going on? I can't get hold of Liam and that uniformed copper that's prowling around said he'd been killed."

"Surely that can't be right," Dave Hilton added. "I haven't heard anything, and anyway, who'd want to harm Liam?"

Alice was saying nothing about the murder until she had spoken to Maxine Hamilton. "You shouldn't listen to gossip, any of you."

"Odd that no one's seen him though. He was in here Saturday at about six as I was closing up. He wasn't through the door before Mrs Hamilton collared him about some urgent repairs. He wasn't pleased about having to work late, but he was certainly alive and well," Minty said.

Alice had been about to leave, but on hearing what Minty said, she turned back. "Are you sure about that?"

"Yes, she is," Erica Cross butted in. "I was in here too. We were joking about the golf match that afternoon. Liam missed it and I was telling him how my sister fell into a ditch. Maxine completely spoiled the moment, just stormed in and dragged him off in that van outside."

"Have any of you seen Liam since?"

"No, and that's unusual for him," Minty replied.

"I want the pair of you to give statements to one of my officers. Tell him exactly what you've just told me," Alice said.

"Important, is it then, Liam's whereabouts Saturday evening?" Erica asked.

There was no way Alice was going to get roped into a conversation about the fate of Liam Purvis — it'd be all round the retreat within the hour. "It could be, and just in case it is, your statements could prove vital."

With that, Alice left them to chew over the various theories they'd no doubt float about poor Liam. Out in the open, she tried the number for Maxine, but there was no signal. She'd give her another hour, then get hold of Hawkes and go round to her house.

"You look stressed. Want to come back to ours for a cuppa?"

It was Martin Webb, out walking his dog. The man was everywhere, very much the nosey sort and determined not to miss a thing. She smiled at him. "Thanks for the offer, but I really don't have the time. I've got some serious thinking to do, and I need a quiet hour with my case files."

"No closer to finding the killer then."

What to tell him? Certainly nothing he'd take back to Clare Hilton that would upset her. "I wish it was otherwise, but the person we're after seems always to be one step ahead."

"There's a glint in your eye. I'd say you know the killer's identity but you're short on evidence. That's it, isn't it?"

Astute of him to work that out. "Without cast iron proof, Mr Webb, the CPS won't give what we've got so far the time of day."

"I might be able to help, though of course my input could add up to very little," he said.

After imparting that little gem, he strolled off. Alice darted after him. "What did you mean by that? This isn't a game, you know. If you have information, you must tell me."

"I'm not sure, that's all. It might be a load of circumstantial nonsense but it played on my mind all night."

"What did? Just tell me what's bothering you, Mr Webb," Alice said.

"I'm out a lot around the retreat," he nodded at the dog, "walking this one. We're supposed to keep them on a lead at all times, but there's a field across the road next to Still Waters Two where we can let them run free."

"How is that significant?" she asked.

"Me and Lulu here are over there every day and I see what goes on. Yesterday evening, for instance. We'd gone over there after tea and stayed playing ball until it'd gone dark. We were near the site of those three new lodges they're putting up next to the lake that's being excavated — the ones Mrs Hamilton is charging the earth for. I've seen the plans, huge they are and with all mod cons. Anyway, last evening there was a lot of coming and going around the middle plot. The concrete bases haven't been laid yet and I saw a man dig a hole in the centre of the plot and then dump a rubble bag in it. I got curious, couldn't understand why — there was a bin close by and a skip less than ten metres away but he ignored them both. It struck me that the only reason for burying that bag was because it was supposed to stay that way. Then I find out that the cement bases for those lodges are due to be done today, which got me thinking about what was in the bag that he wanted to hide."

"Did you recognise the bloke?" she asked.

Martin shook his head. "Like I said, it was dark and I couldn't even tell if it was a man or a woman who dumped the bag. I suppose it could have been one of the construction people, but equally it could have been anyone." He tapped his head and grinned. "Suspicious mind. Can't help thinking the worst."

Alice smiled back. "Me too, and that's the problem. Thanks for the information. I'll certainly look into it."

What Martin Webb had told her left Alice in a thoughtful mood. Even though he may have hit on something important she couldn't go poking about on Maxine's land without the appropriate clearance. But what if this person had buried damning evidence of some sort? And why not just burn it? What she needed was a good enough reason to obtain a warrant to search the Still Waters Two site, make whatever they found there official, and therefore usable as evidence. And she had to be quick, otherwise she'd be eaten up with curiosity about what had been hidden, and wouldn't get any rest.

She rang Frank Osbourne and told him what Martin Webb had said. "I want to organise a search, sir. Hamilton was with our victim early yesterday evening and Jack's team have only found his wallet. Just like with Callum, there was no mobile. He must have had other possessions on him when he was killed."

"Speak to the woman first," Osbourne advised her. "Say nothing about what Webb told you, or the possibility of a search, but make it a priority to find out who last saw Liam Purvis alive. If that turns out to be Hamilton, I'll get you that warrant."

That lightened Alice's mood, but she still couldn't understand why Maxine had killed Purvis in the first place. For some reason she must have considered that he'd outlived his usefulness after yesterday. Did the fact that Alice had seen her at the hotel with him have anything to do with it? If it did, the woman had taken a huge risk. She must surely be aware that it would bring Alice running to her door.

Her thoughts were disturbed by Hawkes, who was shouting to her from his car. "All finished at the lay-by. A quick coffee and then on with finding his relatives. Want one?"

Alice nodded and followed him to the lodge. He had the kettle on by the time she got there.

"Mustn't forget to pick up my suit from the cleaners later," he said, looking at his mobile. "Bloody landfill. I just hope poking through all that rubbish hasn't ruined it."

"There's a lesson for you. Never wear anything for work that you can't afford to lose. I meant to ask, while you were poking about did you find anything else — Callum's mobile for instance? I've been looking through the preliminary report and there's no mention."

He handed her a mug of coffee. "Jack Nevin took away the rubble bag the second lot of body parts were found in. There was no phone, but there was a tangle of gaffer tape. He reckoned it had been used to tie Callum up at some point."

She wasn't about to hold her breath. It'd probably turn out to be as useless as everything else they'd found at the various crime scenes. She sighed. "I'll be glad when this case is done. I'm not sure how much more of this I can take."

"I can take over for the rest of the day if you want to go home, ma'am."

He meant well, but Alice didn't want to miss Maxine. "Thanks for offering but I've got something important to do first, and you're coming with me."

"Sounds ominous."

"We have to speak to Maxine Hamilton and I don't want to do it alone."

"Don't blame you. From what I hear she's one fierce woman."

"That's not the reason, Sergeant. I saw her having lunch with Liam at the Needles Hotel on Saturday. Apart from which, she's top of the list for the role of Mad Hatter. But not a word to anyone, understand?"

Hawkes looked taken aback at this. "When did you decide that?"

"She fits the profile, lives central to all the killings — and there is something else which I'm not ready to disclose yet," she said. "We are interviewing her now on the basis that she could have been the last person to see Liam alive. We'll ask her what time they parted company and if she knows where he went. Then we'll decide on our next move based on what she tells us. If we find out that Maxine was indeed the last person to see Liam alive, we get a warrant to do a search."

"Hamilton's not a particularly pleasant woman. The people with lodges here tell me that all she's interested in is the money. Default on the site fees, refuse to upgrade when the time comes and you're out," Hawkes said.

"That simply makes her a hard-headed businesswoman," Alice said patiently, "but I take your point."

"I've found out a little about Liam Purvis, ma'am. He's from Glossop. Before he started working here and took up residence in one of the lodges allocated to staff, he lived there with his parents. Want me to have a word with them?"

Alice was only half listening, she'd just had a text from Minty telling her that Maxine was back. "Yes, but not yet. We have to be quick, get over to Maxine Hamilton's place. I daren't miss her, what I have to say is too important."

CHAPTER THIRTY-FIVE

Maxine Hamilton lived in a large stone farmhouse across the road from Still Waters and in the middle of the site of Still Waters Two, currently under construction. Walking up the driveway, they were assailed by the noise. In close proximity construction vehicles, particularly an earth mover, were busy excavating the area of ground that would eventually be the lake.

A woman Alice didn't know answered her knock. Alice held out her badge and asked to see Mrs Hamilton. "It's urgent," she added, seeing that the woman was about to make some excuse.

"It's all right, Glenda, I've got a few minutes." Maxine Hamilton was standing in the hallway. "I'm about to leave for a meeting with the contractors."

"We'd like to speak to you about Liam Purvis," Alice began.

"What about him?"

"He's been murdered," Alice said bluntly. "His body was found this morning off the Woodhead Road."

That got her attention. "Poor Liam. As you know, he worked here, had done for some time. I'm sorry to lose him." The words sounded sincere enough but then her tone changed. "That's another death associated with the retreat, Ms Rossi. Isn't it about time you found the killer? After all, you've been hanging around here long enough. Surely you must have made some progress by now."

"We're doing our best," Alice said.

"You need results, Ms Rossi, or I'll have no customers left," Maxine said. "Have you seen what's going on next door? How am I expected to sell those lodges when the retreat is fast becoming murder central. Do Liam's family know?"

"We haven't spoken to his parents yet, but that will be dealt with. You were with Liam on Saturday at the Needles Hotel," Alice said.

"His mother will be devastated. She wasn't happy when he left and came to live on the retreat."

"Your lunch date, Mrs Hamilton," Alice prompted.

Maxine gave Alice a coy smile that didn't sit well on her. "I didn't realise you'd spotted us together. We did try to be discreet."

"Sharp eyes," Alice said. "I don't miss much."

"Well, you obviously think I can help, so what can I tell you?"

"What did you do after you left the Needles?" Alice asked.

"We came back here. Liam checked on progress next door and then he left. He told me he was going to see his mother."

"What time was it when you last saw him?" Hawkes asked.

"About five in the afternoon. He popped in to say that they'd had a problem digging out the lake next door. Apparently they'd hit some old pipe works and would have to delay until the surveyor took a look."

"And has he?" Alice asked. "Only I couldn't help noticing that work is still going on."

"Yes, everything is fine. We're on schedule to finish the lake by the end of this week."

"Can I ask what your relationship was with Liam?" Alice asked.

"He was an occasional dalliance, nothing serious." She smiled. "Liam was a good-looking young man and I enjoyed his company."

"D'you know if he had any enemies? Had he said anything about being afraid of anyone?"

Maxine Hamilton looked at Alice and grinned. "He used to say that the most frightening person he knew was me, Ms Rossi. Make of that what you will."

Alice shuddered. She could well believe it. "Did you catch sight of him after five on Saturday?"

"No. After he left I finished some paperwork, made some calls and called it a day. I have a busy week ahead of me," Maxine said.

Alice knew from what Minty had told her earlier that this was a blatant lie and could easily be proved as one, but she said nothing for now. She wanted those statements first, and to speak to Liam's mother. The extra time might also prove useful for forensics.

Hawkes had been busy taking notes. "Nevertheless, we might need to speak to you again," he said.

"I'm here until late tomorrow afternoon, after that I'm off to Birmingham for yet another meeting with the contractors," Maxine said.

If she disappeared now, they might never find her again. Alice knew they were close to a result, all they needed was that vital shred of evidence that would tie her to any one of the killings. She said nothing about the conversation in the office but asked instead, "Mrs Hamilton, would you mind taking a DNA test?"

"What on earth for?" she said. "I've done nothing. I certainly didn't kill Liam, if that's what you're thinking."

"It would be for elimination purposes only," Alice said. "You spent time with him just hours before he met his death, so our forensic people are bound to find your DNA."

Maxine stared at Alice for a moment, appearing to weigh this up. "Yes, of course. Will you send someone round?"

There was no way Alice was going to give her the chance to slip away and had come prepared. She took the sealed swab and container from her bag. "All I need to do is swab the inside of your mouth and we're done."

For a fleeting moment, Alice was sure she saw a look of fear cross Maxine's face. She'd pinned the woman down, put her in a situation she couldn't wriggle out of.

Sample taken and safely packed in an evidence bag, Alice gave the woman a big smile. "All done. I'll pass it on to the lab and we'll be in touch."

"As I said, make it quick. I'm off tomorrow afternoon and I could be away a couple of days," Maxine said.

Alice nudged Hawkes and they made for the front door.

Outside, Alice patted her bag. "I can barely believe that I might actually have a sample of Mad Hatter's DNA."

"That's if you're right about her. Even if you are, there's nothing to match it against as far as we know," Hawkes said.

"There have been a number of killings during the last six years. Jack will trawl through the DNA from every case before we can be sure of that. It only takes one instance, Hawkes. We already have a partial stray sample. Jack gets any sort of match with that and we have her."

Hawkes changed the subject. "Liam was dumped in that lay-by, so he must have been taken there in a vehicle."

"The retreat has a van, it's usually parked outside Minty's office. Ask her who has keys. I'll wait for you at the lodge and then we'll both go and speak to Liam's parents," Alice said.

CHAPTER THIRTY-SIX

On the way to the Purvis home in Glossop, Alice rang Jack Nevin and told him about the DNA. She explained her suspicions about Maxine Hamilton but based them on the fact that she'd been with Liam the day of his murder and no one had seen him since.

"I want you to look at everything. I know it's a long shot, but go through the DNA we've gathered from all the Mad Hatter cases so far. If you identify any piece of stray DNA that was never pinned down, see if it's a match, as well as that partial from the cigarette end. I'm hoping for a good outcome on this, Jack."

"We'll do our best, Alice. If it's there, we'll find it, but you know as well as I do what a long shot that is. We'll give it a go, that's all I can promise."

"That's all I want, Jack. I'll drop it off at your lab in the morning. If it turns out that Maxine was the last person to see Liam alive, if he didn't visit his parents like she suggested, Osbourne will arrange a warrant that will allow us to search part of her property. A resident saw a rubble bag being buried there, and I would dearly like to know what's in it."

"I'll let you know tomorrow what the latest forensic tests have come up with. Dolly will be in touch about the time of Purvis's PM."

Call over, Alice turned to Hawkes. "I'm actually daring to hope that we're getting somewhere at last. Pull a few things together and we could have her."

"I understand what you're saying, ma'am, but it all sounds a bit tenuous to me. So Maxine had lunch with Liam, they might even have been an item, but that doesn't mean she killed him."

"There is more, Sergeant, I'm just not sharing it at present."

"What about Osbourne?"

"He knows, so don't worry. Things go pear-shaped you won't be dragged down with me," Alice said.

Half an hour later, Hawkes pulled into a narrow lane of terraced cottages. The Purvis home was halfway along.

"How d'you think they'll take it, ma'am?"

"Badly. Liam was a young man and their only son. Better get it over with, Sergeant. It never gets any easier, you know."

Diane Purvis stood in the doorway, eyeing the two detectives up and down, before grudgingly inviting them in. Alice gave her the news and waited for the tears, the fallout, but apart from a stray tear that trickled down her cheek, Mrs Purvis appeared to be unmoved.

"Don't get me wrong, we loved Liam dearly but we lost him a while ago. It was always going to end this way. It was that woman, that boss of his. She's poison, no one up at the retreat likes her, she uses people. Liam was a fool, couldn't see past the pretty face and the money she spent. I only met her once but I saw it right away. I tried to tell him but he wouldn't listen. She thinks of nothing but that bloody business of hers, of turning a profit, and she'll do anything to make sure it does."

"Is your husband here?" Alice asked, looking around the empty sitting room.

"Fred's ill, he's in bed upstairs. He has a bad chest and spends his life attached to an oxygen tank."

"I'm sorry," Alice said. "That can't be easy."

"It isn't, running after him all day long and not being able to leave the house for any length of time takes its toll, believe me. Liam said he'd help out but lately we've hardly seen him."

"Did you see him Saturday evening or yesterday?" Alice asked.

"No. He was expected here for a meal Saturday night but he didn't turn up. Instead, he rang me just after six on Saturday to say he was doing a job for that Hamilton woman and not to make him any tea. Really upset Fred that did. We haven't heard from him since and I can't get him on his mobile either."

"Did he say what this job was?"

"Taking her to look at something on the new site. It meant driving the works van over some rough ground and she'd asked him to take her. I got a bit shirty with him. I mean it was Saturday, couldn't someone else have done it? He'd been working all day as it was."

"He was doing a job with Mrs Hamilton," Alice said. "You're quite sure of that?"

"It's what he said," Diane confirmed.

"And you're sure he didn't say anything about seeing anyone else? He wasn't meeting someone later?"

"No, just the job for the Hamilton woman and then back to the lodge for a few cans. He sounded done in, as if he needed an early night."

"Thanks, Mrs Purvis, that's very helpful."

"Will I be able to see him?" Diane asked.

"Yes, of course. I'll arrange for someone to ring you to arrange a time, and then you'll be picked up and taken there. If I send a PC round tomorrow, would you give a statement, tell him what you've just told me?"

"Of course, love. I'll help in any way I can."

Back in the car, Alice turned to Hawkes. "That wasn't what Maxine Hamilton told us, was it?"

Hawkes shook his head. "It's way off. From what his mother says, he must have gone out to lunch, back to hers and then carried on working."

"I'll get on to Osbourne and tell him. It's looking as if Maxine Hamilton was indeed the last person to see him alive. She was certainly lying to us about what he did after leaving the Needles Hotel. We need that warrant."

CHAPTER THIRTY-SEVEN

Alice dropped Hawkes back at Still Waters and then made for home. On the way, she rang Osbourne and brought him up to speed with events. "Hamilton has a meeting in Birmingham tomorrow afternoon so we need that warrant quick."

Osbourne promised he'd have it for her in the morning and he'd organise the search team.

"I'll meet them up there but first I'll drop the DNA sample into the lab. If we find anything on her land, or if her version of events still doesn't correspond with Liam's mother's statement, I'll bring her in."

Osbourne chuckled. "I'll expect fireworks then."

The case was hotting up, and Alice felt better than she had in ages. The only downside was that this was Michael's last night with her. Tomorrow he'd drive back to his family in Edinburgh and she probably wouldn't see him again for ages. Visits from her son were often fraught affairs punctuated by disagreements, but not this time. This time they'd talked through a lot of stuff and for the first time ever, Michael had understood her side of the story. Finally, they could discuss his father without arguing. Michael's absence would also mean her home was empty again. She'd better organise a PC to keep an eye out, just in case things with Hamilton didn't go as planned.

"Want to eat out?" he asked as soon as Alice got in. "Only if you do, I should book. It's a popular place."

"Yes, that'd be nice. Are you all set for the journey? Sure the Lotus will get you there?"

"It'll be fine, Mum. Zandra can't wait to see it. We've agreed to have a trip out this coming weekend and then it's up for sale."

Alice gave him a beaming smile. "Sensible girl, your wife. I'm off for a quick shower and a change of clothes and then I'll be with you." As she climbed the stairs, Alice heard her mobile. It was still in her bag on the dresser in the hallway. "Get that, would you?" she called over her shoulder. "Tell whoever it is I'll ring them back."

Half an hour later, she reappeared and joined her son. He held up her phone. "I'd no idea this had turned up," he said to her. "Dad always said I could have it, give it to Zandra and pass it on down the line." He showed her the photo of the pendant. "Problem was, the thing disappeared and Dad said he'd no idea what had happened to it."

"You recognise it?" Alice asked in surprise.

"Yes. It belonged to some ancestor, it's an heirloom, apparently."

"I must have seen the thing somewhere and photographed it," she said, a bit of a lame excuse. "I can't recall when or what for."

"You saw it this week, Mum. The image is date stamped."

Alice grabbed her coat. She didn't want to discuss the pendant with Michael, it would mean explaining the casket, the dead baby. "We should go, it's getting late. Who was on the phone?"

"A PC Wallis. He wanted to know if you were okay, I said you were." He followed her to the front door. "The pendant, it's connected to your case, isn't it?"

He wasn't going to let it go, he was tenacious like her. And she'd feel guilty lying to Michael, particularly about something so important. If her suspicions were correct, the mite in that casket could have been Paul's child and therefore Michael's half-sister.

She sighed. "We found it with the body of a female infant at Still Waters. She had been buried within the last seven years, which we know because we found a modern teddy bear with her whose date was easily traced."

"I don't get it. Why would Dad put the pendant in a baby's coffin?"

"I think the child was his, Michael, his and Maxine Hamilton's. But as yet I have no proof of that, so until I do, kindly keep the information to yourself."

Michael looked shocked. "Surely Dad wouldn't keep something like that to himself? I could understand him not telling you, but he could have spoken to me about the baby. If it had lived, how did he expect to explain it away? The kid was my sibling for heaven's sake."

"It's becoming increasingly obvious to me that he led two separate lives. He must have believed that the one with Maxine Hamilton had nothing to do with us," Alice said.

"Even so, this is huge."

"Huge or not, we're still investigating, so don't let your imagination run riot."

"Dad used to keep the pendant in a metal box in his desk. He showed me the thing one day and explained where it had come from. Originally it belonged to an ancestor of his, she's the Ruby in the inscription, and it's been passed down the family ever since."

"I'd no idea. Pity he didn't tell me. It would have saved the team a deal of work."

"How is the child connected to the murders?" Michael asked.

"I'm not sure. I'm hoping that it has nothing to do with the case, but I'm still waiting on the forensic results." Talk of the pendant was better left for now, Alice decided. She wanted to enjoy her final night with Michael, and telling him any more details about finding the casket and its contents, would only cloud the evening. Like her, he'd theorise about the baby and its parentage, and no doubt come up with the same questions as she had.

"Want to walk round?" Michael asked. "That way we can both get sloshed with no worries."

Alice no longer had much of an appetite — thinking about the infant and its fate had done that. But it was Michael's last night, so she'd make an effort. "We can walk, but getting sloshed will have to wait. I've got a big day tomorrow and I need my wits about me. And don't forget, you've got a long drive home."

"Going to nail that woman, are you?"

She smiled. "With any luck, and d'you know, Michael, I can't wait. I just hope that forensics has come up with the goods and she'll finally get what's coming to her."

"Want me to hang around in case there's trouble?" he asked.

"No, you should get home to your family. I've taken up enough of your time and anyway, I'll be gone for most of the day."

CHAPTER THIRTY-EIGHT

Tuesday

Alice was up early. She cooked breakfast for herself and Michael, said her goodbyes and left for work by six. Michael had promised to visit again soon, and bring Zandra and little Paul with him. She'd enjoyed having him around so it was something to look forward to once this little lot was sorted.

First on her list was to deliver the sample of Maxine Hamilton's DNA to the lab. Next, she picked up the search warrant and arranged for Martin Webb to be on standby to show them exactly where the rubble bag had been dumped.

Soon, Alice turned into the entrance of Still Waters. The team were waiting for her in the car park, along with Martin. She was excited, eager to get started. This had the potential to be a good day.

She called to the young sergeant. "Hawkes, you and I will go up to the house and speak to Hamilton. The rest of you will assemble across the road at Still Waters Two." She turned to Martin. "Would you go with them and point out the spot in question?"

He didn't look too keen. "I'd prefer to lurk in the background if you've no objection. I'll make sure they search the correct area, but I really don't want Mrs Hamilton to know it was me who gave you the information." He looked sheepish. "Liz really likes it here and she's made a lot of friends. If Mrs Hamilton finds out it's me that snitched to you lot she'll have us out."

Alice nodded. "Don't worry. If things go well this morning she'll be in custody by lunchtime. But please keep quiet about what we're up to. Gossip about possible outcomes won't do the families of the victims any good."

Having said he understood, Martin Webb marched off at the head of the search team.

Alice turned to Hawkes. "There must be something in it. Why bury a rubble bag if what it contains isn't incriminating?"

"Why not just burn it?" he said.

Alice had asked herself the same thing. "Some things don't burn," Alice answered.

"She won't like this at all," Hawkes said as they went. "Hamilton will argue the toss to the very death."

"I don't care. I've been after this woman for too long. We get the evidence we need and her reign of terror stops — today."

"Nice idea, ma'am, but we might find nothing," Hawkes said.

"Then again, we might find all the objects we're missing — a couple of mobile phones for starters, not to mention weapons used in the previous killings. Other things too — personal belongings of the victims, some of it valuable jewellery. And then there's the vehicles. Forensics will go over the retreat van and any others belonging to Hamilton. Liam's body had to be moved in one of them."

"We still don't know where he was killed," Hawkes said.

"Tell the team to keep their eyes peeled. Wherever he was killed, there is bound to be blood."

Hawkes was right. Maxine Hamilton was outraged to find the police turning up unannounced and mob-handed. "You have no right. This is private property."

Alice waved the search warrant at her. "This says we have every right, so I suggest you don't try to obstruct us."

Maxine gave Alice a look of pure evil. "You think you're clever, don't you, Ms Rossi? Well, you've gone too far this time. I'm off to have a word with my solicitor. He's Gerald Meade, the senior partner in Meade and Associates."

"Be my guest, but he won't tell you any different." Alice turned to Hawkes. "I want that vehicle in the drive impounded, along with any others you find, and don't forget the van parked outside Minty's office."

"Problem, ma'am," a uniform called to her. "We've identified the plot in question but the concrete was laid last night."

"Get one of the construction workers on it," she said. "I want it shifted and quick."

"It'll take time."

"Just get it done, Constable."

"My solicitor has advised me to say nothing to you." Maxine Hamilton was back. "Meanwhile make sure you don't take liberties. From what I read of the warrant you have permission to search my land and vehicles only. You are not allowed inside the house."

Alice nodded. "We are if it becomes necessary."

"What are you looking for?" Maxine asked.

Alice gave her a smile. "I'll let you know when we find it." She beckoned to Hawkes and they made their way towards the new site.

"I demand to know what you're after!" Maxine screamed after them.

"You're in no position to make demands, Mrs Hamilton," Alice called back.

But Maxine Hamilton was still ranting. "I need my site back. I've deadlines to meet. Make sure whatever damage you do is put right. You leave my property as you found it or I'll file a complaint." She turned and marched off, back to her house.

"Not happy, is she, ma'am?" Hawkes said with a grin on his face. "I must say, seeing her wound up like that makes coming to work this early in the morning almost worthwhile."

Within ten minutes, two of the construction workers were using pneumatic drills on the concrete base laid the day before. It didn't take them long to break it up and start shifting the pieces to one side.

Alice made her way across the plot and looked back to where Martin Webb was watching from behind the shrubbery. She reached the centre, stuck in a spade and he gave her a thumbs up.

* * *

Jack Nevin and half of the team of CSI people he'd brought with him were tackling the vehicles, starting with the retreat van parked outside the office.

"Bleach," Jack said upon flinging open the rear doors. "This van has been cleaned within the last twenty-four hours." He climbed inside and shone his torch around. The floor was bare metal, if there was once a covering it had been taken away. Minty stood at the door to her office, watching events. Jack called over to her. "You drive this thing, don't you? Was there anything on the floor in the rear?"

Minty nodded. "An old piece of carpet."

"D'you know what happened to it?" Jack asked.

"No idea. It was there on Saturday morning. I collected stock for the shop from the warehouse and I remember placing the boxes on it."

Jack turned to one of his people. "Have a walk round and see if there's any trace of anyone having lit a fire this weekend. If so, take a sample of the ashes. Check the bins and skips too."

Jack climbed back inside the van and continued his inch by inch search. "I reckon we've got a faint blood spatter here," he called to one of his team. "The seam between the right-hand side panel and the roof." He photographed the spot before taking a swab.

"The seats at the front and the controls stink of cleaning fluid," another CSI called to him. "No prints or fibres and not much chance of DNA."

Jack Nevin got out of the van and passed the packaged swab to one of the team. "Get that back to the lab and have it checked against Liam's DNA. If we have a match, then we have the vehicle his body was transported in."

Another of the team was examining the tyres. "There's a lot of mud and what looks like sand and concrete on these."

"Cleaned the interior but didn't bother with the outside." Jack nodded. "Sloppy. Take a sample. We'll see if the dirt matches what's at the building site. I want this van locked away under guard. The blood sample checks out, we'll take it to the lab and give it the works."

He nodded to a uniformed PC hovering nearby. "Don't let this vehicle out of your sight. Next, we'll have a look at Hamilton's car. Let's take a walk over and see what we've got."

CHAPTER THIRTY-NINE

Digging into the compacted earth took a while, but finally one of the search party lifted a black rubble bag from the soil and called out to Alice.

"Hawkes," she shouted. "Looks like we're off."

Alice donned a pair of gloves and went over to a plastic sheet laid out on the grass behind the plot. "I'll do it," she said. The bag was fastened with the same bright yellow rope that had been used on the bag containing body parts retrieved from the lake. "Everything will go to forensics, including this. We can't afford to make any mistakes."

Watched by Hawkes, she carefully untied the rope and gently tipped the contents of the bag out onto the sheet. There was an assortment of items — three mobile phones, several sets of keys, two wallets, a purse and some jewellery. But what immediately caught the eye were the hammers, two of them.

"Quite a haul," Alice said. "Those hammers look dirty. What's the betting that's dried blood? And those phones probably belong to our latest victims."

"I've counted six sets of keys, ma'am," Hawkes said. "We don't have six victims from the retreat."

"Some must be from other killings. Don't worry, Jack will do his best to match everything to its owner."

"There's some nice pieces of jewellery," Hawkes said. "That necklace looks the business."

Wearing gloves, Alice picked it up. It was a chain interlaced with different precious stones. The centre one looked like a diamond. "It's hallmarked platinum so the stones are probably real too." Alice bent down and looked closely at the other items. "I'll have to check the file but Celia West's family described something like this. The day she went missing, Celia was getting ready for a dinner date and was wearing expensive jewellery." She moved a few other items around but couldn't find anything else of any significance. She looked round at the team. "Get this lot bagged up and off to the lab. Good work, everyone." She still had the ring Michael had found in the Lotus. It too was set in platinum, and the diamond was a good match for the one in the necklace.

"What now, ma'am?" Hawkes asked.

"We tell Jack what we've got and then it'll be another word with Maxine Hamilton, this time at the station in Manchester. Although we still have no proof that she has anything to do with what we've just found until we've got the forensics back. If Hamilton maintains she knows nothing about it, we can't say otherwise."

They made their way up the drive towards Hamilton's house. Jack and three of his people were all over her car.

"This one is okay," he said quietly. "But the van has been scrubbed within an inch of its life, and recently too. However, I did find a smear of what I suspect is blood."

"Good, and we've just found a load of stuff in a bag buried under the concrete base for one of the new lodges. Mobiles, keys, things folk have in their pockets, and there was an expensive necklace there too. I suspect Celia West, the woman from Chinley, may have been wearing it when she disappeared. And then there's this." She held up the bag containing the ring. "Please don't ask where it came from, but given it's a good match for the necklace, would you check it out too, please?" She pointed to the prong. "I think that's blood."

"I'll check it for DNA. If it is we'll soon know," Jack said.

"If by chance that ring or the necklace did belong to Celia, I'm also hoping that Mad Hatter couldn't resist trying them on," Alice said.

"I'll get everything back to the lab. Don't forget that Dolly is doing Liam's PM later."

In all the excitement, Alice had forgotten. She looked at her mobile, and right enough there was a message from Dolly. The PM was scheduled to take place in a couple of hours. "That word with Hamilton," she told Hawkes. "And then off to the morgue."

* * *

Maxine Hamilton was expecting them and invited them to come in. She obviously wasn't expecting what Alice had to say.

"We want you to come to the station, Mrs Hamilton, to answer some questions and give a statement. If you wish, you can arrange for your solicitor to meet you there."

"This is ludicrous," Maxine said angrily. "I've done nothing wrong and I've nothing to tell you. You're just wasting my time."

"I don't think so," Alice said. "First off, you can explain why you told us a pack of lies about Liam Purvis yesterday. We know from various witness statements that you were most likely the last person to see him alive."

"Whoever told you that is lying. Liam left me at five. He could have gone anywhere after that."

"I think you're confused, Mrs Hamilton. He was at the retreat at six and you were seen driving off with him in that van. And if you still insist we're wrong, I'm sure the CCTV in your manager's office will tell a different story."

Maxine Hamilton's expression changed. At Alice's words, an initial flicker of doubt quickly became anxiety.

"I don't know what lies you've been told but Liam's death had nothing to do with me," she said quietly.

"We're not accusing you of anything," Alice said. "We simply want you to put your side of things across and give a statement."

"What about my meetings? I'm supposed to be seeing my contractors in Birmingham."

"Sorry, but you'll have to delay your trip."

Maxine stared at Alice. "You're out to get me. You've been digging around on my land. What's to say you didn't plant whatever you found?"

"This isn't about what we did or didn't find — yet. But we did find a number of items that will be taken to the lab to undergo forensic tests. That's all I can tell you."

"What sort of items?" Maxine asked.

"I can't say."

She glared at Alice. "This entire thing is a farce. You've got nothing on me, no evidence that I've committed any crime. I'll come with you but be warned, my solicitor will have me released in no time, and I shall file a complaint about your manner."

"I'm simply following procedure." Alice smiled politely.

CHAPTER FORTY

Alice stood with Hawkes and watched Maxine Hamilton being driven away in a police vehicle. "We'll give them ten minutes and then leave for the morgue."

"You're going to let her sweat it out?" Hawkes asked.

"It won't do her any harm to spend a bit of time sitting around in an uncomfortable interview room." Alice smiled.

It'd been a good morning. Both search teams had made progress and Alice was hopeful that Jack Nevin would find something useful. There was the blood from the van and the two hammers — a favoured weapon of Mad Hatter's.

"Another PM," Hawkes said. "But if we have Mad Hatter, at least it'll be the last."

"A nice thought, but don't tempt fate, Sergeant."

"Ma'am!" a PC called out. "We've found something."

Alice and Hawkes went over to the gate that linked Hamilton's property with Still Waters Two. A couple of PCs had been searching around in the sand and cement bags in a wooden store when they'd found a large patch of blood on the ground. Someone had tried to disguise it by throwing sand over it but it was still obvious to anyone who knew what they were looking for.

"Tape off the area and get the CSI people to take samples," Alice told them. "I think we've just found the place where Liam was killed."

"Poor sod, bundled into that van, brought here and done in and then driven to the lay-by and dumped. I won't be sorry to see the back of this place." Hawkes shuddered. "There's just too much death, and the retreat has taken on a weird atmosphere."

It was time to go. "We've still got work to do — the morgue and then the station," Alice said. "But I agree with you about this place. If I never see Still Waters again it can't be too soon."

They drove in silence, Hawkes concentrating on the road and Alice on her paperwork. "If Hamilton toughs it out and refuses to speak to us," she said, "it'll be difficult to hang on to her. That solicitor she mentioned is from one of the best firms in Manchester. If he maintains that Hamilton simply made a mistake about the time she last saw Liam and we can't prove he went with her to the site, she'll walk."

"Isn't there anything we can do?"

"We're in the hands of forensics, I'm afraid, and as you know, everything they do takes time. I do have something up my sleeve but I'll only use it if I absolutely have to."

* * *

"You've had a busy morning," Dolly said when the detectives arrived. "Jack's back and all fired up about what you've found. Fingers crossed."

"I'll second that," Alice said.

Dolly led the way into the examination room. Liam was laid out on a trolley. "I've cleaned him up. The wounds you see on his hands and upper body are the result of a fight. His knuckles are bruised and cut, and we've taken swabs."

"Aha, the possibility of DNA. I like it," Alice said.

"Unless his attacker wore gloves," Dolly said.

"He's in a right state," Hawkes said, his eyes on the body.

"The scrapes and cuts on his legs, arms and face are consistent with having been thrown from a vehicle. I've removed several pieces of grit from them."

"Poor bugger," Hawkes said.

"The cause of death was a blow to the back of his head. Again, it was delivered by a hammer or something similar. See the mark here?" She pointed. "Same as the others. Find it, and it will be smeared with his blood and tissue. The blow was hard, it shattered his skull and caused a catastrophic bleed on his brain."

"Jack found blood in the van belonging to the retreat. If we're lucky it'll prove to be Liam's and then we'll know how he got from where he was killed to that lay-by," Alice said.

"He'll rush the tests, he's well aware of how important they are." Dolly smiled. "His clothing and the places where he had bled were covered in grit from the lay-by, but there were also traces of concrete and sand. It's possible he was killed on a building site."

"We think we've found where," Alice said. "Forensics are looking at it now."

"Concerning the other victims, it was definitely Celia West's pacemaker we removed from the remains in the lake. The serial number checks out."

"Now I can inform her sister, try to explain what happened to her. Not that that'll be easy," Alice said.

"I wonder what she did to get on the wrong side of Mad Hatter?" Dolly asked. "She was the only victim from Chinley."

That had puzzled Alice too. The killing hadn't followed the usual Mad Hatter pattern. One victim, same method — the usual text sent out — but in every other instance there had been multiple victims and not just one. Perhaps it'd been personal, something to consider.

"I've looked closely at all the photos from the post-mortems of the other victims," Dolly said. "Some were too far gone but it does look as if a patch of skin was taken from any that had a tattoo."

"And if they didn't?" Hawkes asked.

"Nothing. The skin was intact, Neil Lewis being a case in point."

"What sick plan would she have for squares of tattooed skin?" Alice wondered.

"Until she's caught and you ask her, we'll never know," Dolly said.

That day couldn't come soon enough for Alice. "Liam's mother will come and formally identify him. I'll make the arrangements and let you know when." She turned to Hawkes. "We have an appointment with Maxine Hamilton at the station." She checked her watch. "I think we've kept her waiting long enough by now."

CHAPTER FORTY-ONE

Alice, accompanied by DS Hawkes, entered the interview room and sat down opposite Maxine Hamilton and her solicitor, Gerald Meade. "Sorry to keep you waiting."

"Am I under arrest?" Maxine asked.

"No, you're simply helping us with our enquiries," Alice said. The words almost choked her — how she wished it were different and they had the badly needed evidence to bring a charge. "It's important that we clear up the matter of the last person to see Liam Purvis alive. So far, that would seem to be you."

"You've got that wrong," Maxine retorted. "He left my house at about five after we'd had lunch at the Needles." She paused for a moment. "I did see him briefly after that, in the office. I wanted him to shift some rubbish left behind by the builders on the new site. Liam said he couldn't, he had to get off to see his parents, so that was that."

"Are you sure he didn't get in the van and accompany you to the Still Waters Two site?" Alice asked.

"Quite sure. I'm not stupid, I can recall what happened."

"Did you see where he went after he left the office?" Alice said.

"True, Liam did drive off in the retreat van but I wasn't with him. He is allowed to use it, as is Minty. I assumed he was going to his parents' house."

She sounded convincing enough — the words flowed effortlessly out of her mouth — but Alice knew she was lying. "Are you quite sure you've not got that wrong?" she asked.

"Positive." Maxine glared at Alice. "What happened to Liam is terrible, but it had nothing to do with me."

"Liam was beaten and his skull smashed in with a hammer," Alice said. "His body was then taken in a vehicle to a lay-by off the Woodhead Road and dumped there."

Stark as they were, the words appeared to have little effect on Maxine Hamilton. She wasn't going to admit to anything — not that Alice expected her to. The woman was as hard as nails. It was time to try a different tack.

"Do you know anything about an infant called Ruby?" Alice asked.

But Maxine remained impassive. She stared at Alice from eyes dark and unemotional. "Should I?"

"I'm not sure. My team found a white casket containing the remains of a baby under one of the flagstones in the boathouse. We think it'd been there for anything up to seven years."

Maxine Hamilton shrugged. "Sorry, but I can't help."

"That's a shame. I was trusting you could. I had hoped to find her parents. No matter, we'll have her DNA results soon, and that will help us find them." She looked the woman in the eyes. "There's no arguing with DNA, is there, Mrs Hamilton?"

"If I recall anything about an infant or its possible parents, I'll let you know," Hamilton responded coolly.

"What about a Mark Johnson? You do know him. You were regulars at the Needles for a while. The staff remember the pair of you."

Hamilton shook her head. "Doesn't ring a bell."

"What about Celia West? Ever met her?"

She got to her feet. "I've had enough. I've never met this West woman or the man you mentioned. You have no reason to hold me here. You've got no proof that I've done anything wrong."

She was right. Until that game-changing piece of forensic evidence was found, there was nothing Alice could do. But it would do no harm to press her a little further about Paul.

"You did know Johnson. The staff at the Needles all vouch for the fact that you and he spent time together there, so why deny it?" Alice said.

"I find it painful to think of him," Hamilton muttered.

"Why is that? Did he dump you?"

The look she gave Alice was glacial. "Of course not. Mark was murdered — a dreadful business — and to this day no one's been charged."

"Mark had another name too, didn't he? Paul Hunter," Alice said.

"So? It makes no odds what we call him, the man was lured to his death."

"Are you talking about the accident, when Paul Hunter fell and was killed in the pothole on Needle Crag?"

Hamilton said nothing for several long moments. She sat down again and stared at Alice. "You know very well what I mean," she spat. "And it was no accident, as well you know. Look, Ms Rossi, you've got nothing, so I'm leaving now. And I'll thank you not to come knocking at my door armed only with innuendo and gossip in future."

"No worries, Mrs Hamilton. Rest assured, next time we talk I'll have everything I need to put whoever killed Liam and the others behind bars for a long time."

* * *

Back in the main office, Alice helped herself to a mug of coffee. By bringing up the accident on Needle Crag, she'd shown Maxine Hamilton her hand, virtually told her that she knew she was Mad Hatter. Now she wondered if that had been wise.

Hawkes appeared at her side. "That Hamilton woman is a piece of work, isn't she? She lies like an expert."

"I wish we had something positive to throw at her," Alice said.

"Who's this Mark Johnson, ma'am?" Hawkes said. "I haven't heard the name before, and it isn't on the incident board either."

"Don't fret, Sergeant, it's something and nothing," Alice said.

"She didn't so much as flinch when you told her about the baby. If she knew about it, or even worse if she's the mother, what sort of woman could deny her own child like that?"

"The Hamilton sort, but I admit that surprised me too." Alice looked out over the city. It was about to rain and darkness was falling. "I'm going home. I've had enough for today. Hopefully, Jack will have something for us tomorrow."

"He's got a whole bag full of stuff to have a go at, surely by the law of averages there must be something in there," Hawkes said.

"Agreed, but this woman is an expert, she has been since day one."

"Odd that. I wonder what her background is. People who kill are not usually so forensically aware, and Hamilton is certainly that all right."

He had a point, but Alice was too tired to dwell on the remark. She picked up the phone and rang the lab. "Dare I hope for a result anytime soon?" she asked.

"So far we've got very little," Jack said.

Alice heard the fatigue in his voice. This case was getting to him every bit as much as it was her. And everyone else.

"The hammers are coated with dried blood and tissue, and no attempt has been made to clean them. I should be able to match them to the victims. The mobiles, on the other hand, have been soaked in a solution of soapy water and bleach and the sim cards have been removed. Various other items in the bag may yield something, but with each one we've looked at so far it's the same story. You know, Alice, there are times when I think we're chasing a ghost. But that being impossible, I'll continue the good work and give you an update in the morning."

Alice gathered her stuff and made for her car. She had hoped the day would have given her a breakthrough, but a solution to the case was as elusive as ever.

CHAPTER FORTY-TWO

Whether it was her tiredness or something else, tonight the house was not the welcoming haven Alice loved to come home to. It was shrouded in darkness, the tall trees at the front casting eerie shadows across the driveway. As she put her key in the lock, Alice shivered. She felt wary for some reason. Something about the house had changed, and not for the better, but Alice couldn't work out what or why.

The smell hit her the moment she was through the front door, a sickening mixture of cigarette smoke and the expensive French aftershave Paul always wore. Possibly the smoke had drifted in from outside, but how to explain the aftershave? Maybe her son had been rooting through his father's stuff and found it. He'd worn his father's tie to the Needles Hotel so he knew there were still a number of his belongings in the house.

Michael had left a note on the kitchen table to say he'd bought some food and replenished her wine. He also promised to visit again soon. Alice would miss him. She'd enjoyed the last few days with him here, having someone around to talk to. She checked her mobile. There was a text from him to say he'd got back safely and that Zandra was over the moon with the car. Alice smiled. So she should be, the thing was valuable, and the money they got from selling it would make a significant difference to their family finances.

Alice had deliberately not brought any work home tonight. There was no point. Everything was in Jack's lap now. Until he came up with something she could use, the case was at a standstill.

She poured herself a glass of red and went upstairs to change. Still feeling nervous, she turned on all the lights as she went. She reached automatically for her dressing gown, which she always left on a hook on the back of her bedroom door. It wasn't there. Michael again, she thought, when she saw it lying in a crumpled heap on the floor. She was on the landing making for the bathroom when another waft of the French aftershave stopped her in her tracks.

When Paul died she'd put everything of his into the spare bedroom. Eventually, she'd sort it out and give what Michael didn't want to the charity shop. But until there was a let-up in her workload there wasn't much chance of that happening. The room was kept shut up, and had become something of a no go area. But tonight she went in, wanting to find out what Michael had been up to. What she found came as a shock. There was no way her son would have left the room in this mess.

The wardrobe doors were wide open and Paul's clothes lay strewn everywhere. The drawers from a chest had been pulled free and the contents littered the floor. Someone had been looking for something all right, something belonging to Paul. Then she saw it — a cigarette stubbed out in a silver pin tray on the windowsill. So it definitely wasn't Michael who'd ransacked the room, he didn't smoke and neither did she. Someone had been in her home.

With her heart hammering against her chest, she hurried downstairs and picked up her mobile. She rang Osbourne, her voice shaky and her mind full of wild suspicions. "Someone has been in my house while I've been at work," she said the moment he picked up. "The room I keep Paul's stuff in has been rifled and there's the smell of cigarettes all over the house. I don't know if anything is missing, but mixed with the smoke I could smell the aftershave Paul used to wear. It was expensive and distinctive, I'd know it anywhere. It's scared the hell out of me."

"It wasn't your husband who broke in, Alice," Osbourne said, reasonably. "He's been dead for six years. This is down to our old friend pressing buttons again."

"Mad Hatter?"

"Why not? Hamilton knows she's been released pending us finding more evidence. She's going to fight back. Doing nothing isn't her style. This thing she has against you is as much psychological as anything else. Are there signs that someone actually did break in?"

It hadn't occurred to Alice to even check, and she should have done so. She quickly went to the front and back doors and then into the workshop. Everything was locked up tight. "There's nothing," she told Osbourne. "The doors haven't been tampered with, nor the windows. If this is down to Hamilton she could have a key, kept one of Paul's."

"Any other people have keys?" he asked.

Alice had only given keys to two people — Dilys, and Michael while he'd been staying with her. She went into the hallway and saw that he'd posted his key back through the letterbox when he left. "My cleaning woman, Dilys, has one, but I'm sure she wouldn't have done it. Anyway, why would she be interested in Paul's stuff? She never even met him."

"We're back to Hamilton in that case. I'll get the CSI people round to dust for prints. Meanwhile, don't touch anything, particularly not that cigarette you found. With luck, Jack Nevin might get DNA from it."

"I'm terrified, Frank. If you're right and this is Mad Hatter paying me back for the trouble I'm putting her way, she won't stop at simply frightening me." Alice took a swallow of her wine. Osbourne was right, it must have been Hamilton, but it didn't help knowing who was responsible. She had got in once and could easily do so again.

“I’ll get someone to come over and spend the night with you,” he suggested. “Longer, if you want. A female officer who’s recently done the FLO training.”

Ordinarily Alice would have refused. Her home was her safe place, and that had always been enough, but not any longer. “Thanks, Frank, I’d appreciate it.”

CHAPTER FORTY-THREE

Wednesday

The FLO was a woman called Debra Myers. She'd arrived an hour after Alice's call to Osbourne. Myers was a DS, had been in the job as long as Alice had and knew the ropes.

"I'll be here all day, ma'am, and I'll sleep over. You needn't worry, I've got a black belt in Judo. Anyone tries to get in and I'll have them."

Her presence was reassuring. Debra Myers was a big woman and looked more than capable of taking care of herself.

"There's plenty of food in the fridge, help yourself," Alice said. "And please call me Alice. You're doing me a huge favour by staying here, and I'm grateful. Sometime today the CSI people will turn up, let's hope they get something."

Alice gathered her stuff together and left for the station. She didn't want to return to the retreat unless it became absolutely necessary — to arrest Maxine Hamilton for example. Would it be today? That was in Jack's hands. She and her team could only play the waiting game until he came up with the goods.

* * *

The main office was as busy as ever. Alice spotted PC Roger Wallis seated at one of the computers. The moment he saw her, he lowered his head, avoiding her gaze. "Don't worry, you did the right thing," Alice said as she passed his desk.

He glanced up, sheepish. "I tried to contact you first, ma'am, but the mobile reception was dreadful. I knew it was important, so I had no choice but to go to the super."

Alice nodded. "I'd have done the same. Has anything else come in?"

"Dr Nevin rang earlier, he wants to speak to you."

This could be it. Alice darted into her office, her nerves jangling again. "Jack, what've you got?"

"The blood and tissue on one of those hammers belongs to Liam Purvis, that on the other one to Celia West. The blood spot I found in the retreat's van is also Liam's."

That meant he had been moved in that vehicle. "Celia West was killed over six years ago. There have been other victims since, I don't understand."

"So she hangs onto the weapons. I suspect some of the other stuff will be Celia's too. We're still doing tests on most of it but everything apart from the hammers has been thoroughly washed."

"Washed, put in a black bag and buried under concrete foundations, hopefully never to be found. And then Martin Webb ambles along," she said.

"Just as well he did, or where would we have looked?"

He was right, that had been a bit of luck.

Jack chuckled. "Now for the exciting bit. And I should tell you that I've been up all night processing this little gem — quite literally as it happens."

Alice felt her stomach lurch. Would this be the breakthrough they so desperately needed? "Just tell me, Jack, my delicate mental state can't take the strain."

"The ring with the broken prong. I got two different sets of DNA from it. One matches Celia West, same as on the necklace, and I suspect they were bought as a set. But the other result from the ring is what you've been waiting for.

The DNA I got from the blood on the prong matched the sample you took from Maxine Hamilton."

Alice said nothing. Her mind was racing. This was it, a way to crack Hamilton. "You're sure?" she asked quietly. "There is no mistake? If I go and get her, she can't wriggle out of it?"

"Not this time, Alice. That ring belonged to Celia West and it has Hamilton's blood on it. That means they met, interacted, possibly fought. At the very least, it needs investigating and gives you a good reason to search her property."

"Thank you, Jack. You have no idea what this means to me."

"My team are at your house this morning and they'll go over everything."

"The cigarette end in the pin tray — I haven't touched it."

"Leave it with me. As soon as I have anything useful, I'll be in touch."

Alice could barely believe it. Six years she'd been after Mad Hatter, and finally it looked as if she'd slipped up, left that vital piece of evidence giving Alice the break she needed.

She rang Hawkes at Still Waters. "Keep your eyes open. If Maxine Hamilton shows any sign of leaving, arrest her. Jack has finally worked his magic and found something we can use. Don't say a word to any of the residents, even if they ask. Give me an hour and I'll join you."

Alice went along the corridor to tell Osbourne. "We've finally got a lever against Hamilton. I intend to arrest her and bring her here for questioning. As you know, we found certain items buried in the black bag, but there may be more. She's a psychopath, very often they keep personal mementoes of their crimes. We have reason to believe that Hamilton has some that are a tad gruesome." She was thinking of the tattooed patches of skin.

"A warrant will be needed to search her house. And you're right, we have no idea what else she may have squirrelled away," he said.

"It'll have to be quick, Frank. I want her arrested and in custody today."

"Give me an hour, Alice," he said. "But as far as you're concerned, this is where it ends. From this point on, you can't be involved. I'm sure you understand. We have to do the next bit by the book. I've looked carefully at the case file and the report you emailed me last night. You needn't worry, I am up to speed. I know what questions to ask, what buttons to press."

Alice saw the look on his face, he didn't want to have to do this, but it was to be expected.

"Hawkes is at Still Waters, he'll keep watch on Hamilton and make the arrest once the search team arrive. I'll wait here and prepare for the interview."

"Am I to play no part in this at all, sir?"

"You can observe the search team, see what they turn up, but you must stay on the sidelines. I don't want you involved in interviewing Hamilton either. D'you understand?"

Alice nodded. After years of chasing this woman, not to be in at the finish was a blow. The case — her case — was about to be snatched from her just when she was getting somewhere. But there was no other way, the relationship between Paul and Maxine Hamilton would come up during the interview. Still, watching events unfold and not taking part wouldn't be easy. It was going to be a long day.

Returning to her office, she found the Celia West file and carefully went through it. It was clearly logged that three items of jewellery had been missing since the day she disappeared — the ring, a necklace, and a pair of matching earrings which hadn't been found. When the ring had been identified as Celia's, Alice realised that she must have been killed before Paul had his accident. How else could that ring have ended up in the Lotus?

CHAPTER FORTY-FOUR

Getting the search warrant took longer than Alice had hoped. By the time she reached Still Waters with the search team, it was getting dark. It couldn't be helped, all that mattered was putting Maxine Hamilton behind bars, where she could do no more harm.

The team made directly for Hamilton's house and Alice, mindful of not compromising what was happening in any way, went to the lodge to speak to Hawkes. "Is she still at her house?"

"I've had a PC watching and he hasn't seen her leave."

"You'd better get over there, the search team will have made a start. Keep them on their toes. And you are to make the arrest."

"Not you, ma'am? Why? This is your case."

"I can't be involved, the reasons are complicated but all will become clear during the interviews. It'll be Osbourne and you conducting those."

Hawkes looked genuinely perplexed. "Well, I'm sorry, ma'am. After all your hard work too."

She smiled at him. "I knew all along it would come to this, Sergeant. What matters is that we now have a piece of evidence that gives us the opportunity to search her home. Let's see her wriggle out of this one."

Alice and Hawkes walked the short distance through the retreat and across the road to Hamilton's house. But the young PC left on watch had let her slip away. Hamilton wasn't at home and no one seemed to know where she'd gone. Alice was livid, the job had been simple enough. "Her car is on the drive, she can't have gone far. Split up," she told the team, "scour the retreat, I want her found. Once we have her, you can serve the warrant and search the house."

Alice made her way over to Still Waters.

"Want me to come with you, ma'am?" Hawkes asked.

"It's a large area and there aren't enough of us. You look around the Still Waters Two construction site. The others can search the lodges. I'll go and see if she's in the office with Minty."

Alice took the main path via the burnt-out boathouse. She had a lot to think about — Paul, Hamilton, and everything that entailed. On her way, Alice tried to work out why Celia West had become a victim prior to Paul's accident. It didn't make sense. She'd always believed that Mad Hatter was playing this evil game with her in order to get some sort of twisted revenge for Paul's death. But Paul had been alive and well when Celia had been murdered. So what motive did Hamilton have for killing her?

The walk took Alice past Ash Lake. She stopped for a moment and looked up. Needle Crag was shrouded in black clouds. Alice shuddered, it was a dreadful place. She wished she could forget that day, but the memory was as sharp as ever. There was nothing she could have done to save Paul, even if she'd wanted to, and that was part of the problem. When Paul had got himself trapped, part of her had hoped it would be the end of him, the end of their life together.

"A wicked place that peak. There's been many accidents up there, some of them fatal, but then you know that. Look what happened to your husband."

Alice stiffened, almost too afraid to turn around because she knew exactly who had spoken. "Paul ran out of luck. He'd been warned, told the weather was wild that day. He took a risk and paid the price, there was no stopping him."

"You could have helped him, got a rescue party organised in time. But you did nothing, did you, Alice?"

"What I did or didn't do is no concern of yours," Alice retorted, spinning round to face Maxine Hamilton. "You're finished. We finally have evidence to put you behind bars where you belong."

Hamilton laughed. "What evidence? There's nothing. I've made sure of that. You are no threat, Alice. You are merely a thorn in my side, but you won't be for much longer."

Alice looked Maxine Hamilton in the eye. "Your threats don't scare me. I'm about to search your house and arrest you. Slap you in handcuffs and cart you off to the station for questioning."

Hamilton shook her head. "Oh, Alice, what good would that do? It would achieve nothing. You're deluded, you have no evidence, no forensics, you can't prove a thing. The CPS will simply laugh at you."

"This time you're wrong."

Hamilton moved closer and poked Alice in the chest. "I know about the bag you dug up, I know about all the other things you've got too. There is nothing there, I made sure of that."

Alice gave her a smile. "What we have didn't come from the bodies of those you murdered here, or from that bag. They might yield evidence in time but for now what we have is from another source."

Maxine's face clouded while she considered this. "You're bluffing."

"Unfortunately for you, I'm not. You should come clean, tell us what you did and why. Why kill innocent people just to get at me?"

"You have to be punished for what you did. Paul would want that too. I kill to lure you into the game, Alice. You investigate, you get nowhere, the case remains open, a blot on your reputation and not good for your career prospects. But very soon it's you who'll become the victim, and you have no idea when that will be. How else can I communicate with you if not through your work?"

"There's always email," Alice said flippantly.

"Don't get smart with me, it doesn't suit you."

"None of the victims had done anything to you. Callum, for example, he was harmless, a young man with his entire life in front of him."

"I was sorry about Callum. I liked him. But I needed a victim to tempt you into the game, you know how it is, the opportunity presented itself and I couldn't resist."

"And Liam, what did he do to deserve being bludgeoned to death?"

"He got on my nerves, asking questions, voicing his suspicions. I was fond of that young man. He turned heads, I'll give him that, but he was hard work. He had to go, he saw something the night he died and threatened to tell you lot. Shame, but for that we could still be having a good time."

"You're a murdering psychopath," Alice levelled at her. "But you will get what's coming to you. You've slipped up and given us the break we need."

"No, Alice, you're bluffing. I don't do mistakes, but you do, like wandering around in the dark alone." She laughed. "You've stuck your nose into my business once too often and now it's become imperative that I get rid of you, once and for all."

Alice backed off, her eyes still fixed on Hamilton's face. If the woman took her on, could she defend herself? Possibly, but it wasn't guaranteed. "Don't be stupid. I have people all over the retreat."

"But they're not here right now, are they, Alice?" she taunted.

"That's where you're wrong. Get away from her now!"

The voice booming out of the darkness was Hawkes's. Alice had never been more pleased to see him. "See?" she said to Hamilton, "Your time is up. Accept it and make things easier for yourself."

Alice nodded at Hawkes. "Arrest and cuff her. Get her back to the station and lock her up for the night. You can do the interview tomorrow."

CHAPTER FORTY-FIVE

Thursday

Alice awoke in a state of hopeful anticipation, confident that today the case would finally come to an end. As if the world was smiling upon her, the rain had cleared away and the sun was shining. She'd no sooner got out of bed than her mobile rang. It was Hawkes.

"Sorry to ring so early, ma'am, but I wanted you to know. The search team carried on into the night, and they found a secret drawer in an antique cabinet in one of the spare bedrooms. There were several items of old furniture stacked against one of the walls. The housekeeper said they were going off to auction. The cabinet was almost hidden under an old rug. We were lucky, one of the CSI team had seen one like it and knew where to look. The drawer went off to forensics, and it's full of stuff — jewellery, watches, wallets, all sorts of things. I reckon it was where Hamilton stashed her trophies."

Alice smiled to herself. "Was there by any chance a pair of diamond earrings?"

"Yes, they were in a small plastic bag with a handwritten label on it that read 'Celia West.'"

"Thanks, Sergeant, that's brilliant news. Hamilton can't talk her way around that little lot. What about the squares of tattooed skin? Any sign of them?"

"We found a large square of what looks likes human skin in a freezer in the cellar. It looked as if she'd stitched the squares together to make a patchwork. Each one has part of a tattoo on it."

Alice shuddered. The woman had to be mad. "Well done. The evidence is compelling, let's see how she tries to talk herself out of that one."

Feeling better than she had in days, Alice went downstairs to grab some breakfast. "Looks like you can get back to your own life," she said to Debra Myers. "Maxine Hamilton is under arrest and we've got solid evidence against her. She won't be released this time."

"Well done, the team will be pleased."

"I know I certainly am. I've lived under the shadow of that woman for long enough."

Their conversation was interrupted by the trill of her mobile. It was Jack Nevin.

"The preliminary results are back from the DNA analysis of the baby. My colleague in Germany was able to get a trace of bone marrow, which made the process a lot quicker."

"Anything significant? Is Hamilton the mother, like we thought?"

"I've got a DNA profile for the mother and a partial for the father. Like you, my money was on Hamilton for the mother, but we were both wrong."

"Go on, Jack, don't keep me in suspense."

"Celia West."

This was certainly out of the blue. Alice didn't know what to think. "Her sister didn't say anything about her being pregnant. I'll have to speak to her again."

"Given the child had nothing to do with Hamilton, why bury her at Still Waters, and with such care?" Jack wondered.

Alice had a growing suspicion but she said nothing. "I'll ring the sister when I get into the office and see what she has to say. I'll get back to you later, Jack."

Alice had to leave. Maxine Hamilton's interview was scheduled for this morning and she needed to speak to Osbourne and Hawkes before they started.

* * *

Superintendent Osbourne was a happy man. He'd looked through the evidence file, and given the findings from the search could see no reason why the CPS would argue with what they had. "I've read everything thoroughly, by now I know the case almost as well as you," he assured Alice.

"Even the personal stuff? You got the text I sent earlier about Celia West's baby? Jack has only got a partial DNA profile but I'll lay odds that if he checks it against Paul's he'll find similarities."

"You believe that Paul fathered the baby in the casket?" Osbourne asked.

"Yes, that's why he left the pendant in there with her. It was a family piece."

Osbourne nodded. "I know what I have to do. We have a sound case. Don't worry, she isn't going to walk away from this. She collared you yesterday at the retreat. What with that and the break-in, I'm just grateful that you won't be taking any more risks."

She smiled. "I dropped my guard there, but Hawkes had my back. He's a first-class officer, sir."

He lifted the file from his desk. "What concerns me about the interview is that I'll have to bring up certain facts — that your husband and Maxine Hamilton were lovers for instance, and about Celia West. Does that bother you? I doubt you've said anything to Hawkes."

"It only bothers me inasmuch as it means I have to stay out of it. I've gone so far, and at the last hurdle have been forced to hand over," she said. "But I know it has to be this way. Even though Paul has been dead six years, being his wife compromises me. You can bring up anything you have to. Our relationship was far from perfect. Even if Paul had lived,

I doubt we'd be together now. All that matters is that you nail her, sir. Face her with what we've got and hopefully she'll tell you about the others she's killed. As for Hawkes, I think he suspects there are things I've held back, so he shouldn't be too surprised."

Alice and Osbourne left his office and went to collect Hawkes, who was waiting in the main office.

"It'll be you and the super doing the interview," Alice said. "For reasons that will become apparent, I have to keep out of it from this point on." She saw the curiosity on his face but ignored it. "Good luck, Frank. Give her both barrels."

* * *

"Follow my lead, Sergeant. If you're confused about anything, go with the flow and check the file."

The two of them made for the interview room one floor down. Maxine Hamilton was sitting with her solicitor, Gerald Meade. She looked surprised when the two men entered the room.

"Where's Rossi? Not got the balls for it?" She grinned.

Osbourne ignored the comment, made the introductions for the recording and got straight down to business.

"In a previous interview you were asked about Celia West," he began.

"Never heard of her," Maxine said.

"We found her body dumped in one of the lakes on your retreat, Still Waters."

"Well, I didn't put her there."

"You still maintain you didn't know Celia West and have never met her?" Osbourne asked.

"I've already said so. This West woman is completely unknown to me," Maxine said.

"How about Mark Johnson? D'you know him?" he asked.

"Never met him."

"Okay, in that case tell me about Paul Hunter."

Maxine Hamilton stiffened and her eyes narrowed but she made no response.

"Do you know that Paul Hunter also used the name Mark Johnson?" He gave Maxine a few seconds. "Of course you do, you and Hunter were very close."

"You've got it all wrong. I don't know the man," she said.

"Paul Hunter, or Mark Johnson as he called himself, was your lover for a number of years. We have statements from people who saw you together."

"Liars, the lot of them. I bet Rossi has paid them to spout this rubbish about me," she said.

Time to draw her out, let Hamilton know what they had and see her reaction. "I bet it really upset you when Paul took a fancy to Celia West. Is that why you killed her? Was that first murder motivated by jealousy?"

For the first time Maxine seemed unsure of herself, a lot less self-satisfied. "What is this? Why isn't Rossi conducting this interview? All these stupid questions are doing my head in."

"DCI Rossi is otherwise engaged," Osbourne said.

Gerald Meade cleared his throat. "I must insist that you present any proof you have, so that Mrs Hamilton can put her side of this across."

"I can't imagine what Hunter said to you when he found out what you'd done to Celia, but I bet he wasn't happy. He and West were lovers, and she was expecting his child," Osbourne continued.

"This is nothing but fantasy, Superintendent."

"You took a ring from Celia West, that and a matching necklace and earrings. We found them all." Osbourne waited, watching Hamilton's reaction.

"No, the ring was lost," she said after a long silence.

Osbourne smiled. She'd admitted to knowing about the ring, it was a start. "You're right, it was, but Alice Rossi found it. And d'you know what else we found? That ring has your blood on it."

She frowned. "You're lying. Rossi can't have found it. It wasn't on the body, or in that bag of rubbish you dug up. It was gone, lost, and I've no idea where."

"It was found on the floor of a classic car, a Lotus Elan belonging to Paul Hunter. Ring any bells?"

Maxine Hamilton appeared to deflate. She shrank back into the chair. This talk of the ring and the car had her worried.

"There was supposed to be no comeback, no evidence, no proof that I'd done anything." She looked from one detective to the other. "How does finding that ring prove that I killed the West woman?"

"I told you, it had your blood on it. That means you lied about knowing her, and makes one wonder what else you've lied about."

"I don't lie, you've got this all wrong."

"We found your hidden drawer in the cabinet, the one with your trophies in it. They are being checked for DNA as we speak. I'll lay odds that everything in there belonged to one or another of your victims."

Osbourne gave Hamilton a moment or two for this to sink in. He could see from the look on Hawkes's face that he was struggling too. "So what happened, Maxine? How come you slipped up so badly? You must have known the risk you took in keeping those things."

"It was supposed to be okay. They were well hidden, no one was supposed to find them." Her voice had dropped.

"Did someone tell you that, perhaps help you?" Osbourne asked.

"I'm not saying. I don't want to say anything else."

"Now is the time to come clean, it'll make things easier for you when you get to court. We also found that hideous patchwork you made out of squares of your victims' skin. No attempt was made to hide that either, it was simply lying in the freezer."

Hamilton gave the men a puzzled look, took a sip of water and sat back in the chair. "I was told it was a good idea, a memento of what I did. I have no sympathy for any of them. West especially deserved everything she got. She was a first-class bitch, always making eyes at Paul, flirting with him at every opportunity. She hounded the poor man. What was he supposed to do?"

"You were upset at their behaviour?" Hawkes asked.

"Yes, I was livid with the pair of them, particularly when she got pregnant. Paul wanted her to move in with us. The absolute nerve of the man. He wanted to look after her, pay her money and have him and me raise the child when it was born." She shook her head. "I couldn't have that. I had no intention of raising some other woman's bastard. I loved Paul, he belonged to me not some chancer with a bun in the oven."

"What happened?" Osbourne asked.

"He got his own way, as usual. The arrangement was that West would stay with us until the birth and then go back to her old life. She had no interest in being a mother. But the infant was stillborn, never even drew breath." She gave the men a big grin. "Served the pair of them right. I was ecstatic. Paul put the brat in that silly little box and I sorted West. He never did ask what became of her and I never mentioned her name again."

"You killed her?" Osbourne asked.

Gerald Meade reached across and said something to Hamilton. She simply batted him away like a fly.

"It's too bloody late, Gerald." She turned back to Osbourne. "Yes, I slammed a hammer into her head. Very good it felt too. After that, I got a taste for it, you've seen my handiwork over the years. I'm not to blame though. None of it is my fault. You can't pin any of the killings on me. The one you should have down for all this is Alice Rossi. It's all her fault. She's the one who should be sitting here, not me."

CHAPTER FORTY-SIX

Alice had watched the whole thing from a side room. None of it surprised her, not even Hamilton's accusations. Following her rant, Osbourne had called a halt to proceedings and Alice went to meet them in the office.

"She's admitted to the killings," Osbourne said. "I'll ring the CPS, tell them what we've got and we can charge her later."

"Blimey, that was tense," Hawkes said. "The woman is unhinged."

Alice smiled. "Now you know how I've felt all these years — shadowed by an unhinged psychopath with me in her sights."

"She'll do you no more harm, Alice, or cause you sleepless nights again. Hamilton will be behind bars for the rest of her days," Osbourne said.

"I can barely believe it's over," Alice said. "That woman has virtually run my life ever since Paul's death. It's been like having a black cloud constantly above my head."

Osbourne tucked the case file under his arm and made for the door. "We'll resume this afternoon," he told Hawkes. "I'll ring you."

"What now, ma'am?" Hawkes asked Alice.

"Well, there's a bit of tidying up to do. I must speak to Celia West's sister, ask if she knew about the baby." She looked across at PC Wallis. "Would you check if the infant's birth was ever registered? There is a register of stillbirths somewhere."

"I checked as part of my original research, ma'am," he said, "and it wasn't there."

Alice nodded. She'd thought as much. With Celia dead, Paul and Hamilton would have put the entire episode behind them. "Anyone wants me, I'm in my office."

Sitting at her desk, she found the contact number she had for Celia West. "Miss West, Celia's sister?"

"Celia is dead, what d'you want?"

"This is DCI Rossi. We spoke shortly after your sister originally disappeared. I wonder if I could clarify something with you."

"I know you've found her remains if that's what you mean. I'm busy arranging her funeral now."

"Did you know that Celia was pregnant?" Alice asked.

There was a slight pause. "I'd no idea, but then Celia never told me anything."

"You must have known, you lived in the same house," Alice challenged.

"Look, I didn't say anything because I was ashamed. My own sister with child and no husband."

"A rather old-fashioned attitude, Miss West. Did you never consider that Celia needed help?"

"No, I wanted her to get rid of it."

"You got your wish. The infant went to full term but was stillborn."

"A blessing, saved a lot of heartache all round."

Alice wanted to blast her for that but held back. There was information she needed. "Did she ever say anything to you about the man she was seeing at that time?" she said.

"Look, I've just told you, Celia was a closed book. Yes, we were sisters but we weren't particularly close. Sad, I know, but that's how it was."

Either this woman really didn't know or she wasn't prepared to drag it all up again. Alice gave up and rang Jack Nevin. "Hamilton is making a statement admitting the lot," she told him gleefully. "She'll be charged later and then my work is done. I just wanted to thank you, Jack, for all your hard work. These last couple of days you went above and beyond."

"You deserve to be free of her, Alice. She was still playing games with you right up to the end. That cigarette end you found in the pin tray — bet you can't guess whose DNA was on it?"

"Hamilton's?" Alice said, knowing that was too obvious.

"Nope. The only DNA found on it belonged to Liam Purvis."

"That's impossible, he's lying in the morgue," Alice said.

"As I said, still playing games. The woman is evil, we must all be thankful there'll be no more now."

"I'll second that."

* * *

There was nothing else Alice could do at the station, so she decided to take a last drive out to Still Waters and speak to the families of Maxine Hamilton's victims. Clare Hilton had been emailing her daily, asking if there'd been any progress, and deserved to know they were about to make an arrest. Alice knew they'd push her for a name, but she wasn't in a position to reveal that yet. No doubt Osbourne would brief the press when he was ready.

Sadie Fox was still at the lodge. She greeted Alice with a smile. "I thought you'd all forgotten about me. There was a lot of speculation yesterday. Martin Webb saw Maxine Hamilton being taken away in a police car and the gossip hasn't stopped since. I'm being bombarded with questions I can't answer."

Alice had anticipated nothing less of Martin Webb. He had been useful to the investigation but he couldn't help giving anyone who'd listen information he'd been asked to keep to himself.

"I'll speak to those involved. Don't worry, your stint here will soon be over."

"Can't wait. I don't know what this lot see in the place, it gives me the creeps," Sadie said.

Alice smiled. "Me too, and not just because of this case."

She left Sadie and walked across to the Hiltons', both of whom were in.

"I hope you've got something to tell us," Clare said as soon as she saw her. "I've heard all sorts, not least that it was Maxine Hamilton who killed Callum. That can't be right, surely?"

Alice took a breath. This was going to be tricky. These people deserved answers, but all in good time. "We have arrested someone for Callum's murder. They'll be formally charged later today."

"It's that bloody Hamilton woman," Dave said, looking up from his newspaper. "Where does that leave us lot? She's the sole owner of Still Waters, if you bang her up the retreat could close."

Clare snatched the paper from him. "Will you at least have the decency to listen to what the detective is telling us?"

He sniffed. "All I want is a name. I never did think much of the woman, but I don't want to lose our place."

"I can't help, I'm afraid," Alice said. "All will become clear in the coming days but right now I simply wanted you to know that the person who killed Callum, Neil and Liam is behind bars."

"Glad to hear it," Clare said. "Gemma's planning to sell the lodge, can't stand to be in the place."

"We'll make sure she gets the news," Alice said.

Alice left the Hiltons and made her way to the office. A word with Minty about the gossip was needed.

"You got her then."

It was Martin Webb and his dog. "I saw Maxine Hamilton being bundled into the police car and as far as I know, she hasn't returned."

"She's helping us with our investigations," Alice said. "But what would really help us is for the gossip to stop. There will be an announcement from my superintendent soon enough and then it'll be all over the press."

"But she is the killer, there's no one else, is there? She did for Neil, Callum and finally poor Liam," he said.

"And if it turns out she didn't?" Alice watched Martin's expression. He looked uncertain. "See what I mean? If it turns out Mrs Hamilton is innocent, she won't take kindly to people spreading rumours like that."

He smiled. "Okay, my lips are sealed. But this is a tight-knit community, nothing is kept quiet for long."

Alice left him staring after her, scratching his head. A quick word with Minty and then she was off home. She'd had just about all she could take of Still Waters.

CHAPTER FORTY-SEVEN

If Alice never saw Still Waters and the hills that surrounded it again, it would be too soon. She headed for home, driving out through the gates without a backward glance. Sadie Fox would wrap up tomorrow and give the lodge keys back to Minty.

On her way, she got a call from Osbourne to say that they had charged Maxine Hamilton. There was a press briefing scheduled for the following day.

"I've organised a little get-together in the pub across from the station. We deserve a celebration drink, and there'll be food too. I've invited Dolly and Jack, and I know they'd love to see you there."

"I'll be there, Frank," she promised, although all she really wanted to do was flop in front of the fire. Still, she couldn't let everyone down. And in any case, they all deserved a chance to let their hair down. The Mad Hatter case was over, Maxine Hamilton was locked up and they had enough evidence to ensure a conviction and a hefty jail sentence. And there was the added bonus that Alice would never again have to look up and see Needle Crag looming above her. A good result all round.

But there were still questions. Who had been in her home was one. The cigarette end had obviously been deliberately placed for her to find, but someone had been smoking and had used Paul's aftershave. Was that someone Maxine Hamilton? It could have been, she'd been interviewed at the station that same afternoon and a detour via Alice's house wouldn't have taken her long. Alice couldn't face the thought that Hamilton had an accomplice, it sent an icy shiver through her body. It was a crazy idea which she put down to her imagination running riot — tiredness no doubt.

Alice arrived home to find Dilys in the kitchen unpacking bags of groceries.

"I'm a day early. Hope you don't mind but I'm off to Scarborough tomorrow with my sister."

"No, it's fine." Alice smiled at her, helping herself to a bottle of red. "Any calls?"

"Your son. He said would you ring him."

Alice disappeared into the sitting room with her mobile. "Michael, everything okay?"

"Yes, Mum. You?"

"More than okay, son. We've wrapped up the case and Maxine Hamilton is in custody."

"Brilliant. You must be so relieved, that woman was driving you insane. Look, Zandra has suggested that we come down next week, the three of us. Think you could cope with that?"

"That's a grand idea, I'll cope just fine."

"We should be with you about teatime on Tuesday. We'll eat out, no need to cook," he said.

"Lovely. I'm looking forward to it."

Alice hadn't seen Zandra and little Paul for almost a year. What with her job and life in general, time flew. A catch up would be great.

"I'm off now," Dilys said. "I'll be back next week. Think you'll manage?"

"Yes. The pressure's off at work for the time being, so I'll be fine." '*The pressure's off* . . .' It didn't hit her until Dilys had gone and she was alone. No more chasing shadows, wondering if there'd be a tweet from her old enemy today. Alice was finally free. At last, she could put Mad Hatter behind her and move on.

She'd enjoy tonight, the team and other colleagues from the station didn't often mix socially. Time to put her glad rags on, fix her hair and order a taxi. She had every intention of enjoying the evening.

* * *

The Crown was a large, popular pub that served food. By the time Alice arrived, the party was well under way. Dolly pounced on Alice the minute she spotted her. "We never did have that chat," she said, "and now I'm too bloody pissed." She held up her glass. "That's what fizz does to me."

Alice took a glass from the tray on the counter. "I'll join you. Frank's put his hand in his wallet, so why not make the most of it?"

"Have you seen the man he's brought with him?" Dolly said.

Alice looked over at them. The stranger was tall with greying fair hair, about her age, she guessed. "Is he a friend, a colleague?" she asked Dolly.

"No idea, but Frank's been touting him around the room since he got here," Dolly said.

"Ma'am, I almost didn't recognise you."

It was Hawkes. "That'll be the posh frock and the odd curl I've managed to persuade into my hair, Sergeant," she said with a grin. "We're socialising tonight, so call me Alice." She looked at him. "Remind me, Sergeant, what's your name?"

Dolly burst out laughing. "Jason, idiot, and give him some credit, he's got the making of a bloody good detective."

"That's because I've been busy training him. Seriously, Jason, you saved my bacon back there by the lake. If you hadn't stepped in, I'm pretty certain Hamilton would have gone for me."

"Alice." Osbourne was approaching with the stranger in tow. "I'd like you to meet Leo Monk. He's a superintendent from the North of England serial murder squad, and he's on a mission."

Alice looked up at him. "Sounds intriguing. Anything we can help you with?"

"Very possibly. How about we have a chat tomorrow at the station?" Leo Monk said.

Alice nodded. She liked him already — he had a nice smile, a firm handshake and a twinkle in his blue eyes.

"I saw that look," Dolly said, once he and Osbourne had wandered away.

"Don't be daft, I'm well past all that."

"Now it's you being daft. There hasn't been a man in your life for ages. It's about time that situation changed."

"I never told you the truth about Paul, did I?" Alice pulled a face. "It'll probably come out at the trial anyway, but he wasn't a nice man at all, and it put me off romance for good."

Before Dolly had a chance to respond, Alice felt a hand on her shoulder. "What did you think of Leo?" Osbourne said.

"I've hardly said two words to him, Frank. It certainly wasn't long enough to form an opinion."

"Only he's asked for you specifically," Osbourne said.

"Me? Whatever for?"

"To liaise with the squad on a case. He is the SIO and the case is Manchester-based," Osbourne said.

"I'll give him what help I can, but why me?" she asked.

"Your name came up in conversation, and Leo wanted to meet you," he said.

"Why on earth would he be interested in me, Frank? I'm practically retired — or have you forgotten?" She grinned.

He returned the smile. "You've got a good few years left in you yet, Alice. Working with Leo Monk could be good for you. Get you the promotion to super that you deserve. The case he's working on is high profile. It certainly wouldn't do your career any harm."

"So, you want to get rid of me, do you?" Alice laughed.

"Not at all. The case Leo is working on concerns serial murders that've been going on for years. Ring any bells?"

"Similar to the Mad Hatter case, you mean?" she asked.

"Which is why your name came up."

"Well, given the case is local, am I likely to have heard of it?" she asked.

"Does 'Operation Dream Catcher' mean anything to you?" Osbourne said.

Alice knew the name. "That's a cold case, surely? There's been no killings for a while as far as I know."

"The killings involved teenage girls, and you're right, there has been a gap, but during the past month two more girls have gone missing, same MO as all the others. So it's not a cold case. On the contrary, it's very much an active one, I'm afraid."

Alice knew very little about the case except that it was the stuff of nightmares, concerning as it did missing teens. She tried to dismiss the entire idea from her mind, but she couldn't deny the spark of excitement.

CHAPTER FORTY-EIGHT

Friday

Alice woke late the following morning, but that didn't matter. The only thing waiting for her at the station was a day at her desk, a stack of paperwork and a meeting with Leo Monk. She was in the kitchen making coffee when her mobile rang. It was Osbourne. Expecting him to rattle on about the impending press briefing for the Mad Hatter case, she was totally unprepared for what came next.

"There's been . . . another one." His voice was shaking. "It was spotted early this morning."

For several seconds, Alice had no idea what he was talking about. Then it hit her like a fist to the guts. "A Mad Hatter tweet? Are you sure? How can she tweet anything? She's locked up."

"It follows the same format — same hashtag and was sent from the same mobile as the last one," he said.

It was possible, the mobile had never been found. Panic began to get its grip on her. How could this be? Hamilton was Mad Hatter, they had the evidence, there hadn't been any mistake. "Please tell me this is some kind of sick joke, Frank. I couldn't cope with any more. For years, I was convinced it was Paul's woman and now we know that woman is definitely Maxine Hamilton."

"Hamilton is guilty all right," Osbourne said. "She confessed to the lot in yesterday's interview. We have her signed statement. But she didn't send the tweet, Alice, someone else did. Maxine Hamilton must have an accomplice."

Alice remembered this same thought crossing her mind at some point. Was it the person who'd been in her house, smoked the cigarette and used Paul's aftershave? Alice couldn't for the life of her think who that person could possibly be.

Gone was the Alice who got up that morning relaxed and cheerful. Alice was back where she had been — nervous, twitchy, weighed down by a black cloud. She finished the call and dressed quickly. She grabbed her stuff, ensured she'd locked all the doors properly and climbed into her car. Within fifteen minutes she was pulling into the station car park and running up the stairs.

Osborne and Hawkes were in the main office, staring at the whiteboard. Written across it was the tweet.

Osbourne nodded. "What d'you make of that?"

Alice read the words and went cold. *Double, double, toil and trouble. Fire burn and cauldron bubble.* It ended with, '*See you soon, Alice*' and the Mad Hatter hashtag.

"It's Shakespeare," Hawkes said. "The witches' chant from *Macbeth*."

"I know what it is, Sergeant. But it has nothing to do with *Macbeth*. Whoever sent the tweet is referring to Allegra's Cauldron, the pothole on Needle Crag," Alice said.

"Well, whoever sent it is out of luck," Osbourne said firmly. "This time you won't be involved. Hawkes here and another officer will investigate."

He was trying to protect her. Osbourne knew how afraid she was of that peak. It was no good. "I am involved, Frank. And if we don't follow the usual routine, whoever sent this will go to ground and we'll never find them. Do we know what's happened?"

"We've had no reports of anything untoward," he said. "It was the same when we were first made aware of Still Waters, we didn't know Callum Hilton was already dead." A sobering thought that sent a chill down Alice's spine. The last thing they wanted was a new set of victims and to have to chase another killer.

She turned to Hawkes. "Who d'you reckon is in the frame for the role of Hamilton's right-hand man?"

"Or woman, ma'am," he said. "Think about it. Erica Cross was a suspect for Mad Hatter originally, Minty too, and we still don't have any history for her prior to Still Waters."

Hawkes could be right, especially about Minty. Alice had also been suspicious about her at one time. "I'm not sure that Erica Cross is even at the retreat anymore. I haven't seen her since that day in Gemma's lodge, but we'll check. We should talk to a few of the others while we're at it."

"What about Martin Webb?" Hawkes asked.

"Nosey. Helpful. Why? What're you thinking?"

"That he's always there, whatever's happening, and he always seems to know exactly what's going on," Hawkes said.

"He did point out to us where the bag was buried. And as I recall, he couldn't be sure if it was a man or a woman who dumped it."

"That could have been deliberate, to take the heat off himself."

But Alice didn't think so. "You up for a trip back there?" she asked him.

"I'm not happy about this, Alice," Osbourne said. "You've no idea what you'll be walking into."

"I have no choice. I get twitchy, I'll ring and you send in a team. Meanwhile, a chat with some of the residents will do no harm. I want to get a feel for the atmosphere, listen to the gossip. But more important, to find out if anyone is missing."

CHAPTER FORTY-NINE

"I had hoped never to see this place again," Alice said to Hawkes as they drove through the main gates of the retreat. She cast her eyes upwards. "There it is, laughing at us. Needle Crag in all its glory."

"Given the cauldron was referenced in the tweet, you do realise we might have to go up there, don't you, ma'am?"

Alice shook her head. "Only if I have to, Sergeant, and I won't be hanging around on that hillside for long, that's for sure."

Hawkes pulled a face. "I'm not much of a walker but I wouldn't mind having a trek up there."

"Well, I'd happily give it a miss. Me and that bloody pothole have history."

"I heard something about that during Hamilton's interview. I wasn't sure what to make of it," he said.

"Don't be coy, Sergeant. Hamilton accused me of murdering my husband up there. According to her, I shoved him down that bloody pothole and left him. That's what all this has been about. All the murders she committed over these last years were her getting at me for killing Paul. But the facts are there and everyone agrees, it was an accident and his own stupid fault."

"That's what Osbourne said."

"There is a coroner's report. If you have any doubts about what happened that day, I suggest you read it." It was a touchy subject and Alice's nerves were tattered enough.

Hawkes pulled up outside the office. "A word with Minty first," Alice said, "find out what, if anything, the people at the retreat know. Plus, it's about time she came clean about her life before Still Waters."

Alice had barely got out of the car before Liz Webb and Clare Hilton were on her.

"Gemma's gone missing," Liz said, looking worried. "She went off to get a paper from the shop at about eight last night and she's not been seen since."

Alice's heart sank. "Have you tried ringing her?"

"Yes, of course." Clare glared at her. "It's the same as with my Callum. She'll be found dead just like him, I know it."

"We have no evidence of that. She'll still be upset after Neil, she might have gone home. Don't worry, I'll check and let you know."

"I doubt she'd go home. The funeral isn't for ten days. And she's got no one in Stockport to be with. We've been looking after her, poor cow."

"I'm sure Gemma is fine." Alice said with a conviction she didn't feel. Clare was right, this was history repeating itself.

Leaving the two women outside, they went into the office. "Not good," Hawkes whispered. "That crag is looming ever closer, ma'am."

He meant it as a joke but Alice wasn't amused. This case had no end to it, and it was getting her down.

"Back again," Minty said when she saw them. "You've heard about Gemma? I hope she turns up okay, but with everything that's been going on recently people are bound to worry, me included."

"With regard to the killings, we have made an arrest," Alice said. "You might like to remind people of that when they come to you with their worries."

"So, why is Gemma missing then?" Minty said.

Alice didn't have time to skirt round the issue, so she came straight out with it. Gemma was missing and needed finding quick. "Minty, why have you got no history prior to working here?"

Minty looked away, avoiding her gaze. "I'd have thought finding Gemma was more important than my past. Who's pointed the finger? Mrs Hamilton?"

"No, we've been doing background research on everyone who works here."

Minty sighed. "I changed my name. I didn't do it official or anything, just started using the new one."

So that was why there was no record. She should have realised, Alice thought.

"I used to be Jane Beddows. You see, I did a stint in prison for working the streets. I'm not proud of it, but I was a different person back then. When I got out, Mrs Hamilton gave me a chance — this job, somewhere to live, a completely new start. Of course, I grabbed it with both hands. She suggested I got myself a new identity to go with it, and she helped with that too." She smiled. "So. Enter Jessica Minto, or Minty as I came to be known."

"You have plenty to be grateful to Maxine Hamilton for," Hawkes said.

"Yes, plenty. But I'd no idea she was a killer. You can dance around it all you like but everyone knows it was her you arrested." She leaned forward. "And know this. If I had been aware of what she was up to, I'd have come forward in a heartbeat."

"But you must still feel you owe her, Minty," Hawkes said.

She looked at Hawkes as if he was mad. "Not enough that I'd help her kill people. I've done some shady things in my time — prostitution, a bit of dealing — but I've never knowingly hurt anyone."

She was telling the truth. Her sincerity was palpable. "Thanks for being honest with us," Alice said.

"Look, this doesn't have to get out, does it? If this place stays open, I want to keep my job, along with the respect of the people who come here. I've nowhere else to go."

"Your secret is safe with us, Minty," Alice said.

"Have there been any strangers hanging around in the last day or so?" asked Hawkes.

Minty shook her head. "Just the usual folk, most of whom you've already met."

"What about Hamilton's house? Anyone staying up there?" Alice asked.

"That bloke she sees sometimes, but seeing as how there's been police all over the place he's probably gone by now."

"Does this bloke have a name?" Alice asked.

"Mrs Hamilton never introduced us. He was just another of the men she'd have staying from time to time."

"Thanks, Minty. If you hear anything from Gemma, ring my mobile," Alice said, and they left.

"What d'you think?" Hawkes asked at once.

"I think we should find out who's been staying at the big house, Sergeant. Meanwhile, I want a team up on that hillside. I hope I'm wrong but I have a dreadful feeling we'll find Gemma or her body in Allegra's Cauldron."

CHAPTER FIFTY

A quick look round Hamilton's house proved fruitless. The place was empty with no sign that anyone had been living there since Hamilton's arrest. If there had ever been a man there, he was long gone.

"The crag it is then," Hawkes teased. "Brought your climbing boots?"

"I have suitable footwear in the boot of the car," Alice said, unsmiling. "You?"

"I've still got some boots in the lodge. I reckon we should get kitted up and go take a look."

Alice knew he was right. The team she'd asked for would take a while to get here, meanwhile Gemma could be up there in dire distress.

"We'll take a look but no heroics, got it? And we don't even try to go inside that pothole. It might look like an easy climb down but it isn't, not even with the right equipment, which we haven't got. The sides are slippery and the rocks are sharp."

"Just a quick peek, see if we can spot any sign of activity up there and then we'll wait for the experts," Hawkes said.

Alice nodded. She didn't want to go up there at all, but what choice did they have? The tweet had specifically mentioned the cauldron. She'd just have to grit her teeth.

They went back to the lodge they'd stayed in during the original investigation. Hawkes still had his key, along with his overnight bag and his boots stashed in a corner. "I'd told Minty I'd pick my stuff up sometime, but what with catching up on the paperwork and the childcare at home I've not had the chance."

"I do hope we don't have to move back in. I couldn't take many more days in this place," Alice said.

"Not top of your list for a holiday then." Hawkes grinned, pulling on his boots.

"Absolutely not. It's a sunny beach with little or no activity for me."

"Got anything planned?"

"I'm considering going somewhere with my son and his family this summer," she said. "I've got time owed, so the sooner the better. They're visiting this weekend so I'll talk to them about it then."

* * *

There was a path up Needle Crag but it fizzled out halfway up. After that you had to pick your way carefully over boulders and through thick undergrowth. If you weren't careful, a step in the wrong place could see your leg disappear up to the knee in the boggy moss and bracken.

Alice was surprised at how quickly she ran out of puff. She'd done nothing like this since Paul's death and was out of practice. Hawkes, on the other hand, had youth on his side and was way ahead of her, almost at the top already.

She stood for a moment getting her breath back, then shouted for him to wait. But he'd disappeared. He'd reached the summit and had gone round the other side, and was now out of sight.

Alice struggled on until several minutes later, she hauled herself up the stone ledge at the top of the crag. She sat down and took several gulps from her water bottle.

"Sergeant! Where've you gone?" she called out. She half expected him to jump out from behind the rocks in a childish attempt to frighten her, but there was nothing but silence. The only sound came from a noisy raven that swooped around the peak before finally settling on a rocky outcrop along with some of his mates.

"D'you know what they call a gathering of ravens?"

The tone was casual, as if between friends, but an ice-cold fear froze her veins. Alice was so shocked that she didn't even dare turn round and confront the speaker.

"An unkindness of ravens, Alice. What d'you think of that?"

She was aware of him sitting down beside her on the ledge, but still she could not look. This was insane. It couldn't be him. Reason told her Paul was dead, yet here he was, no ghost, a solid presence who was sitting here talking to her as if nothing had ever happened.

"I think it's very fitting. They can be nasty buggers, ravens. A lot like some people."

"Where's my sergeant?"

"Oh, him. He's resting. Don't worry. I haven't done him any permanent damage, but he won't be much use to you for a while."

Shaking, Alice got to her feet. They were high up and it was slippery underfoot. Holding onto a rock, she finally summoned up the courage to turn and look. Was she hallucinating? Had the strenuous walk up here and her shortness of breath done something to her brain? She blinked, but he remained as solid as before.

He sat on the ledge, staring at her, looking much as he always had. Her husband, Paul Hunter, and very much alive.

CHAPTER FIFTY-ONE

"We had a funeral. Your ashes are buried in the crem next to your parents. What happened, Paul? Everyone thinks you're dead."

"Believe me, that's given me and Maxine a great deal of freedom. We've had a ball these last years, spent most of it on a beach in Spain."

"When she wasn't killing people."

"Maxine blamed you for that. She hated you for what you did to me and was determined to make you pay." He chuckled. "Who was I to argue with her? I was pretty pissed off with you myself back then. I admit, watching you run around like a scalded cat getting nowhere amused me no end. Both Maxine and I thoroughly enjoyed playing with your head. Shame it can't continue, but things have got tricky."

"We found the evidence we needed to charge her, you mean," Alice said.

"Oh, that wasn't down to any great skill on your part, Alice. I had a hand in that too," he said.

His words shocked Alice but she wasn't sure why. He was a vicious bastard. "Why would you want to shop your girlfriend?"

"Maxine is a complicated woman, jealous too. I knew a while ago that the time would come to rid myself of her and I prepared."

Alice's mind was reeling. She'd not only been battling Maxine all this time but Paul too. "You and Maxine planned this whole thing. Between you, you orchestrated everything — the killings, the lack of evidence — and all just to get at me."

"Maxine said you deserved it and who was I to object? The idea of getting back at you through your work was born one hot night in Marbella over a jug of sangria."

"I had no hand in what happened to you that day, you know that. Why didn't you tell her the truth about the accident?" Alice said.

"Maxine's complicated, she thrives on hate and needed someone to blame. Besides, I had to take the heat from me after the Celia West incident."

"You had an affair with her and she had your baby. We found the casket and the pendant. I bet Maxine didn't like that," Alice said.

"True, Maxine is insanely jealous, but then she killed Celia and that made it all better." He looked at her. "You will make sure the infant has a proper resting place, won't you?"

Alice nodded. "I will, but not for you. The infant would have been Michael's sister."

"You owe me, Alice. I could have been killed that day."

"The world thinks you were."

"I didn't get away scot free, you know. I was badly injured. I've got a metal plate in one arm and had to have my right leg pinned. I was a mess for months. I couldn't walk properly for weeks, never mind climb."

"Well, you appear to have recovered now. You should have put Maxine right, told her what really happened. It could have saved a lot of lives."

"It wasn't that simple. I told you, Maxine is a jealous woman. After Celia the woman she feared the most was you."

That surprised Alice. "Why would she fear me? She always had the upper hand."

"She was terrified that one day I'd leave her and return to you." He grinned. "I played on that fear too. Over the years she became more and more paranoid about the influence she imagined you had over me."

"You're a louse."

"I enjoyed the ride. Maxine does revenge well. When I told her you were nearing retirement and how much I missed you, our son and his family, there was no stopping her. The woman's a psychopath. A born killer. I couldn't have stopped her even if I'd wanted to."

"I thought you were dead, that her hatred of me was because she believed I was responsible for the accident and wanted revenge."

"Maxine didn't like how you simply got away without paying for my injuries. All the pain I suffered during my recovery really got to her. I must admit I did nothing to put her right."

"You fell. It was an accident, Paul. You chanced your luck and it failed you. It had nothing to do with me."

"That wasn't how Maxine saw it. I was injured and you left me in that hole to rot."

"But you didn't rot, did you? How did you get out?"

"You forget I know this hill and that pothole like the back of my hand, but I was lucky as well. I managed to crawl to the path that runs down the inside and leads to a hidden entrance on the other side of the hill. It wasn't easy, not in my condition, and it took hours. Partway along I got a mobile signal and rang Maxine. She organised some of her people to get me out. She sent me to a private hospital to get fixed up, and when I was well enough to travel I convalesced at her villa in Spain."

"Then you came back to England and resumed the identity of Mark Johnson. Didn't you think to contact me? And what about Michael? He was grief-stricken."

"No, I was free of my old life and glad of it. I was missing, presumed dead, which suited Maxine and me just fine. Maxine is a world away from you. She's wealthy, and exciting to be with. She doesn't give a toss for the rules or people's finer feelings. If someone has to die, she's happy to see to it. She's wonderful to watch, so skilful, and doesn't feel a shred of remorse."

He was as mad as Hamilton. "So, whose was the body? It was found three years later wearing your clothes and with your stuff in the pockets."

"He was a casual worker at the retreat. He upset Maxine, so she decided to use him to end the uncertainty about what had happened to me. She killed him, dressed him in my clothes, left him to decompose a bit and then put him in a remote part of the cauldron to be found at some later date. It was an excellent idea. When he was found, he'd rotted away to nothing but bones."

Shame Jack hadn't had his Berlin contact back then. Alice couldn't believe this was actually happening. Here was Paul, casually narrating his and Maxine's antics of the last six years in all their horror as if they were simple everyday events.

"She went to my home, rummaged through your things. Did you know?"

"I suggested it. Spooked you, I bet." He laughed.

"What was she looking for?"

"Nothing, but she did bring back some of that aftershave I always liked so much. I'm touched that you kept my stuff."

Ignoring the comment, Alice asked, "Did you help Hamilton murder those people?"

He laughed. "Only inasmuch as I taught her about forensics. How not to leave any trace behind. She'd never have made such a good job of it if I hadn't provided the expertise."

"Then you're as guilty as she is."

"Has she named me? Dropped me in it? Has she even said I'm still alive? No, she hasn't and she won't. I don't exist, and you'll never get Maxine to say otherwise, whatever questions you ask. Maxine tells you about me and in her mind we're practically back together again. She'd never risk that. And think about it, Alice. You start going on about seeing me and what will people think?" He leaned closer to her. "That you've finally lost it, that's what."

"She'll talk, we can be pretty persuasive," Alice said.

"You have no evidence that I took part in any of it."

He was right. Alice was thinking about that cigarette end found at the lakeside, and the boot prints. "You still smoke. You left a stub behind when Callum Hilton was killed. We've got casts of boot prints too."

"I'll lay odds that the cigarette end is too degraded, and the casts could match any number of boots. There's plenty of people fish that lake." He stood up. "Admit it, Alice, you've got sod all."

"I'll still have to arrest you."

"Arrest who, exactly? I don't exist, I'm dead, remember?"

Alice got to her feet and looked around. She could really do with Hawkes right now but there was still no sign of him. Paul was tall and strong. He was bound to resist, and she was no match for him.

"Don't make this difficult, Paul."

He laughed again. "You don't stand a chance, so don't even try. But you're in luck. I promised Maxine that if I ever got you up here again, I'd throw you down that pothole myself, but I'm feeling generous today."

Alice took a step back. Where the hell was Hawkes?

"As much as I enjoyed being with Maxine, she got too intense towards the end. The killing spree and her hatred of you took over, warped her mind. You've done me a favour by arresting her, so I owe you."

This took Alice aback. "You wanted her gone?"

"Yes, and so I made sure you found what you needed."

"It was you who buried that bag," she said.

"Yes. I also suggested she save trophies from the kills, particularly the tattooed skin. I knew they'd come in useful one day."

Hamilton couldn't have suspected a thing. She'd said nothing about him being alive, not even hinted at it.

"I'll tell Maxine you double-crossed her. Are you sure she'll be so loyal once she knows the truth?"

"Yes. I'm her world, you see. But it doesn't matter anyway. Very soon she'll get word that I've dropped dead from a heart attack. She'll mourn me for a while, then live on her memories. So, don't waste your time, Alice."

"Got it all worked out, haven't you?"

"It's what I do best. Well, I've enjoyed our little chat, Alice, but I'm off now. I know we didn't always get on but things have changed. With Maxine locked up, I've got my freedom, money and a safe place to go."

"You won't get away, you will be found."

"I doubt that. Anyway, just ask yourself, why would you want that? I've got my freedom but so have you. Enjoy it, Alice. Get on with your life and forget all about me."

"What d'you know about Gemma Lewis?" she asked.

"Nothing."

"You sent a tweet out this morning luring me up here."

"Not me, Alice. That was down to Maxine giving me the opportunity to kill you. She knew you wouldn't be able to resist, knew you'd come up here and I'd be waiting. I suggest you have a word with that manager of hers, see what she has to say."

CHAPTER FIFTY-TWO

Alice would have attempted to take him on but at that moment she heard Hawkes call out her name. He was on the other side of the crag and needed help. "Don't move," she said to Paul. "You can't get away with this. You're an accessory to murder."

A waste of words, but she had to try. She turned her back on him and started to inch her way round the crag. She found Hawkes lying face down in the heather, a nasty cut on the side of his head.

"I must have tripped," he said, struggling to get up. "One minute I'm looking around and the next my head hits a rock."

Alice knew that wasn't what happened. Paul had clobbered him one. "Did someone attack you?"

"I don't think so, ma'am. There's only you and me up here."

"Look, try not to move. That's a nasty wound you've got and you could be concussed."

Hawkes rubbed his head and pointed to a rock lying half buried in the moss. "I tripped over that bugger there, fell heavily and cracked my head on these boulders to the side of me."

No mention of anyone else. Fair enough, he obviously didn't remember. He'd suffered a heavy blow and had been out of it for several minutes. The cut was bleeding, leaving a trail down his face.

She dabbed his face with a tissue. "From the state of your head, it must've been some fall."

He nodded and winced. "I know. I went out with a bang. Everything went black until I came round a few seconds ago. To be honest, I still feel groggy."

"You'd better stay here. Don't try to get up. You're injured and I need to get you looked at." She took her mobile from her jacket pocket and rang Minty. "My sergeant's been injured. We need mountain rescue to get him off the crag, and medics."

"I'll sort it right away," Minty said. "And Gemma's turned up by the way, so panic over. The silly woman went off to the pub without telling anyone where she was going, had too much to drink and ended up spending the night in one of their rooms."

That was something at least, and it meant that Paul hadn't been involved in her disappearance after all. "Help's coming," she told Hawkes. She took off her jacket and put it under his head. "Just lie there and don't move until you're rescued."

Alice went back to speak to Paul but of course he was nowhere to be seen. She hadn't expected him to hang around while she saw to Hawkes, that was too much to ask. She couldn't see him anywhere on the hillside or the path they had come up by, so he had to have used another way. She went up to the entrance to the cauldron, which these days had a metal mesh covering. It had been moved. Alice knew that just inside and to the left was the difficult but navigable pathway that Paul knew only too well. It led to the bottom of the crag and the road on the other side. She would never attempt to use it herself — too steep and dark — but Paul could. Maybe he'd parked up by the road and used that path to come up and down so he wouldn't be seen. If she was right, he could be anywhere by now.

* * *

It was nearly an hour before the rescue team turned up, but then they had Hawkes and Alice off the mountain in record time. Waiting at the bottom, in the Still Waters car park, was an ambulance and a couple of paramedics.

"We'll take him to the hospital in Glossop, get him looked at," one of them told Alice. "It was a nasty bang on the head and it'll need stitching."

Alice watched them leave and then went for a word with Minty. She was in the shop with a group of the residents, discussing the latest events.

"Good about Gemma, isn't it?" Clare Hilton said. "I don't think I could have stood any more horror."

Alice doubted she could have either. "I need a private word, Minty."

Taking the hint, the others left. "That tweet we got this morning. You sent it, didn't you?"

Minty looked back at her, her eyes wide in fear. "I didn't write it. I'd no idea what it meant. The day before you carted Mrs Hamilton away, she gave me a mobile and told me to send off a tweet she'd written and when to post it."

"D'you still have the phone?" Alice asked.

Minty reached under the counter and handed it over. "If I've done anything wrong, I'm sorry. I didn't think it was anything important. Mrs Hamilton said it was for a joke."

Some joke. Alice had nearly had a heart attack when she'd been told about it this morning. Donning nitrile gloves, she took a quick look at it, hoping there might be something about Paul there — a text sent to or from him — but there was nothing. The only number in the call log was hers. Apart from that, it had been used to send the tweets and nothing else. Alice put the phone safely in an evidence bag. It was the last piece of the puzzle.

She left Still Waters for the station in Manchester, glad to be out of the place. She couldn't make up her mind whether or not to tell anyone about Paul. And who could she tell anyway? Hawkes didn't recall what had happened, so as it stood she was the only person who knew Paul had been up there at all, or that it had been him who hit Hawkes. It was unlikely that anyone would believe her. She could hear Osbourne's reasonable voice now, telling her that it was simply a figment of her imagination, and the whole thing was due to stress and being back on that peak. He'd probably put her on sick leave, and that wouldn't do her any good at all. Paul had covered his tracks well. It wouldn't be easy to prove he was still alive.

She really wanted to come clean, tell Osbourne, but unless Maxine backed her up no one was going to believe her. And anyway, was anyone likely to believe what Maxine herself said about Paul? No, she was on her own in this. Her best bet was to forget about Paul and say nothing.

EPILOGUE

The super was relieved that both the tweet received that morning and Gemma's disappearance had come to nothing.

"We now have Hamilton's mobile too. I'll give it to Jack to look at, see what he can find," Alice said.

"You've done well, Alice," Osbourne said. "The Mad Hatter case is finally resolved, due in no small part to your tenacity."

"Don't forget the officers who've worked with me, particularly Hawkes." She gave Osbourne one of her charming smiles. "He wants to transfer to this station, and he'd be an asset. He's young, keen and bright."

"I'll think about it, Alice. I agree, he does have potential. Let's see what he has to say for himself when he gets back to work."

Alice was just about to leave Osbourne's office when they were joined by Leo Monk.

"I was keeping my fingers crossed that you'd make it back before I had to leave." He sat down next to Alice and passed her a file. "Operation Dream Catcher. I'd like you to read it. Then, if you're interested, you can join the team as the new SIO."

"I don't understand, sir. I thought that was you," Alice said.

"Only because I have no one else experienced enough to do it. However, your recent involvement in the Mad Hatter case more than qualifies you for the job."

Alice knew very little about the case apart from what Osbourne had told her, that it involved the disappearance of young teenage girls. "Can I take this and read it over the weekend?"

Monk nodded. "Please do, and give me a ring early next week." He handed her a card. "We are about to move offices. From next week we'll be based on the fifth floor here, so you'll still see the usual faces. I do hope you will decide to join us, Alice. The case desperately needs new input."

From the size of the file, Alice could see that. It was another mammoth case that had been ongoing for at least three years. A quick flick through the pages, seeing the photos of the young girls who'd gone missing and Alice knew she had no choice but to give it her best shot.

THE END

ALSO BY HELEN H. DURRANT

DETECTIVE ALICE ROSSI
Book 1: THE ASH LAKE MURDERS

DETECTIVE RACHEL KING
Book 1: NEXT VICTIM
Book 2: TWO VICTIMS
Book 3: WRONG VICTIM
Book 4: FORGOTTEN VICTIM
Book 5: LAST VICTIM

THE DCI GRECO BOOKS
Book 1: DARK MURDER
Book 2: DARK HOUSES
Book 3: DARK TRADE
Book 4: DARK ANGEL

THE CALLADINE & BAYLISS MYSTERY SERIES
Book 1: DEAD WRONG
Book 2: DEAD SILENT
Book 3: DEAD LIST
Book 4: DEAD LOST
Book 5: DEAD & BURIED
Book 6: DEAD NASTY
Book 7: DEAD JEALOUS
Book 8: DEAD BAD
Book 9: DEAD GUILTY
Book 10: DEAD WICKED
Book 11: DEAD SORRY

DETECTIVE MATT BRINDLE
Book 1: HIS THIRD VICTIM
Book 2: THE OTHER VICTIM

DETECTIVES LENNOX & WILDE
Book 1: THE GUILTY MAN
Book 2: THE FACELESS MAN

Thank you for reading this book.

If you enjoyed it please leave feedback on Amazon or Goodreads, and if there is anything we missed or you have a question about, then please get in touch. We appreciate you choosing our book.

Founded in 2014 in Shoreditch, London, we at Joffe Books pride ourselves on our history of innovative publishing. We were thrilled to be shortlisted for Independent Publisher of the Year at the British Book Awards.

www.joffebooks.com

We're very grateful to eagle-eyed readers who take the time to contact us. Please send any errors you find to corrections@joffebooks.com. We'll get them fixed ASAP.

Milton Keynes UK
Ingram Content Group UK Ltd.
UKHW011816221223
434844UK00003B/145